C000068569

THE THIN BLUE LINE

CHRISTOFFER CARLSSON has a PhD in criminology, and is a university lecturer in the subject. He has written five crime novels, including the bestselling *The Invisible Man from Salem* and the Young Adult noir *October is the Coldest Month*.

THE THIN BLUE LINE

Christoffer Carlsson

Translated by Michael Gallagher

SCRIBE

Melbourne • London

Scribe Publications
2 John Street, Clerkenwell, London, WC1N 2ES, United Kingdom
18–20 Edward St, Brunswick, Victoria 3056, Australia

Originally published in Swedish as *Den Tunna Blå Linjen* by Piratförlagets 2017
Published by agreement with Pontas Literary & Film Agency
First published in English by Scribe 2018

Copyright © Christoffer Carlsson 2017
Translation copyright © Michael Gallagher 2018

All rights reserved. Without limiting the rights under copyright reserved
above, no part of this publication may be reproduced, stored in or introduced
into a retrieval system, or transmitted, in any form or by any means
(electronic, mechanical, photocopying, recording or otherwise) without the
prior written permission of the publishers of this book.

The moral rights of the author and translator have been asserted.

Typeset in 12.35/16.75pt Dante MT by the publisher

Printed and bound in the UK by CPI Group (UK) Ltd, Croydon CR0 4YY

Scribe Publications is committed to the sustainable use of natural resources
and the use of paper products made responsibly from those resources.

9781911617211 (UK edition)
9781925322897 (Australian edition)
9781925693041 (e-book)

CiP data records for this title are available from the National Library
of Australia and the British Library.

scribepublications.co.uk
scribepublications.com.au

For my parents

PART I

The Friend Who Went Up in Smoke
Stockholm
November 2015

1

A letter arrives in the post.

The envelope is white, postcard-sized, and postmarked Stockholm. My name and address are written in anonymous block capitals in black ink.

It's lunchtime, and for once I happen to be at home when it gets pushed through the letterbox along with the rest of the day's post. I'm about to head back to work, so I just pick it up, slip it in my pocket, and leave.

Then I forget all about it.

Sitting in the passenger seat next to Gabriel Birck, my hand finds its way into my inside pocket, and there it is, crumpled and creased after having spent a few hours inside my clothes.

Birck squints as he leans forward.

'Here comes another one.'

I leave the letter in my pocket and reach for the camera, put my eye to the viewfinder, and take two photos of the woman approaching the entrance. Outside, the hum of Stockholm surrounds us, but it's quiet in here, save for the sporadic crackling of the police radio.

'Can't we listen to normal radio?' I ask.

'I prefer it like this.'

'But …'

'No. This is my car.' He looks pissed off. 'Fucking hell, what a waste of time this is. If time is money, we must be paying up big right now.'

He's probably right.

Restructuring within Swedish Police has been going on for almost a year. Everything's supposed to be more efficient, but instead no one has any idea what anyone else is doing — what's termed 'a crisis'. Officers are shuffled back and forth between divisions, and no one ever achieves anything. Chiefs are engaged in constant struggle to fill the gaps, yet the directives from above are said to be so vague that they don't even know what their budgets are.

I can't remember things ever being this bad. Clear-up rates are falling, resentment is rising, and all the money that was ploughed into the reorganisation seems to have disappeared.

'Every day feels like a fucking holiday,' Birck goes on, and it's true.

That's why we find ourselves close to the large square of Odenplan, having been seconded out to Surveillance. They were short of people to cover the night shift. Our task is to record anyone arriving or leaving Västmannagatan 66 between eight p.m. and three a.m. According to the duty officer, the address is being used to fence stolen goods, but the Anti-Theft Unit haven't been able to prove it.

Birck puts his hand on the door handle.

'I need a piss. Call me if anything happens.'

It's twenty-five past eight, it's November, and it's cold. As Birck crosses the street to use the toilets over at Hotel Oden, his breath looks like puffs of thin white smoke. He hunkers down against the cold and turns up the collar on his winter coat. The rain that fell a few hours ago has left the roads with a glistening sheen of moisture. In the distance, the neon signs around Odenplan are just visible, pools of light in all this blackness. A bus sweeps across Karlbergsvägen, but silhouettes are all I can make out, no faces.

It's been a long year for the police, and a long year for me. I forced myself off the pills, despite being convinced for a long time that it was impossible.

That was three hundred and seventy days ago today. It feels like more.

I took it a minute, an hour, at a time. Days felt like weeks, which felt like months, and I started to feel older than I was. When there's nowhere to escape to, you age quickly.

I reach for the letter again, inspect it from all angles, then rip the envelope open with my front-door key.

It contains a photograph printed on thin paper, folded in two. That's it.

The photo feels slippery and cool between my fingers; it depicts a dark-haired woman with a thin face and large, almond-shaped eyes. She's wearing a dark-green waist-length jacket, a black shirt, and equally black drainpipe trousers. She's waiting on a street corner — impossible to determine which — and is staring out at the road as if waiting for someone.

On the back of the photograph, a handwritten telephone number and two words:

Help me

I get my mobile out, dial the number, and press the phone to my ear. No answer. I hang up, and open the phone's web browser, do a search for the number: no hits.

It's not unheard of for people to just mess the police around, often for no good reason at all, so I'm used to it. One thing about this is confusing, though. I recognise the woman.

As Birck emerges from the hotel, I fold up the photo and put it in the envelope before slipping it back into my inside pocket.

The police radio crackles: someone has found a dead man's body in a flat on Karlbergsvägen, a kilometre from where we're sitting. My first thought is to head over there, to get out of this if nothing else, but we'd have to clear it with Surveillance first. And if we did find our way to the body, we'd only have to turn around and come back, because someone else would've got there first.

A man stops outside Västmannagatan 66, then enters the building. Dutifully, we take our photos. Monday the second of November will be remembered for nothing whatsoever.

My phone buzzes with an incoming text. It's from the number I just called, the one on the back of the photo.

Tomorrow, 10pm

That, and an address in Södermalm, is all.

who is this? I reply. *and why didn't you answer?*

'Who's that?' says Birck.

'Why do you ask?'

'You look weird.'

'It's nothing.'

Sitting in that car, the hours drag by.

I think about the dead man in the flat on Karlbergsvägen. The city just lost another soul, but Stockholm stopped caring a long time ago.

2

It's been a year and a half since my old boss, Charles Levin, died. My tablets have been taken from me. John Grimberg, who was my best friend long ago, is missing.

The emptiness inside me keeps growing. I'm still working as a detective at the Violent Crime Unit in central Stockholm, but it's hard to stay in the same place, and the same role, when everything else has changed. I know I need something to take the place of the tablets; addictions don't disappear just like that. More often than not they'll mutate: former drunks become workaholics, clean junkies become gambling addicts, flat-broke casino punters turn to booze. For those who do actually manage to get free, it's easy to lose their way.

Freedom. A strange word, when you think about it.

I wake from a nap brought on by the fruitless Surveillance night shift. Darkness has once again enveloped the city, and it's getting on for half-nine. I grab my coat and scarf. I've looked at the photo a few times during the course of the day, as well as studying the handwriting and the envelope it was sent in.

I walk to Kungsholmstorg. The southbound bus snorts its way towards me through the cold. I get on, taking a seat on my own right at the back, where I can feel the warmth and the vibration from the engine. As we sweep along the Södermalm waterfront, I can almost make out the frozen silhouettes of the Gröna Lund amusement park on the far side.

I get off at Tjärhovsplan and check the address in the text message, then peel off onto Tjärhovsgatan, where I find the entrance and try the door. It's locked, and it's as black as the bottom of a well in there. All I can see is a spindly spiral staircase winding its way upwards.

A man appears from the shadows. He's wearing dark clothes and a cap when he steps out of the entrance.

'Leo,' the man says and calmly takes hold of my arm. 'I'm not going to hurt you. Come with me.'

Then something flashes in his hand: a little knife, with the blade pointing towards me.

'Grim,' I say.

3

I must have crossed over to the other side. Him touching me feels unreal. Like he's a ghost.

'So?' Grim says. 'What do you think?'

'If it wasn't for your voice, I would never have recognised you.'

This is how he makes his living: helping people to disappear and giving them new identities. He disappeared himself, over a year ago.

The hair peeking out from under his cap is no longer blond but dark brown, and his blue eyes are now brown. Yes, *it is him*, but he's put on weight, his face is puffier and his cheekbones are less defined than they used to be. He looks a bit swollen — ill, almost.

He's wearing a pair of baggy jeans and a thick, dark-brown jacket over a knitted jumper — the kind of thing you imagine dockers might wear. The clothes fit badly, as if they weren't his.

'Are you going to hurt me?'

'I'm not going to do you any harm. That was the first thing I said.'

'Can I trust you on that?'

'What do you think?'

'I have no idea anymore.'

That makes him laugh.

'Well I can hardly blame you.'

Grim had always been my best friend. A friend who had then

9

tried to kill me. Things like that tie people together, whether they like it or not.

I change the subject. 'Where are we going?'

'Nowhere, really. It's just safer, meeting like this.'

'Safer?'

'We can turn right here.'

We leave Tjärhovsgatan and head up towards Katarina Church. Illuminated and whitewashed, it shines brightly in the November night.

'I need your help,' says Grim.

'With what?'

'You got my letter, right?'

'Well I wouldn't be here otherwise.'

An elderly man makes his way down the hill with the aid of his walking stick. His gut is the size of a beach ball, stretching the fabric of his coat taut. He grunts his way towards us.

'You saw who the woman in the picture was,' he continues, quietly, once the man has gone past us.

'Yes.'

'I need to know who did it.'

'Why?'

'That would take a long time to explain.'

'Well make a start then.'

'Not tonight. We haven't got time.'

Some distance away, perhaps down on Medborgarplatsen, someone's setting off fireworks. They explode against the black sky, the sound muffled and satisfying.

We get to the church. Close by, you can hear the bustle and hum of the bars along Mosebacke.

'I don't know who did it,' I say. 'Nobody does. Why is that so important?'

Grim, more impatient now, insists:

'Can you help me or not?'

'This isn't okay — contacting me out of the blue after a year and a half, then asking me about something like this without telling me why!' Suddenly I can feel my insides burning with rage. I don't know where it came from. 'It's an insult.'

'I will explain, but you can start by having another look at the investigation. That's all I ask.'

'That's asking too much.'

He stops.

'I'll be in touch again soon.'

'Grim,' I say, in a harsher tone than I intended. 'What's going on? How long have you been back?'

'A week or so. I'll be able to tell you more soon. Listen.'

'Yes?'

'Thanks for coming. It's good to see you.'

Right there, for a split-second, his mask slips, and I recognise him.

Another firework whistles skywards and explodes somewhere over Götgatan. I stand watching it for a second before I turn to Grim, but he's disappeared, swallowed up by the ground as if he'd never been there at all.

4

I stay close in to the stone frontages of Södermalm's old buildings as I walk, then place my hand flat against one of them. Somehow it's as if I can feel the stones' age against my skin. The city fills my view. Another firework explodes in the distance.

Grim's been missing for a year and a half. I've learnt to live without him, without the need for him, and without the threat I still felt I was under when he was around.

And then he turns up.

I'm standing outside that entrance on Tjärhovsgatan again. *This is where he appeared from, out of the darkness.* Is he holed up in this building? I cross the road and lift my gaze upwards to study the windows in the facade. In a few of them, the lights are on, but the vast majority are in darkness.

I wait, but he doesn't show up. Maybe he's already there, inside the building, or perhaps this place has no significance whatsoever. That might be exactly why he chose it, so that I won't have a relevant address to link him to, should I decide not to do as he says.

If I chose to betray him. That's what it feels like, weirdly enough.

I flop onto a seat on the metro.

The woman in the picture. That's why he got in touch. Not to let me know he was okay, not because he wanted to meet me. He contacted me because he *needed* me. That's all people are to Grim. Tools.

I pull out the photo. She's oblivious to the picture being taken; there's something quite natural about the whole scene. It's as if the camera has captured her in an instant where she seems to be at one with her world, serene. She is very beautiful.

I know who she is. It was awful, what happened. Everyone thought so. Tragic.

She's been dead for over five years, and a connection with Grim would never have occurred to me.

Is there a connection? What did he actually say?

It's not until I get off at Fridhemsplan that it strikes me. Aiding and abetting a criminal. That's what I'm making myself guilty of, as of now, if I keep this to myself — a serious crime, although not uncommon among police officers. A lot of the time it can be explained away, but almost as often it ends up with officers being convicted — destroying their careers. What the fuck am I going to say to Birck? Or Morovi?

And Sam? Well ... what am I going to say to Sam?

I stop at a 7-Eleven to get some ice cream and cigarettes. Then I head home to Alströmergatan and take the lift to the third floor.

Whichever way you look at it, the faded apartment on Chapmansgatan was a loner's place. I was pleased to see the back of it. The two-bedroom place on Alströmergatan has been ours — mine and Sam's — for six months. The windows are huge, and the lighting's always warm. The parquet floors creak underfoot, and the fireplace radiates a gentle wood smell. Occasionally, when Sam and I are both off work, we go to auctions together to buy antiques. We're gradually furnishing our first home together. It feels good, feels right.

Tonight, I'm coming home with a feeling that's close to shame in my chest.

'You're awake,' I say. 'It's gone eleven.'

'Mm,' Sam mumbles slowly from under the blanket, stretched out on the sofa. 'I happened to fall asleep.' She adjusts the cushion under her head. 'What were you doing out?'

The lie comes more easily than it ought to, and there, without thinking about it, I've made a decision.

'A late interrogation. It overran.'

I'd rather not think about it.

Kit, our two-year-old cat, slinks along the wall and tips his head to one side before pushing himself against my calves.

'But I did buy ice cream.'

She smiles sleepily and runs a hand through her hair. Her left hand, with four fingers, thanks to Grim. Scarred for life.

'Grab two spoons,' she says.

5

The days that follow are different, but not really. Daily life goes on at a pace I'm starting to get used to, and yet everything has changed.

I sleep less well than I used to; I'm more distracted. When I'm with Sam, or at work, I avoid having my phone out, despite the chances of him contacting me again so soon after meeting up being pretty small. I don't know why I'm so sure of that, but I am. He's not going to contact me. There's an invisible bond between us now, I can almost feel it in my hands.

I avoid topics of conversation that might lead to Grim. People at work occasionally ask me about him, and what happened. Whether I've heard anything. I don't want to have to lie — I've told so many lies to so many people over the last few years.

Despite that, I know that I would lie if anyone asked. Grim — or was it me — has driven an invisible wedge between me and Sam. I cannot justify the fact that I'm protecting him, that I'm protecting *us*. I think he's the only person who's ever understood me. We grew up in Salem together. He was almost a mirror image of me. That might be it. He's the only one who truly knows me. And now we're sharing a secret once again.

On the radio, news: fire at a refugee centre last night, no suspects. No end in sight to the war in Syria, in fact an escalation seems more likely. The number of refugees arriving in Sweden from war-torn regions is increasing every week. The situation is acute. 'The police are under great strain. They have requested extra resources.'

I'll remember this, later on. Was it an omen? Possibly.

The woman in the picture. I can't stop thinking about her, or Grim. I really don't know why it's burrowed its way into my head, whether it's for Grim's sake, or whether I'm actually interested in the case. It's not often you really can't tell whose behalf you're acting on.

Doing a simple search would be calming. That's the way I try and justify it to myself, but I still hesitate for a long time. On the morning of the third day, I finally do a search on her name.

It all revolves around a murder, in the early hours of the thirteenth of October 2010, and the collapsed investigation that was put to sleep the following year and remains in hibernation. Straight after New Year, I note, the case is going to be transferred to the Investigations Unit at what used to be the Regional Detective Branch — the cold-case department. In less than two months, the case will no longer be ours.

Anja Morovi is one of the sharpest shooters in the Stockholm Police, has a Masters in Criminology, and knows how to run a place like Violent Crime. Her office is smaller than you'd expect, but well-furnished and light, and beyond her large window Stockholm is slowly waking into life. She's sitting behind her desk in a high-backed chair studying something on her screen, which just bleeped.

'Robbery on Barnhusgatan,' she mutters. 'Haven't people got anything better to do?'

I look down at the coffee cup in my hands. There isn't much that feels right here.

She switches off her monitor and turns to face me.

'You wanted a word.'

'Yes …'

Even now, I hesitate. It's my one last chance to not do this. To walk out of here and tell myself that everything is as it was.

'Do you remember Angelica Reyes?'

'Yes.'

'I saw that the case is being transferred soon.'

'Yes, that should please the stark raving archivists.'

I hesitate again.

'It's for the best, I suppose,' Morovi continues. 'The last time any of us touched that case was 2011, as I recall. But still.'

'I was thinking maybe I could take it on.'

'You? Haven't you got anything else to do?'

'I'd be able to give it a week.'

'You weren't even on that case, were you?'

'Not really, no.' I squirm on my chair, and sip some coffee. 'But that could be a good thing.'

Morovi leans back, folding her arms across her chest.

'This whole department is on its knees from being overworked, we don't even have time to investigate new cases properly. And you want to look at one that's five years old?'

'Yes.'

'But why? Why Angelica Reyes?'

'It's unsolved. It'd look good if we solved it, and I'll have time to have a go. As long as nothing big comes up, in which case you can move me on.'

Morovi smiles faintly.

'You're a much worse liar than you think. You can tell me what this is really all about next week.'

'You're giving me permission, then?'

'You need some help, there's too much material for one pair of eyes. Take Gabriel. But don't talk to anyone other than me, officially I'm assigning you one of tonight's assaults. It would look

17

good if we solved it — I'll buy that — but I don't want us to get a reputation for scrabbling around at the very last minute trying to save face. Even if it's true.'

Her computer bleeps once more. She rolls her eyes and wakes the screen.

'Assault, in Vanadislunden Park. Jesus, how do they keep it up.'

I stand up and head for the door.

'Listen, Leo,' I hear her voice from behind me.

I turn around.

'Yes?'

'Be careful. They're real mazes, unsolved murders.'

6

The case files for the Angelica Reyes murder are packed in boxes. They cover an entire wall of the large archive room, and on the outside of each one someone has written the case number in felt-tip. I run my fingers along them as I stand there under the stark fluorescent lights.

Grim might be trying to trick me. That would be no surprise. In that case, I'm getting dragged into a five-year-old murder with no solution, a maze with no opening.

I identify the boxes containing the case's earliest material and load them onto a trolley, which I then wheel off into one of the offices in the archive. It's the newer type, with glass doors and large windows — more a transparent cube than a room. Since no one is to find out that we've started looking at the case, it's probably best to stay down here, at least to begin with.

The room is bare, save for a plain table and a few chairs. I pull one out, sit down, and stare at the boxes. The past is coming back, in fragments.

I have them, these memories of Angelica Reyes, even though I wasn't really on that case. I found myself on the periphery of it all, doing a few interrogations with the odd witness and checking out an alibi or two. Lots of us ended up having to do stuff like that, and we were all pleased not to be any more involved than that.

It's a few minutes to ten in the morning, on Friday the sixth of

November. I want to wait for Birck, but something about the boxes is drawing me to them. An impatience all of a sudden, a desire to get to work.

The perpetrator's name is in those files, I remember everyone saying, despite them never getting anywhere with it. One out of all those hundreds, possibly thousands, of names belongs to the person who took her life.

Perhaps Grim's in there, too? What's his connection to the Angelica murder? Did they know each other? Probably not — I would've found that out by now. Why does he need to know who the murderer was?

Birck pushes the glass door open.

'Angelica Reyes?' is the first thing he says. 'What for? On a Friday and everything.'

'It's getting handed over soon. Morovi wants it cleared up.'

'She said it was your idea.'

'I want to see it cleared up, too.'

'Why?'

'I … I'm a police officer. Isn't that enough?'

'But why the Angelica murder, though?'

'I just told you. It's going to be transferred soon. Can we get started now?'

'Can't we do this on Monday?'

'No.'

That's how it starts.

7

It almost always starts off the same way, with a dead body somewhere, indoors in this case. An unsuspecting patrol is called to the scene, and they get out of the car. A nasty autumn downpour has just begun. They rush over to the entrance, about to make a home visit they will never forget.

Within a few minutes — that's all it takes — the phone rings at the Violent Crime Unit, and on the night in question, in the small hours of the thirteenth of October 2010, the man who answers is Chief Inspector Charles Levin — my boss at the time.

According to the entry log, drawn up and filled in by the first patrol, Levin gets to John Ericssonsgatan 16 at thirty-five minutes after midnight. Another five minutes pass before another officer from Violent Crime, this time a detective inspector, arrives at the scene.

The fact that Levin was in charge of the case is a real stroke of luck for us. Everything was done properly: the cordon was expansive, the forensic investigation of Angelica Reyes' home was conducted without delay, and filmed in its entirety, and a team of officers knocked on doors and spoke to potential witnesses in the area. Both desk-bound and field intelligence officers were deployed to scour databases and CCTV footage, a prosecutor was assigned the case immediately, and — most importantly of all — everything was properly documented.

Birck and I find ourselves five years, almost two thousand days, away from the centre of events. This is a colossal distance for any murder investigation, and yet ... getting to grips with the case feels a little like lifting a shroud. Someone has made a tear in the fabric of time and when you put your finger through it, stretch its thin surface, you move close to another world.

John Ericssonsgatan is a broad, leafy strip of a street on the island of Kungsholmen. It slopes steeply, as though it were trying to pull itself down to the water. Down there, the frontages have been restored, there are bars, bakeries, and balconies. Further up, the buildings are only beautiful from a distance, with ageing, heavy stairwells and lots of grotty, musty old flats. The rents are lower here, and not just because you're further from the water. Lots of the buildings are home to clients of Social Services.

It is one such building that is home to Angelica Reyes. Her apartment is on the third floor, a studio and kitchenette, and the front door is open. One officer is standing by the threshold while the other is further in, alongside the bed.

There she is.

The stills from the forensic investigation show her on her back with her limbs at incongruous angles. The total number of injuries inflicted by the perpetrator is twenty-three, including the odd hack and scratch marks on her upper arms and legs, as well as countless parrying injuries to her hands. The blows that killed her are four deep stab wounds to her chest and abdomen, with the knife striking her liver, one kidney, and her right lung.

At that moment, Levin steps into the apartment where Angelica Reyes has lain dead for a little less than an hour, and flipping through the case files I can almost feel it — he and the others gradually realising that they arrived shortly after the moment of death. It's an intimate scene.

The film from the crime scene starts a few minutes before one a.m., recorded by one of the technicians. When Birck and I start watching the film, we both do so holding a cup of coffee.

'Weird,' I say. 'Feels different.'

'Compared to the stills, you mean?'

Yes. Still images from a crime scene freeze time. Moving pictures make it unnaturally drawn-out. It feels odd, witnessing a five-year-old reality, like catching a glimpse of someone else's dream.

'Puncture marks on her arms,' Levin's voice says from inside the flat.

We start in the doorway. The camera's just been switched on and it wobbles slightly before steadying up. Someone in the background is on the phone; you can hear a female voice reading Angelica Reyes' date of birth aloud. Somewhere in the flat, it's not clear where, a radio is playing 'Be My Baby' by the Ronettes. You catch a glimpse of the window, a streetlamp beyond it, and the rain pouring down.

'Pretty old, though,' Levin goes on. 'I'll ask the coroner to have a look at the back of her knees, and her groin. She might have quit. Look at this, parrying injuries on her hands and forearms. Lots of them.'

The hallway is narrow and short, with a hat shelf on one side, complete with hooks for coats and jackets. A jumble of scarves and gloves is piled on top of it, and on the floor beneath it a dirty rug lined with well-worn boots, light-coloured trainers, and three or four pairs of heels, one of which has wooden wedge heels that look pretty heavy.

Immediately on the right is the bathroom, and at the end of the hall is the only other room. Part of the left-hand wall is given over to the kitchenette: a stovetop and a microwave. The rest of the wall is occupied by a black bookshelf dotted with a few books, photographs, and a wilting pot plant. In the centre of the room is a grey three-piece lounge suite, but no one is paying any attention to it yet. Because opposite, on the right-hand side, is the bed. Angelica Reyes is lying in it, just like in the photographs, but not quite.

'Sorry,' Levin says from out of shot, moving away from the technician's camera. 'Can we turn the radio off?'

'Not yet,' someone says. 'We haven't got that far.'

There's a bedside table with a lamp on. There's also a copy of *Vogue* magazine, Jens Lapidus' *Easy Money*, a packet of Marlboro reds, a lighter, and what looks to be about two thousand kronor in hundred and five-hundred notes.

The camera films Angelica Reyes' body. It feels too close, as if you ought to avert your eyes. A phone rings in the background. The coroner arrives. It's five past one in the morning on the thirteenth of October.

The only window in the flat overlooks John Ericssonsgatan, and you can almost make out the building opposite, along with a dark, cloudy strip of sky. No moon.

I note the blood splattered on the bed, the floor, and the victim's skin. What was Grim's involvement with this?

In front of us, lying on the table next to the computer, is some of the introductory material; Birck studies the files, plastic wallets, and reports with a tired look in his eyes, and asks how we're supposed to get through all this, where we should start.

I haven't really got that far.

'We'll follow the investigation's original direction, so that we know what they did and didn't do. When that doesn't get us anywhere, as we know it won't, we can go back and see what they missed.'

Birck nods despondently.

'What's up?' I ask.

'Would they have missed anything? Levin was the one in charge then.'

'Otherwise they would've found the perpetrator.'

'Yeah, but ...'

'I know what you're getting at.' Old secrets. Some of which had caught up with Charles Levin in the end.

'Okay. Good. That's all I'm asking for.' A weary chuckle. 'So, Levin arrives at five past one in the morning on the thirteenth of October. When do they find out who she is?'

'They know as soon as they lay eyes on her. She was known to us.'

'There must be a biography or something in the notes of the preliminary investigation,' Birck says. 'Can you dig it out?'

I get out of my chair and sift through the rest of the first box. Birck hauls a second one onto the table, opens it, and, under a series of binders containing transcripts of interviews with the deceased's family, just waiting there: the story of Angelica Reyes.

8

Who was she? That's the thing about dead people — they can't speak for themselves. The story of her life has to be told through bureaucratic records, diary entries, and the testimonies of people whom, one way or another, she knew.

'Born 1986,' Birck reads from the biography. 'In Santiago, Chile. Only child. At three, she and her family move to Stockholm, and to one of the tower blocks out in Hallunda. Her dad works as a mechanic, her mother as a cleaner at Huddinge Hospital.'

Hallunda can be a tough place for a little kid, but Angelica Reyes managed pretty well. She learnt to read and write early; teachers wrote about her projects, her thirst for knowledge, how much she enjoyed school. At junior and middle school, she was a very good pupil. Several of her teachers mentioned how pupils had to switch desks and change neighbours once a month, and from this it became clear she was also very generous.

'Listen to this,' Birck says, tapping the paper with his fingertip. *'You could see that whoever happened to be sitting next to Angelica Reyes was bolstered by her. Her peers' performances improved for as long as they were still alongside Angelica.'*

Birck looks up.

'Lovely,' I say. 'And a bit sad.'

She trained regularly at the local gymnastics club, and early on she finished third in a competition. She dreamed of becoming an air hostess. An unusual dream for a little girl in one of Hallunda's tower blocks, but perhaps not that surprising. Angelica Reyes wanted to see the world. In her teens, she'd developed a wanderlust that had never really waned.

It's not easy to follow those incremental changes after so much time has passed; it's more a case of feeling your way to them. Her wanderlust remained, but apparently started to manifest itself in other ways. A friend explained how Angelica loved smoking marijuana, even at the age of fifteen. Is that true? Could be, you have to assume.

A little while later, Birck and I listen to the sound recordings placed at the heart of the preliminary investigation. They were considered crucial to the overall picture of her. The interviews are stored as digital sound files on a thumb drive, and Birck clicks between them with a confused look on his face.

'They're not in any kind of order,' he mutters. 'Jeez, I can't find anything here. There's no way this is Levin's doing.'

'It probably isn't,' I say. 'He didn't like computers. I'd guess it was an assistant who put this together.'

The files are of various people talking about Angelica Reyes, and as she approaches her teens they describe a person who is changing, changing in ways that are seemingly difficult to pin down.

'She became, you know,' one of her classmates from middle and high school says, 'well, things started to happen around her. Everything was fine until we started in sixth grade, I think it was. She started smoking — cigarettes, I mean — and drinking. She went to parties with older guys, that sort of thing. She was skiving off all the fucking time, you know, and then before long she was in the smoking area every day, if she even made it to school. Then, in sixth or seventh grade I think, this thing happened. She claimed that she'd been at a party and these two guys had raped her. I think that's what pushed her over the edge, or whatever you say, because no one believed her. By then there were all sorts of rumours flying around about her. She was a whore, a slut, this, that, and the other. Maybe she'd had sex with them, but rape? Everyone laughed at the idea. She didn't report it to the police, and it was her word against theirs anyway. When a few months later it turned out that she was still hanging out with them — the guys who raped her — getting stoned with them and even staying over at one of their places, everyone saw that as evidence that it had never happened. And anyway, whichever version was the truth, she still looked like a nutter — who the fuck hangs out with people they've been raped by? If, on the other hand, she hadn't been raped, who the fuck falsely accuses people of crimes that serious? She was after attention, that was it. That was our take on it.'

Then the classmate on the tape goes quiet, before adding:

'I haven't ever given it much thought. In fact, it's only just occurred to me, but by then she might not have had anyone else to turn to except them.'

Birck stares at the computer screen.

'Jesus Christ.' He turns his attention to the rest of the material. 'Is the rape in the records?'

It isn't. There was never a formal complaint, and no witnesses, just hearsay. A crime that disappears, like so many others.

Before long, her parents could no longer cope. They received comprehensive support from Social Services, without any significant impact. She developed a benzo addiction and in September 2003 she was remanded into a secure juvenile care home. When she emerged a few months later, she picked up exactly where she'd left off.

According to Stockholm's Prostitution Unit, it was about then that she started guzzling increasing quantities of alcohol and tablets.

'Autumn 2007,' I read aloud. 'She's placed into care, and when she's due for release, Social Services are notified. They write: *Reyes reports that she is currently of no fixed abode and has been staying with friends and acquaintances. Crosschecks with the Prostitution Unit and the Vice Squad reveal that the individuals concerned are known prostitutes and suspected fences.'*

'Well I'll be …' Birck says drily.

The subsequent twists and turns in Angelica Reyes' life are rather predictable: first a conviction for possession, then discovered inside an apartment that was known to house a brothel and instructed to leave. She received treatment for her amphetamine addiction, but before long she was combining speed and opiates, so-called *speedballing*, according to her medical records. Somewhere along the line, her social worker, who was interviewed on countless occasions after the murder, managed to secure Angelica an apartment at John Ericssonsgatan 16, her registered address from the first of March 2009.

It's at that address, in her bed in that apartment, that she was found stabbed to death in the early hours of the thirteenth of October 2010.

Hallunda, Norsborg, Salem. The three vast concrete housing estates are different places, yet not really, and I recognise myself in Angelica Reyes' biography. I can see us there, me and Grim, almost passing through the scenes where it all played out. We're a few years older, but not many.

I think about Angelica Reyes, being thirteen or fourteen and being raped. That was the kind of story you'd hear out round our way, about people getting into trouble. And bad jokes of course. Someone once said that Norsborg's county bird emblem is a fucking police helicopter. Someone else, better read than his mates, didn't get it and protested: 'Norsborg isn't a county, you idiot.'

'Right,' Birck says, rounding up. 'So they realise straightaway that they're looking at a dead prostitute. The money lying on the bedside table, two thousand kronor, suggests that she'd recently had a client. They think they're looking for a punter.'

'Or a pimp.'

'It's almost never the pimp. The girls are worth too much to them. My money's on a punter. He pays up, and Reyes puts the money on table. Then they get on with it, until something happens to make this punter see red.'

'Like what?'

'Well, what do you reckon? Like he's struggling to get it up, and Reyes makes some comment? He might think it's a dig, sometimes that's all it takes. I think it happens quite a lot — that when they do get the chance to perform, they can't. She has the misfortune to meet a client who has violent tendencies that night, someone who is convinced that his fragile masculinity is inextricably linked to the equipment between his legs.'

'I think that was the working theory that emerged then,' I say as I flip though the material in front of us, looking for the surveillance memo written before the first briefing.

'Probably because that's what happened. It nearly always is in cases like this. They never managed to find the right punter, that's all. What this is — and you'll have to excuse my lack of political correctness here, because I don't give a shit — is a typical whore-murder, which they have the misfortune of not being able to solve.' He looks at me. 'But you don't believe that.'

'I don't know.' I stop looking through the material, and check the time. 'But it is nearly lunch.'

'Which reminds me, I'm having lunch with an acquaintance from the National Board of Forensic Medicine. He's a real demon when it comes to DNA, perhaps he can help us with this.' He laughs sarcastically. 'I mean, we're going to need all the help we can get. What are you doing?'

I'm meeting Sam.

9

You have to learn to live with each other, I think to myself, sitting opposite her at one of the window tables in Mäster Anders' restaurant, halfway through lunch. If you do that, you can do anything, I think.

Learning to live with someone else. That's the hardest part.

'I'm not saying we have to have kids now,' I say, 'but maybe we should be talking about it.'

'We *have* talked about it.'

'Don't you want to?'

Sam puts a bit of pork schnitzel into her mouth and chews slowly.

'I was the one who brought it up in the first place,' she says.

'Exactly. What's changed?'

'I ...' She sips her low-alcohol beer. 'I don't know.'

'Is it something to do with me?'

'I've never liked your shoes.'

'My *shoes?*'

She laughs.

'Kidding.'

'Dead funny.'

'Sorry.' She reaches for my hand. The palm of her hand is smooth and warm. 'I do that when I'm nervous.'

'I know.'

She *was* the one who brought up the subject of kids. That's how we ended up getting Kit, our cat, who is basically useless in terms of doing anything other than wandering around looking gormless. The idea, I think, was to see whether we could manage to share the responsibility of anything more alive than pot plants. Until a while back, I was scared of it, but then, I don't know, something changed. Something inside me.

We spent a week together in Athens at the end of the summer. We were going to sunbathe, go swimming, and visit the city's ancient worlds, admire its art and architecture. But then the Greek economy collapsed, and not long afterwards came the reports of the refugee disasters in the Aegean Sea. We couldn't cancel the trip, so we decided to go anyway and see whether we could do anything to help. We handed out toys and bottled water to the few refugee families we saw, but that was the most disturbing thing about the whole experience: just how few refugee families we saw. You didn't notice them at all. They'd hit the mainland and then — *poof* — disappear.

Exploring a city where people disappear like that isn't terribly appealing, so for the most part we stayed in our hotel room and had sex. One time, Sam emerged from the bathroom afterwards with a troubled look on her face, and with her slim, tattooed body glistening in the warmth of the room.

'I think I'm ovulating,' she said.

For the rest of our time in Athens, I was walking around with something in my chest, a feeling I couldn't put into words. She didn't get pregnant, to her obvious relief, while I was ... well, what was I? Not disappointed, that's not the right word. I don't know ...

'What are you up to at the moment, anyway?' Sam asks, breaking my train of thought. 'At work, I mean.'

'Are we finished talking about kids?'

'Leo. Give me a bit of time. What are you doing at work?'

'I'm on an old case. It's going to be transferred soon, which Morovi sees as a personal defeat. We've got a week to solve it.'

'Who had the case to begin with?'

'Levin.'

Sam's lips form a little 'o'.

'I understand,' she says.

We carry on eating, not talking about kids or work. It's nice, but I still feel a bit down. I spent so long working so close to Levin, first at Violent Crime and then during his short spell in charge of Internal Affairs, yet there was so much that he never told me.

Then he died.

Levin died. Was murdered. And I was injured in the operation to arrest the perpetrator. Which was how I ended up in hospital, which was when Grim disappeared.

For a few days that summer, the tabloids and broadsheets all ran the extensive search for the missing John Grimberg as their top story. Several times I heard the chopping of rotor blades outside my hospital window. I would convince myself that the whirr was accompanied by sirens, yet each time I had to accept that although the rotors were real, the sirens were coming from inside my own head. A desperate search was in progress, and hundreds of officers from across Greater Stockholm had been tasked with finding him. They had Stockholm's Central Station under surveillance, as well as the two main airports, and were attempting to deploy everything at their disposal, from dog units to mobile-phone records, but to no avail.

I lay there smiling to myself in my hospital bed, while no one was looking. He stayed disappeared, I didn't hear a peep out of him.

Christ, I need to tell her.

'There's something I think I'd ...'

'I'm not really hungry,' she interrupted.

'Huh. Me neither.'

'And we live pretty close to here,' she went on. 'And I don't need to be at the gallery for another half an hour.'

'And?' I say, confused, my thoughts elsewhere.

'Leo.' She leans across the table. 'I'm asking to go back to ours so that you can fuck me.'

When I arrive back at HQ afterwards, Birck gives me a funny look.

'What's up with you then? You look ... high, almost.'

'How was lunch at National Forensics?'

'Not a patch on yours, by the looks of it.'

10

The room down in the archive soon feels like a whole different world. Above ground, it's November, and 2015, but down here, behind the glass walls, it's October, and 2010. The serial rapist in Örebro has been arrested, and wherever you go you hear 'Dancing on My Own' by Robyn, or Eminem and Rihanna's 'Love the Way You Lie'. The Swedish election results are just a few weeks old. The financial crisis lies draped over the globe like a sodden blanket.

It's in that world that news of the murder of Angelica Reyes arrives, and it does so carefully and discreetly. On day one, a half-page story in the paper; day three, a single paragraph; day four, nothing. She is forgotten.

The next week, Birck and I work on the case from first thing till late, day after day. There are no signs of any errors or mistakes in the investigation. It was unsuccessful nonetheless.

The crime scene itself reveals less than might've been hoped for. This ought to be a cause for concern, yet the documents show no signs of that, not at first.

A few textile fibres are recovered from the rug, the bed, and Angelica Reyes' abdomen — by her navel. They are likely to have come from the perpetrator, but they cannot be linked to anyone or anything. Not only that, one of the bloodstains comes from someone other than the victim. This is also presumed to have come from the assailant, but repeated trawls of the DNA register draw only blanks.

What ought to be helpful is the mobile phone. It belongs to Angelica Reyes and is discovered in Kronoberg Park in the early hours of the thirteenth of October. A mother taking her five-year-old to preschool stops and picks the phone up off the ground. It's soon handed over to the police, lifeless and dirty, rendered useless by a night out in the rain. No fingerprints, but traces of blood. Angelica's blood.

My pulse is quickening. Kronoberg Park is sealed off while an extensive search for forensic evidence is conducted. Nothing is recovered. The rain along with the hundreds or perhaps even thousands of people who have moved through the area since the time of the crime have destroyed the little evidence it might have been possible to recover.

A strange article from her home captures the imagination. A little USB thumb drive, black, matt finish, no cap.

It contains seventy-two childhood images, from 1986 to 2001, many of them scanned: Angelica Reyes, whose roots spread from Santiago to Hallunda; photos of a sunny Chile, a smiling family in a courtyard somewhere; in another, indoors this time, a chubby little child crawling across the floor. Pictures from a first bike ride with training wheels, a family dinner, and then — all of a sudden — we're in Sweden. You can tell by the light — colder, not as close. From there on, it's images of growing up amidst the concrete, rows of tower blocks, a last-day-of-school photo showing Angelica Reyes laughing, revealing her white teeth. She has slight acne. It's 1998. She's rarely on her own in a photo; you'd probably never guess what lay ahead for her. But perhaps there was a clue there — the look in her eyes, a longing to get away.

Interviews with her relatives reveal nothing more than this: in 2006, she went through the photo album in her parents' flat, picked out a few pictures, and had them digitised. She wanted to be able to keep them with her, she said. Further investigations confirm this — she used to keep the USB stick in her handbag.

That's not where it was found. Instead, it was discovered behind Angelica Reyes' bed, in a hole in the wall just big enough to hide it in. She probably made the hole herself — the estate agent who inspected the flat before she moved in failed to mention it.

Angelica Reyes doesn't own a computer, which makes it all that little bit more confusing. Since there are no signs that the USB has been used or moved, it's unlikely to be linked to the crime itself, yet in the files Levin has added lots of notes and question marks about that particular detail. *Perhaps she wanted to store it in a more secure place than her handbag?* he proposes tentatively. Then: *Pictures can often be very important to people — sometimes it's all they have.*

Birck turns a page in one of the files, scratches his head, and looks tenderly at the cigarette packet I'm spinning between my fingers.

'A mobile phone, a few fibres, a whole array of blood spatter which cannot be tied to anyone, that can't even be usefully analysed by Forensics — okay, there's a decent DNA sample, but with zero matches in the database — and a USB stick full of pictures of Santiago and Hallunda. That's all they've got?'

'Looks that way,' I say. 'But they seem pretty optimistic anyway.'

'And my contact at National Forensics had nothing for us,' Birck goes on. 'Cold,' he said. 'The Reyes case is ice cold.' Which it is.

It is. But back then, in 2010, it's burning hot.

In the days after the murder, the team chart her last movements. They talk to friends, social workers, and then, later, old classmates and teachers. They are shown the pictures from the USB stick, and asked whether any of them stand out. They don't.

Angelica didn't keep a journal, but they get hold of her diary via one of her friends. Each side is scanned in and stored. It doesn't look as though she used it very much. Perhaps she didn't have that many appointments, at least not of the kind you write in your diary.

Together, Birck and I continue searching through the investigation. He does so with bored nonchalance, while I do so with my own reasons that I have to keep to myself. Grim is here, somewhere. But where? Under what name? I don't know where to start.

On Tuesday afternoon, I get a text from him.

it's been a week, have you started on the investigation?

no

are you lying to me?

no

I stare at the screen, waiting for his response.

why haven't you started yet? That's it.

why is this so important?

10pm, same place

11

At the time of her death, Angelica Reyes has a large social network. She has lots of friends, by no means all of them in the same line of work, as well as a host of pimps and dealers, not to mention the countless punters she has met over the years.

Levin and his colleagues never manage to contact all of them — that would be an almost impossible task — but they do manage to speak to an impressively large number. They concentrate on those closest to her, and above all her clients. *It is one of them*, a female detective declares during the intelligence meeting on the fifteenth of October, three days into the case, a statement noted and underlined by Levin in the minutes. It may be that he trusts her judgement, or that he wants to confirm the theory for himself.

One of the victim's best friends is named Jonna Danielsson. A woman of around the same age, from a similar background, who moves in the same circles. There's a copy of her passport photo in the interview notes, which Birck pulls out. Her face has clean, symmetrical lines, round, deep-set eyes, a small but plump mouth. Her hair is cut in a strict pageboy hairstyle.

'Is she still alive?' he asks.

'Dunno. I've met her twice, but the second time was years ago.'

Once in the Kronoberg remand centre, in 2011, and the second time in a junkie doss house in Vasastan in 2012. On both occasions she looked awful, but not quite as bad as you might expect. I haven't seen or heard from her since.

'I do remember that she was bloody crucial,' I say. 'To the investigation, I mean.'

Jonna Danielsson's account begins about twenty-four hours before the murder. Angelica Reyes sleeps at her place, out in Norsborg. The following day — the day of the murder — they meet up at two in the afternoon for a late lunch in a restaurant not far from Kungsholmstorg. They remain there until about half-three, before going their separate ways. At around midnight, she arrives at the apartment on John Ericssonsgatan to drop off an outfit that belongs to Reyes.

Her voice sounds calm and soft on the tape, the kind of voice you might expect a hostess at a classy country club to have, with an intonation belying many hours of practice:

'She'd told me to come around then — midnight — because we're usually both free at that time. Angelica often has a client between say five and seven, something like that, another about nine, and a third at eleven, if she's lucky.'

According to Jonna Danielsson, the punters contact a pimp, who in turn contacts Angelica Reyes or one of the others in his stable — her word — before getting back to the punter with a time and a place.

Angelica Reyes' mobile phone receives a call at five thirty in the evening. The masts carrying her call indicate that she was at home at the time. Half an hour later, the first client of the evening has arrived, a man investigators manage to track down with the help of Vice Squad and the Prostitution Unit. He has an alibi and is immediately eliminated from inquiries. Same goes for the next punter, who sees Angelica Reyes between nine and half-past.

It's when we come to the evening's possible third client that things start to get interesting. Unfortunately, this is also the point at which the sequence of events and their timings become much more vague.

And confusing.

At about quarter-to eleven, Angelica Reyes' phone rings again. She answers, and it lasts for less than a minute. The call was never successfully traced, but it did come from a mobile phone — that much can be deduced from the type of signal. Presumably it was a call from her pimp, informing her that a third customer would be arriving soon.

After that, it's empty, dark, until Jonna Danielsson arrives at John Ericssonsgatan 16 around midnight. Standing by the lift, she hears an intense tapping sound in the stairwell and spots a man reaching the ground floor before leaving the building in a hurry.

'He didn't see me,' she says. 'That's for sure. He didn't even look in my direction. But I saw him.'

She does find it odd, but doesn't give it much thought. Instead, she takes the lift up to the third floor and walks over to Angelica's door. It's ajar.

At nine minutes past midnight, a call comes in to the police control room. The caller is Jonna Danielsson; she states her name. Then, sounding remarkably composed on the tape, she explains that she has found her friend Angelica Reyes dead in her apartment. At this point, things get confusing, because as Jonna Danielsson is standing there with the phone in her hand, a patrol car arrives in the rain and parks up outside John Ericssonsgatan 16. There's no way they could get there that fast.

Someone else has already had time to contact the police and inform them that a dead woman is lying on the third floor of that same address.

How anyone other than the murderer could know that?

That's the question.

12

'Hold on,' Birck says, his eyes skipping back and forth between two pieces of paper, one in each hand. 'Control get the call about a dead person at nine minutes past twelve. That's when Jonna Danielsson calls. Confusion ensues, because operators have already sent a car to the scene, after a previous alarm from an unknown person four minutes *earlier* — which would make it five past.'

'That's right. Danielsson's call is the second one to come in.'

'Who makes the *first?*'

It could be the same man that Jonna Danielsson noticed while waiting for the lift, the one hurrying down the steps at full pelt and who might be the murderer. Subsequently Levin dedicates a large tranche of the investigation's budget on tracking him down, while an audio technician spends hours analysing the recording.

'Dead woman at John Ericssonsgatan 16,' the first call begins. 'Third floor. Hurry.'

'John Ericssonsgatan 16,' the operator recaps in a neutral tone.

In the background, you can hear the operator typing commands into the computer, and saying:

'Dead woman. Are you there … ?'

'Hurry,' the voice interrupts.

'And you, what is your name …'

That's as far as the operator gets. The call ends.

Birck stares at the screen.

'Weird,' he says, then takes a swig of coffee from his mug. 'I think the voice sounds a bit … unnatural.'

'That occurred to me, too. A bit strained, almost. Play it back again.'

The same words, and sounds. Tones reverberate off the glass walls as we listen. It's taken a long time to go through all of it, even focusing only on the most obvious material. In a few hours' time, I'm meeting Grim.

'Yes, definitely something,' Birck says. 'Why does he want to disguise his voice?'

'They assume this is the perpetrator,' I say.

'Exactly. Me, too. This is our man, I think.'

'But that's a weird assumption. Why would the perpetrator contact the police?'

'They often do.'

'Sure, but why in this case?'

'Because this is some terrified punter who only realises what he's done after the fact and is racked with guilt at seeing her lying there, dead and bloody and fucked up, and who wants someone to come and clear it all up as quickly as possible. It's happened before.'

'He hardly sounds shaken, though.'

'Right, how about this,' Birck says. 'Let's say that the person making the call to the police has nothing whatsoever to do with this. Why wouldn't he say who he is?'

That's a good question. And a tough one.

'Because he has something else to hide?'

Birck rolls his eyes.

'That's your imagination.'

I press play, listen to the short call again.

'He doesn't sound like a man who's just taken someone's life. Admittedly he is distorting his voice — but he's calm enough to do so. He sounds cool and collected.'

'That's what you're hearing,' says Birck. 'What I'm hearing

43

is someone *straining* to sound like that. It's reasonable to assume that this is the same person that Jonna Danielsson sees in the stairwell. There are no reports of anyone else moving around the building immediately after the crime. You're on board with that, right?'

'Yes.'

'So what if we start from the other end? With the man on the stairs. Who is that?'

At that end, it turns out, everything gets weirder still, and perhaps we're just taking another step further into the maze.

Jonna Danielsson is at the base of the stairwell. She presses the button that slowly sends the lift down its shaft. As she waits, the man makes his way down the stairs, and the tapping of footsteps echoes around her. He's about 180-centimetres tall, with short, dark hair; he's pale and skinny, with defined cheek- and jawbones and a pointy nose. Dark-blue jeans and a light-green unbuttoned military jacket. Inside that, Jonna Danielsson catches a glimpse of a white T-shirt. His clothes are clean and his hands are empty. Without looking around, the man makes for the door and leaves. She doesn't see which direction he takes.

'*When one person kills another, as in this case, with repeated knife blows,*' Birck reads aloud from meeting notes made by my old boss, '*it is impossible for the assailant to avoid blood spatter. It gets everywhere. Of course, it is possible that Danielsson doesn't notice spatter on his jeans, since blood on dark-blue denim is easy to miss, but the light-green coat is clean, too. As, crucially, is the white T-shirt. Blood on a light-green coat becomes dark purple, and you might, from a distance, not pick it up. But dark red spatter on a white T-shirt stands out crimson and clear.*'

The man has no rucksack or bag, according to Jonna Danielsson, which rules out him having got changed afterwards.

'But he might not have had any clothes on when he did it?'

Birck ventures. 'If this is a punter we're talking about then it would be logical for him to be naked.'

'That's the theory they work from,' I say, tapping further down on the page Birck has in front of him, where Levin notes that this has been pointed out to him by one of the detectives. 'Or else it's not the perpetrator she sees, but someone else.'

'And who would that be?' Birck puts the sheet of paper down and opens his arms wide. 'A punter pays Reyes for sex. Perhaps he doesn't have an awful lot to work with, if you get my drift. Reyes points this out, which badly wounds his fragile masculinity — and he loses it. Only afterwards does he realise what he's done, at which point he gets dressed, calls the police, and rushes off down the stairs.' Birck looks at me. 'Something like that.'

'That's what they arrive at in 2010, too.'

'One last little problem — finding him.' Birck yawns. 'And they never do.'

They didn't. But perhaps they came close.

A promising moment arises ten days after the murder, on the twenty-second of October, as Levin is eating lunch down in the canteen with parts of the preliminary investigation on the table in front of him.

A colleague from Vice Squad approaches him and asks if he'd like some company. Levin puts his file to one side, but once they've finished and are about to head off, his colleague asks what he was grimacing about when she arrived. He hands the plastic wallet over: the first page details Jonna Danielsson's description of the unknown stranger in the stairwell.

'Oh,' the colleague from Vice Squad says. 'Sounds like the guy I saw at a party a few weeks back.'

The party, she goes on, was held in a basement in Nacka, and hosted a collection of Stockholm's finest shady characters: musicians, authors, criminals, addicts, and troublemakers. She was there along with a duo from Surveillance because three of the guests were suspected punters with connections to a particular pimp who they were keen to bring in. The problem was, they had no idea what this pimp looked like. At the bar, she started talking to a man she thought might be the one they were looking for, but before long she realised she'd got it wrong and left him to it. What he was doing there, she doesn't know, but he did give a name: Karl Hamberg.

'This is the man who matches the description?' Levin asks.

'I don't know whether or not it's the same person. But it's a small world we're talking about, and the description is bang on. Right down to the military jacket, which, if I remember rightly, was unbuttoned then, too.'

Over the next few days, Levin and his colleagues conduct extensive searches for a man named Karl Hamberg, but find nothing, apart from a collection of namesakes who can all be eliminated from their inquiries.

That name is a cul-de-sac, or rather a little corner somewhere in the depths of the maze.

Birck stretches and says he needs the toilet.

'After that I'm going home,' he adds. 'And tomorrow we're going to have to talk to some fucking people, just for a change.'

'Who?'

'The ones who worked on the case, for example.'

'I've promised Morovi that we'll report back to her first thing tomorrow.'

'Right.' Birck's eyelids flutter. 'And what are we going to say?'

'I don't know. But I'll see you at eight.'

He heads off. It's getting on for ten; time for my second meeting with Grim.

I flip through the papers without finding anything that might be able to help us. Karl Hamberg. A dark-haired, pale man. *Dead woman at John Ericssonsgatan 16. Third floor. Hurry.* Someone doesn't want to reveal themselves, yet contacts the police to tell them what he's seen. Who would do such a thing, and why?

13

It's about one minute to ten when the text arrives: four digits, and the words *top floor*.

I'm already here. Maybe he knows that. Next to the door on Tjärhovsgatan is a little keypad, and after I've entered the number the lock buzzes. I open the door and step inside.

The sound of my footsteps cracks between the walls of the stairwell. On the top floor, I search for any sign of movement in the gloom, but find none. Instead, I see a lone sliver of light on the floor from a door left ajar.

I push it with my foot. The sliver of light widens, weak, as if from a useless table lamp.

'Come in, and close the door behind you, please.'

I do as he says and try to get my bearings inside the flat. It feels as though someone's just moved out, having left behind all the furniture they wanted rid of: an old IKEA desk over on my left. On it, sure enough, is a table lamp, next to which there's a bottle of whisky and two glasses. In front of the desk is an office chair on castors. At the far end of the room, there's a mattress and a blanket, a faded fridge, and a little table with electric cooking rings on it.

Grim is sitting on the chair by the desk, and he pours a dram of whisky into each glass.

'Do you live here?'

'It's a long story. Want some? Don't stand over there by the door, come in and sit yourself down.'

I guess he's referring to the mattress; there's nowhere else to sit. It's more comfortable than it looks. When I get close to my friend, it's all I can do to resist the sudden impulse to touch him. I take the glass from his outstretched hand and take a little sip. The whisky brings a pleasant heat to my chest.

'Have you started looking at the investigation?' he asks.

'Why is it so important?'

'Because ...' Grim runs a hand through his hair. 'It's hard to explain. *Have* you started?'

'Not yet.'

'Why not?'

'I wanted to talk to you first.'

'About what?'

'Do I really need to say it again? I want to know what you've got to do with the Angelica murder.'

'You think I was involved.'

'Well, weren't you?'

Grim sighs and leans back on his chair. He looks so different now. And something about that hurts.

'Weird,' Grim says. 'Me and you, sitting here like this. Isn't it?'

'You're acting as if it was perfectly natural. *That's* weird.'

'I know.' Grim bites his bottom lip. 'It's ... I don't know where to start. I don't know what to say.'

'You escaped.'

He puts the bottle down and raises an unnaturally dark eyebrow, which nevertheless suits his face.

'I escaped. And?'

I look down at my hands, trying to work out whether there's a question of some sort hiding in my thoughts.

'Why?'

'If you knew what it was like to be deprived of your liberty, you wouldn't be asking that question.'

Grim gets up from the office chair. It creaks horribly. He pushes his hands into the pockets of his jeans and stretches his back with a grimace.

'It's not easy, putting on weight. I'm so stiff nowadays. It's the cortisone, you just swell up and it distorts your appearance. Very effective.'

'How did you get hold of it?'

'Well, safe to say I didn't buy it at the chemist's.'

I look around. There's no wardrobe or chest in here, I wonder where he keeps his clothes. Maybe he doesn't have any. Something isn't right here. The walls are thick, and cold.

'No windows,' I say, when I realise.

'Great, isn't it?'

'So do you live here now?'

Grim laughs, as though it's an absurd question, but it isn't. The only absurd thing here is that no one has seen as much as a hair off his head for a year and a half and then, suddenly one autumn evening, he's here again, talking about a five-year-old murder.

'It was like this,' he says.

He had to get out of Sweden. He doesn't want to tell me how he did it, and I don't really know why he had to.

He made his way through Denmark to Germany, then spent the summer laying low in a little town south of Berlin. He enjoyed his freedom and kept his nose clean, not even crossing the street on red unless everyone around him did; then he went with the flow to avoid sticking out. Someone too well behaved is just as conspicuous as a severe delinquent. For those on the run, it's all about being as visible as everyone else, because that way you don't get seen. That worked for a while, but then in the autumn the local drugs squad raided the block where Grim was holed up. Despite it being nothing to do with him, it was enough to scare him away and get his thoughts ticking.

He had enjoyed his freedom. That raid made him feel like a little rat. A rat who ended up in Munich, then Warsaw, Amsterdam, and finally Copenhagen. False documents all the way. By this point, it had been a year and three months since he'd escaped from St Göran's, and something was wrong.

'You can't stay on the run forever,' he says. 'It will send you round the bend. If I've learnt one thing, it's that. I would never have thought that way five years ago. I don't know, though, I'm the fucking wrong side of thirty-five and I'll be forty in a few years. Something about the passage of time has made me … Oh, I don't fucking know. Everything's started to feel different.'

'So you came back.'

A weak smile, impossible to decipher.

'I came back.'

Aiding and abetting, I think to myself again. That's what this is. That's what I'm guilty of, unless I do something about it.

'I'm trying …' He laughs. 'I'm trying to sort my life out. What little is left of it. If possible.' He slumps back into the chair. 'And that's tied to Angelica Reyes.'

'How?'

'If we're going to be able to talk about that, you're going to have to have looked at the files.'

I take a deep breath, as if readying myself, but it sounds more like a sigh.

'What if I tell you that I have started looking at them then?'

A new smile spreads its way across Grim's lips.

'I knew it.'

'So tell me.'

'Why didn't you want to admit that you'd started?'

I stand up from the mattress.

'I'm not up for this, Grim.'

'Eh?'

'This ... whatever this is. The game, the sport. Friendship, if that's what we have, is so tightly bound up with loyalty, and you are constantly testing my loyalty. I test yours, too, I'm the same, I know that. But I can't be arsed. If you're not planning to tell me what it's all about, then I'll be off.'

I can't say that without looking away, like giving my brother an ultimatum. He's the only one who understands me, and I'm at risk of losing him. Perhaps hearing this feels the same way for him, but I've got no choice. It can't go on the way it always has.

I look down at him. I sense a vulnerability he'd never normally exhibit.

'Have you started looking at the case?'

'Yes, I told you.'

'Well in that case you ought to find me in the files,' he says. 'I don't know where exactly, or what the information points to. I might not be referred to by name, not my own, but I'm sure I'm in there. And when they — or you — find me, it will probably look like I did it. But it wasn't me. I don't want you to think it was.'

It's always so complicated — trying to work out whether Grim's telling the truth or not. He has spent long periods living as someone else, which leaves its mark on a person, makes him perfectly at ease with suppressing the truth. Identifying one of his lies takes something else, a sort of hunch.

Sirens wail, very close by. The sound forces its way through the walls and makes Grim go stiff. He opens one of the desk drawers and pulls out the knife.

'I think we should have a look.'

'Where?'

He grabs the bottle and points the knife blade at the ceiling.

14

Above Stockholm, the winds are sharper. The city extends like a rug of lights in every direction. To the north, the black shimmering waters of Lake Mälaren, to the south, the dome of the Globe Arena glows orange, and beyond that I can almost make out the concrete housing estates on the outskirts of the city.

We've come up through a hole in the roof, and with the bottle in one hand and the knife in the other, Grim is cautiously approaching the edge. Down on the street, the blue lights flash quickly and clearly, and the sirens bounce between the frontages, mixing with the background hum of the traffic.

'What is it?'

'A road accident, I think.'

He puts the knife down and takes a swig from the bottle. The wind catches his hair and our clothes. We sit down on a ledge. He hands me the bottle, and I drink some whisky, more greedily than before, perhaps because of the cold. Something's not right here. Something doesn't add up.

'You came back because you couldn't face being on the run anymore,' I say. 'And the first thing you do is to start asking questions about Angelica Reyes. Why? I just can't get my head round it.'

Grim pulls the zip on his jacket right up, stuffs his hands in his pocket, and pushes his chin against his chest. Aside from that, he doesn't seem bothered by the weather, like he's well used to the cold. Perhaps that's from his time on the streets, as an addict, just one of the many things that I've never asked him about.

'You know you met her, right?' he says. 'One night, a long time ago.'

'Angelica Reyes?'

'She wasn't very old at the time, maybe ten or eleven. It was after a summer party, a gig at the youth centre. We were on our way home, and we saw her waiting for a bus.'

'The one that nearly got run over?'

'Yes.'

'Was that *her*?'

'That was Angelica Reyes.'

Two headlights appear round a corner, tyres squealing until they get a firm grip on the tarmac. The girl is stepping out onto the road, headphones on — big ball-shaped ones. Me and Grim rush over and throw her out of the way.

I'm sixteen and we're drunk, but not in as bad a state as the driver of the car. As the vehicle careens on through Salem, its tail-lights bounce like two red blobs in the darkness. The girl's long dark hair falls in waves around her shoulders. Her headphones have fallen off and are resting awkwardly around her neck. She's tiny, a child, but she's done her best to disguise that fact with her clothes and her makeup. It half works. Her face is symmetrical and beautiful, her features well-defined. Her eyes are wide open and they shimmer in the cold light of the bus shelter.

An ignominious moment. Two kids, stinking of Russian vodka and weed, have just saved a child's life.

'Are you okay?' Grim asks.

The girl's cheeks flush red and she looks at Grim as though he's just asked her to kiss him.

'Good, thanks.'

I ask if she's getting the bus. She says she is.

'Where do you live?' Grim asks.

'Hallunda.'

'What are you doing *here* then?'

She scowls.

'My friend has just moved out here.'

'And you're going home on your own?'

The girl looks down at her shoes, mumbles something about her friend's dad who was supposed to give her a lift but couldn't because his car broke down. Then he fell asleep on the sofa.

The young Angelica Reyes looks up, cockily.

'But I can take care of myself.'

I get nervous, worried that someone might see us standing here talking to a child. We'd get loads of shit for that.

'We're going,' I say.

Grim turns to the girl.

'Do you know how to get there? Hallunda's a fair old trek.'

She rolls her eyes and puts her headphones back on, but her cheeks stay red. We leave her at the bus stop, and by the time we get back to our block I've almost forgotten all about her. It's one summer night of many, almost twenty years ago.

'Yes,' I say. 'I remember.'

I give him back the bottle. Below us, the sirens have fallen silent, but before long new ones can be heard in the distance. An ambulance, approaching from the west.

'How do you know that was her?'

'We bumped into each other every now and then, over the years. We didn't know each other, that's not what I mean, but it is a pretty small world.'

'So you were acquainted with each other.'

'I wouldn't call it that.'

'So what would you call it then? Is this why you're saying that you turn up in the investigation?'

'Think about it now. What's my name? John Grimberg. What's the next letter of the alphabet after J?'

'K.'

'And after G?'

'H.'

'There you go. K and H.'

I just stare at him, flummoxed at first.

The pieces of the puzzle come together in my head. It's only a matter of hours since I saw the name.

'Karl Hamberg,' I say. 'K.H.'

'Born March '81,' says Grim. 'I can't remember the date anymore. He was registered at an address out in Hässelby. Divorced parents, no siblings. He was self-employed, a tradesman. I never bothered with any more detail than that. He was just a thin shell, nothing more. Someone I used in emergencies.'

'You were there. You were at Angelica Reyes' apartment that night.'

'See what I mean? It looks like I did it.'

Is he the one that did it? After looking at the material from 2010, it's pretty obvious that the man in the stairwell is linked to the crime. Could it be him? I'm not sure I want to know.

I reach for the bottle, unscrew the cap, and take a big gulp.

'My job,' Grim says, 'what I was supposed to do, I mean, was to make her disappear.'

'On whose instructions?'

'Hers. She was the one who wanted it.'

And just like that, almost everything pertaining to Angelica Reyes has changed altogether.

15

She contacted him, thinking his name was Karl Hamberg, but realised who he was as soon as they met up. They both remembered that near miss in Salem. Angelica asked Grim if she'd ever thanked him. For saving her life, that is.

That connection between them made him feel uneasy.

'And yet you went along with it anyway,' I say.

'She said that she could pay.'

Grim was short of money, and had had the Fraud Squad sniffing around for a while, so that he'd had to abandon several of the shells he'd used. He was desperate — in that world, everyone gets desperate, sooner or later — so he said yes.

He asked a few questions, did a bit of reconnaissance and a handful of background checks. He took photos of Angelica and her everyday life. That sounds like pretty comprehensive gathering of information, but it wasn't, not compared to his usual approach. Nor did he see any reason to do any more than that — a prostitute wanted to pay to become invisible, to disappear. Fine. Why? She had her reasons, surely. They always do. The fact that he knew of her was no barrier; not many things are if times are sufficiently hard.

He arranged the ID documents and arrived there at the agreed time — at midnight on the twelfth of October — to push them through her letterbox. That was what he usually did.

When he got there, the door was open.

Yes, alarm bells should've rung, he knows that, he should've got straight out of there, but because it was Angelica, well ... Fuck.

He walked over and opened the door a little wider, took a step or perhaps a few inside the apartment, he doesn't remember *those* details. He saw her lying there in the bed.

Then he rushed down the stairs as fast as his legs would carry him.

'And you called the police.'

'I shouldn't have done that either, but seeing her lying there like that was so fucking ... I thought about her, you know, the girl we met that night in Salem. The girl with the big headphones, who nearly got run over by a pisshead. Something inside me just wouldn't ... I had to do it. Yes, I did it, anonymously, as soon as I got out onto the street.' Grim looks at the bottle, which is still in my hand. He reaches for it and takes a swig, before getting to his feet. 'I shouldn't have done it. After that, I went even further under the radar.' He looks out across the city. 'Shall we head back down?'

'Why did she contact you?' I say. 'Why did she want to disappear?'

'She was scared. I think someone was threatening her. "Somebody's out to get me," was what she said.'

'Right. And? Why was someone out to get her?'

Grim shakes his head.

'That's what she said. But I think ...' He hesitates, opening the hatch in the roof. The loft space appears like a big black hole. 'I think she knew something, or perhaps she'd got hold of something she shouldn't have got hold of.'

'What makes you say that?'

Grim shrugs, smiles weakly.

'A feeling.'

Angelica Reyes was going to disappear. She was being threatened. *Somebody was out to get her.* There may be fragments in the preliminary investigation that point to that, notes in the margin that Birck and I haven't had time to digest, but I doubt it. Levin would never have allowed something like that to stay in the margins.

That's if it's even true. If Grim's telling the truth.

'How are things out in Salem, by the way?' he asks once we're back behind the locked door to his hideaway.

The bottle in his hand is now half-full, and he puts it down on the table.

'How do you mean?'

'Just wondering.'

'You're trying to change the subject.'

'No.'

There's a pleasant swaying sensation in my neck. The whisky's gone to my head, and it feels like warm, wet cotton wool.

'I'm hardly ever there.'

'But your mum, and your brother, is everything alright with them?'

'What do you mean?'

'Just wondering,' he repeats.

I'm not sure it's quite that simple. There's almost always something lurking between the lines when Grim asks a question, but on this occasion I can't make out what it might be.

'They're fine. Nothing much has changed.'

'And your dad?'

'As I said, nothing much has changed.'

'Alzheimer's. Fuck.' He looks at me. 'Have I offered my condolences?'

'He's not dead.'

'I didn't say he was. But is that what it feels like?'

'As if he's dead?'

'Yes.'

No, it doesn't. He's disappearing before my eyes. Evaporating into thin air. That's what it feels like.

'I don't want to talk about it,' I say.

'I'm trying to show that I care.'

'When did Angelica Reyes contact you?'

'I do actually care about you, Leo, even if you don't believe it. Even though it might not seem that way.'

'When,' I repeat, 'did she contact you?'

He looks at me for some time. Sighs. Gives up.

'Two weeks earlier, something like that. End of September. She wanted new ID documents and she could pay. But I've told you that?'

'What else did she say?'

'I did actually ask why, even though I wouldn't normally. There was something about her that … Maybe it was because I recognised her. That's when she told me that someone was out to get her, someone who wasn't going to give up. That it was her only way out.'

'A boyfriend?'

'When it comes to women, it nearly always is. But no. I don't think it was this time. Angelica didn't have a boyfriend — I knew that much — and by the sound of it, she had a pretty good relationship with her ex.'

'So,' I say, recalling Birck's theory, 'a punter then.'

'I should think so.'

It must have had something to do with information. She must've known something, or seen something, or heard someone talking. There's a whole myriad of possibilities. Could that memory stick be the answer? Maybe I should have another look at those pictures. No, both the stick and its contents were examined by technicians and declared untouched. It must be something else, but what?

'You say that you were there, then, when Angelica Reyes was

murdered. Five years ago. What significance does it have now? You said that you were trying to sort your life out and that it's tied up with her. In what way?'

Grim unbuttons his jacket and turns around. His posture slouches.

'This is where it gets a bit tricky.'

Grim left the murder alone, even though it really got to him. He'd liked Angelica.

From a distance, he watched the police investigation and the search for a suspect peter out. That was a relief somehow. He had been *there*. Observant eyes might've noticed him. If the investigation had been nearing success, then he could've been in trouble despite his innocence — it would be difficult to explain it all away. That's before you even got to his business: a counterfeiter and a con man suspected of murder is soon out of work. He assumed that the police knew that someone was after her; that sort of thing tends to emerge during an investigation.

'Then,' he says, 'about three years later, as you know, I ended up in St Göran's after ... Well.'

'We don't need to talk about that.'

There wasn't all that much to do at St Göran's, which might be the reason that he spent so much time thinking. His thoughts turned, as they sometimes do, to the past, and as hard as he tried to steer them away from it, they always returned to the same events, on the twelfth of October 2010.

We all have mysteries in our lives.

This was one of his. It gnawed away at him.

'In hindsight, I can't really explain my motivation,' he says. 'I made a few calls anyway. I had a few contacts who I hoped might remember her and who might've known things that they couldn't reveal at the time, when the case was still warm. That's often the way in that world, people do know things but they don't say anything because they're afraid of getting dragged in. None of those conversations led anywhere, though. Or maybe they did, I don't know, because what happened next might have had something to do with them ... I had ...'

Grim weighs the words in his mouth.

'Yes?' I say.

'A visit.'

At the end of May, last year, a man came to St Göran's. He was in his forties, well-dressed in jeans and a shirt, with dark hair, pale-green eyes, and an angular face. The visit lasted just over fifteen minutes, and the man never gave his name or said what he did. Afterwards, when Grim asked the charge nurse who his visitor had been, the logbook revealed a Lukas Bengtsson, Stockholm Police.

Therein lies a problem.

Grim lets go a smile as he says it:

'There was no Lukas Bengtsson with Stockholm Police.'

16

'This Lukas Bengtsson, if that was his name, said that he wanted to know how much I knew. Or why I was interested in Angelica. That's how he referred to her, first name only. I suspected that he'd known her or something. But he told me to keep away from it. Otherwise I risked ending up in trouble.'

Grim's answer to that was, just as one might expect from him, to snigger and shrug his shoulders. Who'd be able to get at him in St Göran's? It was almost harder to get into the place than to get out.

The man had raised his hands.

'It was easy enough for me,' he said.

'Is that a threat?'

'You can take it however you like.'

Which set Grim to wondering just what was so dangerous about Angelica Reyes' death.

'At this point, this is May last year, she'd been dead for over three and a half years. Old murders go cold quickly, and not just as far as the police are concerned. The Angelica investigation was stone dead. I don't know who he was, never seen the man before, and how he'd got word of my conversations about Angelica I have no idea. Anyway, I ignored him. At least to begin with. But when you're sitting in St Göran's, it's easy to start getting paranoid. I barely dared to leave my room. And not long afterwards,' he added,

'I split. I took my chance, and it wasn't because I didn't feel safe, not exactly. I wanted to get out. I was seriously fucking paranoid, right, but I was desperate for freedom, too.'

I sense that he's troubled, suddenly, can't quite put my finger on it.

'What is it?' I ask.

'I have done so many things that were wrong. I've done ... I've hurt people. But I've come back. I've wanted to come back. Maybe, for once, I've got a chance to do something right.'

'Right?' I say. 'You have a punishment left to serve. The right thing to do would be to walk into the nearest police station and hand yourself in.'

'I can't do that.'

'I could make you do that,' I say.

'No. You couldn't. What's up with you?'

'I don't know whether I trust you or not. You might be lying about all this. You might not even have been on John Ericssonsgatan at the time of the murder. Why should I believe that someone was out to get Reyes?'

'For the same reason that you've already started looking at the investigation. Because you do, you do believe me. And,' he adds, more serious now, 'why would I lie about this? I have nothing to gain from doing that.'

I stare at him for ages. *Is there something else there?*

'I've got to go home. I need to sleep. And think.'

'I can imagine,' he says, crestfallen. 'See you soon?'

'That's up to you, isn't it? Again. I really don't have much of a say in this relationship.'

'*You* chose to look at the investigation.'

I know. I did. I regret it. But I don't say so.

'By the way,' says Grim, 'you haven't come across a list of some kind? In the records, I mean.'

'A list? No, what would be on it?'

'I thought that maybe she kept a list of her customers. They sometimes do. That might help you.'

'You think a punter threatened her, scared her so badly that she wanted to cut loose like that?'

That's what it is. That's what's gnawing away at me. The idea that someone like Reyes would let herself be influenced by a simple punter. I don't think so.

'I don't know,' says Grim. 'Maybe it depends on who the punter was.'

17

Wednesday comes, bringing cold and rain. When I get to Violent Crime Unit, I get a coffee from the buzzing drinks machine and head for Morovi's office. I acknowledge my colleagues with a quick glance and the briefest of greetings. That's the curse a secret brings — simply carrying it will change you.

Morovi adjusts a light-blue scarf around her neck and runs a hand through her hair as she looks at herself in the little mirror on the wall.

Concealing a suspect. Concealing a suspect, it is wrong.

'Good morning,' she says, with her back to me. 'Grab a seat.'

Once she's happy with her reflection, she sits down behind the desk herself.

'So then?' she says, once Birck has also arrived. Unlike me, he seems to have managed both a good night's sleep and a shower. 'Angelica Reyes,' she continues, reaching for her notebook. 'How's it going?'

Birck scratches his cheek thoughtfully.

'My take on it is that Levin's people were on the right track from the start. They didn't have enough luck.'

'A punter then.' Morovi turns to me. 'Is that your take on this, too?'

'Yes.'

'The way I see it,' Birck goes on, 'is that we have two possible ways forward, and maybe just the one, really. The first is to try and work out who makes that first call to the police, and the second is to identify the man seen by a witness, Jonna Danielsson, leaving John Ericssonsgatan 16 shortly after the murder. There is a name in the investigation that might be legit, but that didn't lead anywhere. Karl Hamberg.'

'There are also a few people we'd like to talk to,' I say.

'Who are they?'

'The ones who worked on the case, for a start,' Birck says. 'At least the ones it's still possible to talk to.'

Because Levin's dead, I think to myself and feel a stinging pain in my stomach. We could've done with him. Besides Levin, the investigation's core group consisted of six people, four men and two women. Two of those six, Hans Aronsson and Renita Björkman, are still around and on active duty, while the rest have either left Stockholm or retired from the force.

Morovi makes a note on her pad.

'Start with Aronsson and Björkman.'

'After them, we'd like to get hold of Reyes' pimp,' says Birck. 'He was interviewed during the investigation, but they never got anywhere with him.'

'I'd like to talk to the witness,' I say. 'Jonna Danielsson. She was Angelica Reyes' best friend.'

'Today is Wednesday,' says Morovi. 'You've got two days. If you're going to ask me for more time at that point, which I expect you to, then I'm going to want to see some concrete results.'

We leave her office, and Birck gives me a quizzical look, but I keep quiet, don't know what to say.

'Everything okay?' he asks later, when we're outside on the street.

'How do you mean?'

'You seem strange.'

'There's something I have to tell you.'

67

'Okay?'

'I …'

The phone in Birck's hand rings loudly and suddenly.

'Shit, I have to take this.'

'That's okay,' I manage.

18

I see her in Norsborg.

It's rare for me to be at one with the city; there's usually a distance between it and me. Moving alongside, not together with, a stranger. That's how it feels. But in the housing estates, that distance evaporates. I like being here, always have, maybe because I come from one myself. I like the air, the smells, the people.

In Norsborg though, I'm fucking lost.

I haven't been here for ages and I don't know which way I should be heading, don't even know whether Jonna Danielsson actually lives in the area or whether it's just a registered address.

I light a cigarette. Spot a riot van. Four uniformed officers heading towards a jerky man loitering on a corner with his hands in his pockets. An old joke pops into my head, Norsborg's county bird is a fucking police helicop—

That's when I spot her.

She's walking towards the metro and she gives the police a quick, unfazed glance, nothing more. She's got a bag on one shoulder, and is wearing an unbuttoned coat and brown boots. She's preoccupied by the phone in her hand.

When I say her name, she stops.

'You,' she says. 'What do you want?'

'You remember me.'

She looks at her phone again, adjusts her shoulder bag.

'I'm in a hurry. What do you want?'

'To talk.'

'I'm on my way to a lecture.' She looks over at the turnstiles leading to the metro. 'I'm late.'

'We can talk on the way.'

'About what?'

'Angelica.'

Something flashes through her eyes before quickly disappearing again.

'When was it we met?' I say, sitting down on the train. 'I know we have, but I can't narrow it down.'

'We first met during the investigation into Angelica's murder. Then in 2011, and most recently in 2012. In that shithole on Tegnérsgatan. And of course you remember.'

'Do I?'

'You're testing my memory. There's nothing wrong with it, let me tell you.'

Jonna crosses her legs and pushes her hands into the pockets of her coat.

'Where are you studying?'

'The School of Social Work. To be a social worker.'

'Full-time?'

'I've stopped working, if that's what you mean. I haven't done it for years.'

The train strains forward and leaves the station. I lean over, smell the scent of her perfume, or hairspray, or maybe both.

'I want to ask you about Angelica.'

'You said. Why?'

'We're going to hand the case over in two months' time. I'm having a last crack at getting somewhere with it.'

'And what am I going to say about Angelica that you don't

already know?'

'I was thinking you could tell me about her. You were her closest friend, right?'

The train jolts as we glide into Hallunda, the neighbouring estate where Jonna's dead friend spent so much of her childhood and her life. The rain starts falling, lashing against the window.

'Angelica was … full of life. Somehow. Always happy. Always … Yeah, full of life.'

Jonna has clean, white teeth. They might not be her own, could be dentures.

'Why do we say that about the dead?' she says.

'How do you mean?'

'You'd never say that about the living, only the dead. And they're not full of life. The dead are … dead.'

They met on New Year's Eve. In the final hours before 2008 turned into 2009, Jonna and a male friend went to an underground club on Lilla Nygatan in Gamla Stan. They had no gear, had been sitting around at his place earlier that evening and were both completely fucking desperate, but neither of them had anything, and everyone who might've been able to sort them out was busy elsewhere. New Year's Eve is the worst possible date you can choose to try and score.

One of the guy's friends got in touch about nine to say that he was going to a club, and asked whether they'd like to tag along. He wasn't overly keen, but Jonna managed to persuade him, mainly because she didn't want to just stay in all evening. The guy was being overly tactile and he'd been trying it on all day. Besides, it was fucking New Year's Eve.

The place was an old basement, with several rooms and low ceilings, all in brick. There were loads of people, lots of whom she recognised, but most of them she'd never seen before. The guy lost her between the door and the bar. The barman was just charging a customer's card, fiddling with his card terminal. Jonna ordered a cocktail. The clubber next to her said:

'Good choice.'

They'd ordered the same cocktail: that's how she met Angelica Reyes.

'Weird, stuff like that, isn't it?'

'Yes,' I say, casting my mind back to me and Grim in Salem all those years ago, the day we found each other by the water tower.

'Are you here on your own?' Angelica asked.

'That's the idea,' Jonna replied, explaining how she was trying to avoid her male friend.

'I get that,' she said. 'I completely get that.'

'She was there with some friends, and I stayed with them for the rest of the evening, dancing and everything. Angelica was … She was just so open. Easy to talk to, simple to be around.' Jonna lowers her voice. 'It was a good way to avoid thinking about the fact that what I really wanted above all else was to do a line. Angelica didn't seem too interested in that, she seemed a bit too straight-laced. She could party, but she still had this air of being sensible sort of thing? So I just bit my lip and tried to enjoy myself.'

Late in the night, or perhaps early in the morning, something unexpected happened. As the tiredness was setting in, Angelica dragged Jonna into a toilet cubicle and retrieved a little wrap from inside her bra, and chopped up two lines.

Jonna shakes her head at the thought.

'Both me and her were deep in the shit even then, 2009, if you know what I mean. I was crashing on people's sofas and in their beds, I'd been working on the street for a few months. Angelica was in the same boat. You could never tell with us, though. You know, with some people you can see that they're in a state and living in shit. It was never like that with us.'

That may be true, maybe not. That's what they all say. No one wants to admit it; everyone's trying to avoid the stigma.

'So anyway, I had nowhere to live,' Jonna continues, 'and when I mentioned that to Angelica she said straightaway, no hesitation, "No worries, you can stay with me, I've just got a flat." That's what she was like. So when she moved in to John Ericssonsgatan, I followed. We lived together during the spring and summer of 2009, until I managed to get a place of my own. I don't know whether … I mean,' she changes her mind, 'I don't think we were good for each other, me and Angelica.'

'How do you mean?'

'We were both bloody good at making a scene. We were drawn to parties, charlie, nice clothes, and nasty men. When we did it together, it ended up being too much of everything, even if we didn't notice at the time. You know, Jesus, by the end Angelica was seeing three clients a day, I was doing two. And I was jealous. Fucked up, right? She was earning more money for our pimp, which meant that he treated her better.' She shakes her head. 'Tragic. That world is such a fucking sad place. I don't know what else to say. Angelica, she … Well, she was a happy, open person. Always optimistic about stuff. She used to meet her parents as often as she could. They knew that she was using, I think, but not how she was getting the money together for it. She liked going to the cinema, we used to go a lot when we could afford it, and she liked second-hand shops. That's where most of our clothes came from. We'd start out in the posh boutiques in Sturegallerian or along Biblioteksgatan, where we'd choose the clothes we liked, then trawl the second-hand shops for lookalikes.'

In my pocket, my phone vibrates with a new text from Birck: *spoken to Aronsson. boring bloke, nothing new. trying to get hold of Björkman. how's it going?*

'Was Angelica seeing anyone? Did she have a boyfriend when she died?'

'She did not.'

73

'Are you sure about that?'

'She wasn't interested, she said. She had a few ex-boyfriends here and there, but she was tired of the lot of them. She wanted to be free for a while.'

That's the same story the investigation revealed: no known threats. The most recent ex-boyfriend was a small-time pusher and addict with a criminal record the length of a roller blind. Aside from that, he was as meek as a lamb, and also had a robust alibi for the night in question. He died from an overdose in spring 2011. Friends and acquaintances said that he never stopped loving Angelica, and that her death had left him crushed.

Jonna turns her head, glances around the carriage. As we stop in the various estates, more people climb aboard; only a handful get off. The architecture is pretty much the same, but each station brings a new smell, a different feel. It's only from a distance that these places look identical.

'We know she saw three customers that night. The first two have been identified and eliminated. We've got next to nothing on the third one. We suspect that it could be him.'

'That's what you thought at the time, too.'

'But you don't?'

'Afterwards, once the shock and the sorrow had started to settle, I did think about that, of course, who could've wanted to hurt her that badly. She had a few debts, obviously — who doesn't? Nothing big though, mostly drugs she'd bought on tick that she was paying off. And she hadn't fallen out with anyone, as far as I know. While we're on the subject,' she says, lowering her voice, 'I guess the only explanation was that she saw a customer, a twisted sick fucker who for some reason did her in. Who that was, I have no idea.'

She looks down at the floor between our feet, staring at a crumpled Snickers wrapper lying there, gently rocking in time to the motion of the train.

'So pointless,' she says. 'That was what really got me to try and get out of it.'

I ask about Angelica Reyes towards the end, whether there was anything different about her in the days or weeks leading up to the murder. Her mood; what she was talking about; what she was doing. I'm looking for signs that Grim is right, that she was preparing to leave, that someone was out to get her; looking for things that point to it being about something more than a nasty punter who lost his temper. If there aren't any, if our murderer is just a customer with a short fuse, it's going to be difficult to get anywhere.

That last bit I keep to myself.

'I don't know whether she was different, really,' she says. 'They asked me that question at the time, and I didn't know what I was supposed to say. I don't think so. Angelica was her usual self, as I remember, maybe a little bit shakier, but you do get so jumpy from the drugs. Paranoid, almost. Especially if you're wandering around in constant withdrawal.'

'How long had she been doing that?'

'I don't know, the last few weeks maybe? The last time I was round at hers, for example, was the beginning of October, and she was relieved when it turned out to be me at the door. "Oh, it's just you," she said as she opened the door and sort of breathed out, almost. "Who else would it have been?" I asked, and Angelica shook her head and laughed. "Junkie nerves," she said.'

'Did you say that when you were interviewed in 2010?'

'I can't remember. I think so.'

'There wasn't anyone new in her life, no one who ...'

'No,' she cuts in. 'There wasn't. Well, actually, I suppose that depends on how you look at it. There were new punters coming into our lives on a daily basis. None of them meant anything to us though.'

'Are you sure about that? I mean, couldn't Angelica have had some punter after her? Someone following here, harassing her, making her scared and jumpy?'

Yes, I think to myself; and, in fear of her life, she tracks Grim down, because she can hardly go to the police. She's making plans, ways to defend herself against someone or something. Grim thinks she knows something, but that might be overcomplicating things. There's no need: a punter refusing to leave her alone would suffice. Perhaps he gets threatening; it might even already have escalated into physical violence. That's why she needs to get away. A drastic decision, maybe, but who knows what the circumstances were? Who knows how it *felt*? But if that is what happened, why didn't she turn to her pimp? That's the way this sort of thing is normally dealt with.

'She never mentioned ...' I hesitate. 'Anyone being out to get her, or however you might put it?'

'Out to get her? No. Why, is that what you lot think?'

'No,' I say.

We roll past leafy Mälarhöjden. The platform is lined with people busy keeping an appropriate distance from one another, all absorbed in their own lives.

'Did she talk about moving on?'

'Oh yes. Often. We all did. You've got to dream, you know.'

'So what did Angelica say about it?'

'I can't really remember everything that was said, there was so much. She wanted to go travelling, just like everyone else our age. She'd seen a lot of shit and been involved in plenty during those years. So had I, but she was young. She wanted to go to Asia and see the Great Wall of China, she wanted to road-trip across America, go partying in Nice, she wanted to see Chile and Santiago and the place where she was born, all that sort of thing. But it never happened.'

'But it never got any more specific than that?' I say. 'I mean, something a bit closer in time.'

Jonna looks puzzled.

'What would that have been?'

That's what I don't know.

'Anything,' I say.

'She did actually say,' Jonna continues, with a slight frown, 'towards the end, I can't remember exactly when, that she probably wasn't going to be doing this for very much longer. *This* was working on the streets, at least that's what I took it to mean. She said she had other plans.'

'What did that mean?'

'As I said, we all had plans. We were all heading for the big time.' A melancholy smile. 'And just look at me. Thirty-one, training to be a social worker. Big time, eh?'

'Given your background, I'd say it was pretty big, believe me. Did she ever mention the name John Grimberg to you?'

'John Grimberg? What's he got to do with this?'

A familiar searing sting runs down my spine.

'So you know who he is?'

'Doesn't everyone who's been following the news? You mean the guy who escaped a year or so ago?'

'Did you know him?'

Jonna shakes her head.

'I never met him, but I know Angelica did, a long time ago. When she was a kid, like ten, maybe. I seem to remember that he'd saved her life. Not what you'd expect, eh?'

'How do you know he did that?'

'She told me. We must've been pissed, or high — we nearly always were back then. I think we were talking about times we'd nearly got in trouble. Cock and bull stories, quite a few of them in the end — things tend to happen around you when you're involved in those sorts of things. And they matter, you tell them to people, to confirm to yourself and to others that you're a survivor. The kind that the world can't break down. Someone who gets through. This one was from way back, though, she'd been round at a classmate's and was about to get run over or something and he'd saved her life. He was a few years older, and needless to say she fell in love with him a bit. Her first knight in shining armour, that's what she called him. She lived out in Hallunda and he was somewhere else, I don't know where, and she told me how she'd gone back there to meet him again. She was a little girl, you know. She became obsessed in that cute kind of way. Nothing ever happened between them, as I understood it — he was so much older. But she did mention that they'd met a few times over the years.'

'In what circumstances?'

'Couldn't tell you.'

'Were they an item?'

'No. But I think she always had a soft spot for him.'

I look down at my hands. The surface has layers, hiding more layers. *Unsolved murders are mazes.* We're approaching Södermalm. The noise level on the train has risen, and now I have to lean in to make myself heard.

'Did you mention this part, about John Grimberg, in the 2010 interviews?'

'Obviously I can't be sure — it's five years ago — but I don't think I did. Why are you asking about him?'

'It's to do with another case, from around the same time,' I lie. 'Sometimes they're connected.'

A poor lie. She doesn't believe me, I can tell, but we leave it at that. She's used to cops. The train soon rolls over the water, from Slussen in towards Gamla Stan. I give her my number. As I step from the carriage, I find the rain has stopped.

19

In the sky above Vällingby, the clouds roll in like a thick grey blanket. Down here, on the ground, in a parking bay between the tower blocks, Birck's car radio is delivering news: the waves of refugees arriving from Syria and Afghanistan have reached crisis levels. From twelve p.m. tomorrow, Sweden is reinstating border controls. The migration minister is encouraging refugees to head elsewhere. Sweden can no longer guarantee a roof over the head of new arrivals. The border checks will be carried out by the police.

'They will, will they?' Birck looks at the radio as if it has just personally insulted him. 'Not only is everyone on active duty on shit money, and already exhausted from the overtime they're doing, now they're going to be checking passports, too?'

'It's a difficult situation,' I say.

'It isn't at all.'

I turn the radio off, lean back in the seat, and study the entrance across the street.

'Are you sure that this is the right person?' I ask.

'Of course I'm sure.'

Miro Djukic turned forty-six two months ago, and at about the same time moved from a two-bed apartment out in Kista to a studio here in Vällingby. In the original murder investigation, he was identified as Angelica Reyes' pimp, and as such was interviewed on a number of occasions, without any significant results. His phone was confiscated and examined, then cross-referenced with mast records, which is how they managed to identify the first two punters she met that evening. When it came to the third, our prime suspect, the searches led nowhere.

Djukic has been keeping a low profile for a few years, but he turns up every now and then as a familiar friend of some suspect in narcotics and prostitution cases. Despite that, I've never met him.

'I spoke to Aronsson and Björkman,' Birck says, his eyes fixed on the closed door to the building. 'Both are convinced that they were on the right track, that it's all about the third man she sold to that night, the same person who makes the first call to the police and who Jonna Danielsson sees on the stairs.'

They're wrong. It can't be the same person; it's not possible. The person who makes the call and is in the stairwell is Grim.

'Unfortunately, they were pretty convinced that Djukic was telling the truth when he claimed not to know who this guy was.' He turns to me. 'How did you get on? What did she say, this Jonna Danielsson?'

'Nothing we haven't known since 2010,' I say. 'But she's alive, anyway, studying to be a social worker.'

'What did you ask her, though?' Birck says, turning his head as the entrance door opens.

According to Grim, someone was out to get Angelica Reyes. That's too big — keeping that under wraps is a dereliction of duty. I take a deep breath.

'I think there's something I need to te—'

'Hold on.'

'Yes?'

Birck frowns slightly.

'There he is.'

The man emerging into the November gloom is pretty short, with cropped brown hair and beard, and a body that looks like it's used to weightlifting competitions. Birck studies the man's lolloping movements.

'Is he carrying an invisible fridge or something?'

We step out of the car. The air is cold and damp.

'Miro,' Birck says. 'Where are you off to?'

'Gabriel.' Miro flashes a crooked smile. 'To the shops.'

'In town? We'll give you a lift.'

'I was going to get the tube.'

Miro looks around, to establish whether there's anyone else around besides me and Birck. He's wearing baggy jeans and a hoody under an undone white winter coat, and he's standing with his hands in full view, hanging languidly by his sides. He knows what's coming, no point doing anything that might make us nervous.

'I don't recognise you, though.'

'Leo,' I say as I stretch out my hand.

Miro takes it. His grip is surprisingly warm, soft almost. He gets into the back seat of Birck's car, and as we make our way from Vällingby up onto the main road back towards Bromma, he gets his phone out and starts writing a text.

'Don't take this the wrong way,' he says when the telephone buzzes with a reply behind me, 'but my ex-wife calls you *pig cunts*.'

'Oh, to be honest, I've heard much worse,' says Birck.

Miro sits in the middle back there and leans forward between our seats.

'Well I do appreciate the lift, I must say, especially in this weather,' he goes on. 'But what do you want? You've got nothing on me these days. I behave myself. I even go to parents' evening, for fuck's sake.'

'It's about Angelica Reyes,' says Birck.

Miro raises two thick, bushy eyebrows.

'Okay.'

'You remember her.'

'Course I do. She was my girl. Well not like *that*. But she worked for me. Fucking awful business.'

'We'd like you to tell us about the twelfth of October 2010,' I say.

'What's in it for me? Besides getting picked up in a dark car in front of neighbours and acquaintances and then being forced to sit here talking to you, I mean.'

'What's in it for you?' Birck says coldly.

'Yes.'

'You get out of a trip to the bunker.'

Miro sighs.

'You *really are* fucking cunts. I don't even know how much I remember now.'

'We'll find out,' says Birck. 'You sold her, right?'

'I did,' says Miro. 'It's not something I'm proud of, but I can't honestly say I'm particularly ashamed of it either. You know in this town, everyone's fighting everyone else, just to survive. That's what it was like back then, and I'm guessing that's what it's like today, too.'

'How many clients would she normally see in an evening, do you remember?'

'On the nights she was working for me I seem to remember she'd see two or three. Three on the night of the murder, I remember that.'

'You're sure about that.'

'Yes. But it was sort of up to them, really. I pimped them, yes, but they could always say no. If they were tired, sick, or needed a break or whatever, I would respect that.'

'Is that so?' says Birck. 'Not what I've heard.'

'So what have you heard?'

'That your cousin was the one supplying them with drugs. That he was a dealer who'd shut up shop on your say so, if the girls weren't doing what you wanted.'

Birck overtakes a heavy goods vehicle, and Miro stares at it as we pass.

'You mustn't believe everything you hear,' he says.

'Can you tell us,' I cut in, 'what you remember of the night of the murder?'

'I went over this fifteen times straight after the murder, every day for the two weeks you lot were interrogating me.'

'We're looking at the case again,' I say. 'You are involved in it.'

'That colleague of yours thought I was the one who did it.'

She did indeed, and this is where it gets tricky.

The person who interviewed him was Renita Björkman. She'd come from Vice Squad, and the fact that she hated pimps, even more than the average woman on Vice Squad did, was no secret. That also made her completely unsuited to the task, but we were understaffed even then, and she was the one who ended up having to sit with Miro. With hindsight, it doesn't take long to realise that Levin himself ought to have taken care of the interviews with the pimp, but perhaps he didn't know at the time, and afterwards it was too late.

That Miro didn't share what he knew, not *all* of what he knew, is not only conceivable but probable.

The police radio crackles into life: suspected assault on Torsgatan. A patrol car answers the call and is sent to the scene.

'What we want to talk to you about,' I say, 'is the third client.'

'The Third Client,' Miro repeats. 'Sounds like the name of a bad crime thriller.'

It's the evening of the twelfth of October 2010, and Miro Djukic is sitting in his apartment in Kista. He's got three mobile phones to hand: one for private use, one for incoming calls, another for dialling out. It's almost quarter-to eleven when he receives a call from a number he recognises.

'So this was someone who'd called before,' I say.

'It was.'

A man. He doesn't introduce himself. He says:

'I would like to meet Angelica.'

That was it.

'Was it normal for punters to ask for specific girls?'

'Oh yes.'

Miro ends the call with the man, puts the phone down, picks up another, and calls Angelica.

'I asked her if the evening had gone okay so far, checked to make sure they'd treated her nicely. They had, she said. I told her she could have another in about fifteen, twenty minutes. She said fine, no problem.'

'How did she sound then?' I ask. 'If you know what I mean.'

'Well ... I think I remember telling you that she sounded pretty much like she always did.'

'Would you like to change that statement?'

'Not change, exactly.' Miro scratched his cheek. 'But what do you call it, expand. I think she sounded ... I don't know, a bit stressed maybe. I assumed she was tidying up or getting the bed ready or something.'

She *is* stressed, I think to myself. She knows that Grim will be coming later. She's preparing to disappear. You can imagine that she's already left, mentally. Perhaps Angelica Reyes' mind is already somewhere else when the arrangements for the third customer are being made. Maybe she's scared.

Miro ends the call with Angelica and rings the third client, confirms the booking and gives the time and place.

'Good,' says the man.

After that, a click, nothing more.

'Customers want as little contact with the pimp as possible,' says Miro. 'They want to convince themselves we don't exist. They're too shy or discreet to pick someone up off the street, they prefer a helping hand to take care of practicalities, you know. But the pimp reminds them of the shitty side of what they're doing. So

84

that conversation was in no way unusual.'

'You said that Angelica sounded stressed,' says Birck. 'And that you assumed she was tidying up.'

'She sounded like she was in the middle of something. Whether anything was going on there, I honestly couldn't say.'

'Where you aware of any threat to Angelica?' I ask.

'A threat?'

'From a punter, for example. Was she scared, did one of them maybe want to hurt her?'

'Not as far as I know.'

'Is it possible the threat might have existed without you knowing about it?' Birck asks.

'No.' Miro sniggers. 'Not as long as the punters were coming through me.'

'Speaking of which.' Birck turns his head while we wait for the lights to turn green. 'You didn't mention this to the police, did you? That you thought Angelica sounded stressed?'

'No.'

'Why not?'

'That kind of detail would've made them more interested in me and the other girls, I felt, and I didn't want that. Someone being described as stressed shortly before they end up getting murdered doesn't sound great. Perhaps I could've been the one threatening her? Or putting pressure on her in some way? It wouldn't look good. And don't forget, in 2010 I was on it. I wanted them to leave me and my firm in peace, as soon as possible, so that we could get back to what we were doing. Dead whores are bad for business. If you'll excuse my bluntness.'

'Those two calls, with the third man,' I say, 'what do you remember of them?'

'I've told you.'

Birck retrieves his phone from his pocket, clicks through the menus, and then holds it up between us.

'Is this him?' he asks.

'Dead woman at John Ericssonsgatan 16,' Grim's voice streams from the phone's speaker. 'Third floor. Hurry.'

'John Ericssonsgatan 16,' the operator repeats.

'Yes.'

'Dead woman. Are you there ... ?'

'Hurry.'

'And you, what is your name ...'

The call drops. I can hear that it's him now; I can make out Grim's voice. Speaking more slowly than normal, a touch softer. It's enough to make him unrecognisable, unless you know that it's him. I'm ashamed that I do.

'Maybe,' Miro says, hesitantly. 'It was a long time ago, I can't remember exactly what he sounded like. But that could've been him.'

Birck stuffs his phone back in his pocket. We're coming up to Kungsholmen. I can see the high-rise headquarters of *Dagens Nyheter* in the distance.

'Everything I said in those interviews was true,' Miro continues, his gaze fixed on something about where the gearstick is. 'But I didn't exactly say everything. There was one more thing I didn't mention.'

'Which was?' I say.

'During that first call with the third client, I heard a sound in the background. Then it stopped abruptly, I think someone turned it off.'

'A sound?' Birck slows down as the lights ahead of us change from green to amber. The police radio crackles again: suspected theft from a storage room at Åhléns department store. 'What sort of sound?'

'Such weird timing,' Miro says. With a crooked smile he nods towards the police radio. 'It sounded just like that.'

20

Standing in the bathroom at Alströmergatan, I run my hand along my cheekbone, and for a second I catch a glimpse of my grandfather's eyes. When I try and smile, I can just make out my dad's dimples. He got them from his mother.

Your ancestry is always there when you look at yourself in the mirror. It doesn't happen very often, but sometimes they become visible, the men and women who came before. You have to learn to accept it; there is no other way.

I walk out into the hall, check that the door is unlocked, sit down on the sofa, and open the half-full whisky bottle on the table. I pour a few fingers into two glasses and pick up one, then lean back.

It's evening, but Sam's not home, she's working late at the gallery, preparing for tomorrow's show. That's lucky.

On the radio, an interview with a duty officer from Malmö. She explains how she, with little more than fourteen hours left until checks are to be launched, is yet to receive any instructions on how the task at hand is to be carried out.

At ten p.m. on the dot, the door opens.

It's a novel sensation. One second he's not there, the next he has appeared, discreetly and unnoticed.

Grim takes his coat off but keeps his shoes on, and inspects his surroundings.

'Lovely place you've got.'

I reach for the other glass and get to my feet to offer it to Grim.

'I don't think I can take the credit for it.'

He takes the glass.

'Thanks. Is Sam home?'

'Why do you ask?'

Holding the glass in one hand and with a new chill in his stare, Grim starts backing away, towards the door.

'There's someone else here.'

At that moment, I hear footsteps behind me, as he makes his way in from the kitchen, where he's spent the last few minutes waiting.

'Good evening, John,' says Birck.

After dropping Miro Djukic off, Birck and I went to an old dive bar on Vasagatan that's almost always empty. Flying Dog. We sat down in one of the window booths, ready to eat.

'There's something I need to tell you,' I said.

'What?'

I squirmed in the booth.

'The reason I wanted to look at this case again.'

I suspect he already had an idea what it was about. He was neither surprised nor annoyed, at least not outwardly. Instead, he just sat and listened until I'd finished.

'So ... this is all about him.'

'It was, to begin with. Now I actually want to know what happened.'

'Fucking hell, Leo.'

'I know.'

He blinked.

'So someone was out to get her.'

'If he's to be believed.'

Birck didn't reply, and he's been very quiet since then. Not even when we were sitting here, in the flat, ironing out details ahead of Grim turning up, did he say much.

It should've been a relief, finally getting to tell someone. That's what getting something off your chest ought to feel like, but that's not how it feels. All I feel is guilt and shame, and, as much as it hurts me to admit it, that an invisible bond has broken — a secret has been lost — between me and Grim.

'Grim, listen to me,' I say. 'Nothing to worry about. We need to talk.'

'You've tricked me, Leo.'

'That was the only way to get you here.'

'Don't move.'

'I can't do this alone, Grim. Gabriel needs ...'

'No.' Grim is standing with his back to the door. He has the whisky glass in one hand, and his coat in the other. In the gloomy hallway, his eyes seem black. 'You tricked me, Leo.'

Grim lets the glass fall to the floor. The sound is muffled by the rug but the whisky trickles out. He puts his free hand on the door handle. In that same instant I feel a tug on my waistband, a hand grabbing my firearm, which I'd hidden behind my back.

'Stand still, John,' Birck says as he takes a step to one side, the weapon pointed straight at Grim's ribcage.

Grim looks at me, then the weapon. Maybe he's weighing up an attempt anyway. I want to approach him, but I'm worried that the movement might seem too sudden.

Slowly, Grim lifts his hand from the door handle.

21

An awkward silence. We're sitting around my coffee table, Sam's coffee table — me and Birck at either end of the sofa and Grim in an armchair. I've poured another glass of whisky and put it in front of him. Birck is sipping away at his, with the gun lying there on the arm of the sofa.

'Can't you put that thing away?' says Grim. 'It's making me nervous.'

'Yes, I suppose so.'

He stands up and replaces the P226 in its holster, up on the hat stand. Everything has an air of deception about it.

'What you told me,' I say slowly, without looking at him, 'I told Gabriel. This Lukas Bengtsson, who claimed to be with Stockholm Police, has probably got wind of you, directly or indirectly, via one of the people you contacted. If you can give us those names, then with a bit of luck they can lead us to the man we're looking for. That's what we've got.'

'Assuming,' Birck adds, 'that you're telling the truth.'

'Have I given you any reason to doubt that?'

'No, you haven't,' I say. 'The people you contacted for information about Angelica Reyes. Tell us about them.'

Grim chuckles.

'Say I do cooperate. That means that sooner or later you'll be telling your boss about me.'

'That's a risk you're taking whether you cooperate or not,' Birck points out. 'Since we're sitting here, I mean.'

'Exactly.' Grim's eyes burn into me. 'Because you tricked me.'

I put the glass down, get up from the sofa, and walk over to him. Then I haul him up and slam him against the wall.

He lets go a heavy sigh as the air leaves his lungs. The painting on the wall next to him takes a knock and falls to the floor.

Sam and I bought the painting in an antique shop. She hated it, but agreed to let me buy it because I claimed that the scene — a sort of flat, open sea — had a calming effect on me.

'For fuck's sake, *you* were the one who came to *me*. After everything that's happened, all that you've done, you asked me to do this. What the fuck was I supposed to do? If we're going to do this, it's going to be on *my* terms. You've got no right to decide how, when, or why anyone else does anything. You get that?'

Grim doesn't respond. My hands are shaking from the unexpected adrenaline rush.

'Leo,' Birck says calmly behind me. 'Sit down.'

'*You* were the one who came to *me*,' I repeat.

'I needed your help.'

'You make it pretty damn complicated to help you.'

'Leo,' I hear Birck once more. 'Sit down.'

I take a step backwards, vaguely aware that something definitive might just have happened between us. Grim looks sad. He looks down at the painting, stoops to pick it up, and puts it back on the wall.

'I made three calls,' he says, trying to hang the painting back on its little nail. 'One to an old smackhead who knows what's what in prostitution in Stockholm, one to a weapons dealer with loads of contacts, and one to a little gangster with big ears. Lotta Jidhoff, Jorge Grens, and Ludwig Sarac.'

With the painting back in its rightful place, Grim takes a step back and cocks his head to one side as he admires the motif.

'It looks peaceful,' he says.

Birck types the names into his phone.

'Who was the last one again?'

'Ludwig Sarac.'

'Did you contact them in the order you told us?'

'Yes. Do you know who they are?'

'Ludwig Sarac, not the other two,' says Birck. 'I've met Ludwig.'

'But not in the context of being a little gangster, right?'

Birck's stare slides towards me, hesitant.

'No,' I say.

The moon is a thin white shard. I stand over by the window to look at it while Grim returns to his armchair.

'Ludwig Sarac is an informant,' I say. 'Or rather was. He was exposed in connection with a raid at the end of last year, and after that he went to ground. No one knows where he is.' I turn to face Grim. 'Why didn't you contact her best friend, Jonna Danielsson?'

Grim stares coldly at me.

'Best friends don't usually know very much about each other.'

'Okay, okay,' Birck says. 'Calm down. One of them is known to be more of a loudmouth than the others, so we'll start with him.'

'It's not Sarac, though,' says Grim.

'How do you know that?' I ask.

'I've spoken to him today.'

'How can you be sure that it isn't him?'

'Well that's a funny story, too, as it happens,' Grim says, scratching his temple. 'And a bit confused, maybe. *Then*, I was the one who contacted him, from St Göran's. Now, this afternoon, *he* was the one *calling* me.'

'Eh? Sarac called you today?'

Yes. The phone rang, a number he recognised. That's why he answered.

The man on the other end turned out to be a friend from way back: Ludwig Sarac, who'd heard that John Grimberg had been resurrected. *Resurrected*, that's what Sarac said. He's a bit odd. He'd doubted the veracity of the rumours, but he did after all have good reasons for trying to get hold of Grimberg.

'Which are?' Grim asked.

About a week ago, at around eleven in the evening on the second of November, way before he'd heard anything about Grimberg being back, Sarac had a visitor. That was pretty unusual these days, since Sarac was holed up somewhere that only a few people knew about. The man wasted no time on small talk, but wanted Sarac's take on a very specific case. It all centred around John Grimberg.

'Where is he?' the man had wanted to know.

'Grimberg?' Sarac was taken aback. 'You mean the guy who's on the run?'

The very same.

'Well ...' Sarac laughed. 'Well I suppose he's on the run.'

'But where *is he*?'

'I don't know.'

Since Sarac knew nothing, the man accepted his answers. He got to his feet and left without another word.

'Strange,' says Grim. 'Isn't it?'

'Yeah,' I say.

'That's what Ludwig thought, too, hence why he tried to get hold of me.'

He couldn't, because he didn't have Grim's number. He left it, until yesterday when he remembered that he'd brought his old phone when he went underground. He said he hadn't known what to do with it, and leaving it behind was just too risky.

It was a few years old, so it should have Grim's number on it. And it turned out that it did, once he'd got some life into the battery, logged in, and flicked through his contacts, by which time it was late in the evening. So Sarac called his old acquaintance to tell him what had happened.

'Ludwig didn't know who the guy was,' says Grim. 'Just who he claimed to be.'

'Lukas Bengtsson,' I say as it dawns on me. 'Lukas Bengtsson, Stockholm Police.'

'You got it.'

Grim's chat with Ludwig Sarac ended up a short one, since fear got the better of him. If the man claiming to be Lukas Bengtsson really was a policeman and had Sarac under surveillance, then the call meant a chance of Grim being eavesdropped. If that was the case, then Stockholm's countless mobile masts would be able to narrow down his environs and more or less reveal his position.

'So …' Birck says. 'Where's Sarac now?'

'You think I'm going to grass on him? He's managed to stay hidden for a while.'

'Grim,' I say. 'We're not going to …'

He waves his hand dismissively.

'I should think he's sitting where he is, waiting, at home on Västmannagatan. Not for long, I shouldn't think. Someone clearly knows where he's staying, so he's probably busy looking for a new lair to slither into.'

'Västmannagatan, what number?'

'68.'

Birck leans forward on the sofa.

'The visit Sarac had from this Lukas Bengtsson, Stockholm Police, was last Monday then? Second of November?'

'According to Ludwig, yes. In the evening, about eleven. How come?'

Västmannagatan 68. Well blow me.

As the man who claimed to be Lukas Bengtsson, Stockholm Police, arrived at Västmannagatan to ask Ludwig Sarac about Grim's whereabouts, me and Birck were sitting in a car equipped with both still and video cameras, having been seconded to Surveillance and tasked with recording everyone arriving or leaving through the entrance next door, Västmannagatan 66.

'Well blow me,' says Birck. He turns to me. 'How well do you think you can see number 68 in the pictures we took of number 66?'

'I don't know.'

'Well enough?'

'Maybe.'

'What are you on about?' asks Grim.

At that very moment, a text arrives from Sam:

just leaving the gallery now, home soon my little idiot x

Shit.

I get off the sofa.

'You have to leave.'

22

It takes a while to get hold of the material from Surveillance. The guy I speak to perfectly embodies Surveillance's general suspicion of, and unwillingness to help, the other employees inside HQ.

'What a fucking mess. What the fuck happened?' Birck says while we're waiting. Then he changes tack: 'What the fuck is happening?'

'I don't know.'

Lukas Bengtsson, Stockholm Police, first visits Grim at St Göran's, then Ludwig Sarac on Västmannagatan a year and a half later. Is he on the hunt? Why? And who is he?

The picture of Angelica Reyes has changed, too. Why were they out to get her? She must've started some ball rolling, one that is yet to stop.

'It's tough,' I say.

'Tough?' Birck's reclining in a chair with his feet on the desk and a cup of vending-machine coffee in his hands. 'What is?'

'Working out what's significant and what isn't.'

'Oh right, yes. What did you say to Sam?'

'Nothing. But she did wonder why I had my gun on the hat stand. And why the hall carpet smelt of whisky.'

Birck laughs. So do I, despite my embarrassment, because you have to do something.

'You're going to have to tell her.'

'I know.'

'Before she starts getting suspicious.'

'I think she already is.'

'What makes you think that?'

'Sam is Sam,' I say. 'It's really just a feeling I've got.'

She was there in the hall, taking off her winter clothes less than a quarter of an hour after Birck had left. She asked about the weapon on the shelf and the whisky on the carpet and I answered with as few words as I could, since it was so difficult to lie.

'Is everything okay?' she asked later, in bed.

'Yes,' I replied.

'You sure?' She stroked my cheek. 'You seem a bit distant.'

After that, she fell asleep, but I lay there with her words echoing around my head. They mixed with my shame about lying and my anxiety about Grim, the need for some kind of sedative stronger than alcohol, and not until much later did sleep finally arrive, like a wave coming to sweep me away.

'You do know,' Birck says, next to me, 'that this is aiding and abetting.'

'Yes.'

'That's worse than anything you've done thus far.'

'I know.'

'And this has been going on for over a week. Why didn't you say anything? At least to me. You know if this gets out there's going to be hell to pay.'

'What do you want me to say? *I know*. It was wrong.'

For a second, I wish I'd never said anything, that I'd just kept quiet, kept lying, kept it all to myself. That would've been so simple, wouldn't it, to just keep going as if nothing had happened?

It would've been simpler than this at any rate.

'Besides,' says Birck, 'a large part of me still thinks that this is nothing more than a particularly hard to solve whore-murder.'

The computer bleeps. Finally, the material has arrived in my email, via the intranet — a large video file and a smaller folder containing the still images from our surveillance of Västmannagatan 66.

23

I open the computer's media player and play the video. My voice is audible, excited, and impatient in the passenger seat. In the sharp foreground, Västmannagatan 66; and in the background, smaller, more blurred, you can just about make out number 68.

'We'll have to see if luck's on our side for once,' says Birck.

Falling budgets mean that moving pictures are only to be used when something happens, in this case when someone leaves or arrives at Västmannagatan 66. Not just because video files take up so much storage on the little memory cards, which in turn are considered very expensive, but also because whoever has to sit and sift through the material afterwards doesn't need to waste more man-hours than absolutely necessary on an activity that, 98 per cent of the time, generates no results.

We're pinning our hopes on the man having been captured on film outside Västmannagatan 68 at some point when we happened to be documenting someone arriving or leaving the building next door.

This is going to take a fair amount of good fortune.

'About eleven, according to Sarac,' I say. 'Wasn't it?'

'If we're going to believe Grimberg.'

I spool through to quarter-to. The onscreen clock ticks forward a second at a time, 22:45:31, 22:45:32, down in the bottom-right corner. The image freezes for a second, before the clock jumps forward four minutes, then two and a half, then another five, and then four more.

A man leaves Västmannagatan 66, disappears from view. At the same time, a car arrives from the north, its headlights like two white eyes in the darkness. The driver parks outside 68 and then gets out, nothing more than a silhouette in the grainy picture.

It's a man. He glances over his shoulder, first right and then left, and pushes his hands into the pockets of his coat. He looks to be wearing boots, and he reaches to open the door of number 68 with his left hand.

The picture freezes.

When the frames start rolling again, over fifteen minutes have passed and the car that was parked on the street is gone.

I spool back.

'There.' I try and zoom in. 'It's the right time, anyway.'

Birck squints.

'God, this really says it all,' he mumbles. 'While Swedish police officers are sitting and staring at an insignificant building, a suspected murderer slips in through the entrance next door.'

I pull out my phone and take a picture of the man's face on the computer screen. He looks between thirty and fifty — you couldn't be any more specific than that — with an upright posture and broad shoulders. His nose is unobtrusive, while his cheek- and jawbones are slightly more pronounced. Curly or wavy hair. I think he's probably got a few days' worth of stubble on his cheeks, but that could be a trick of the light.

I send the picture to Grim, with the words *lukas bengtsson?*

yes

how sure are you?

sure

it's a shitty picture. how sure are you?

very sure

I study the screen. A police radio crackles in Miro Djukic's ear on the twelfth of October 2010. *Lukas Bengtsson.* Why does this man claim to be someone he is not? Because he's got something to hide. He was the one that was out to get her. It was him she was trying to flee. *A cop*, fuck.

'Lukas Bengtsson as the perpetrator,' Birck says slowly. 'That's the theory. Correct?'

'Yes.'

'A colleague, then. Possibly.'

'Exactly.'

Birck exhales.

'So what the fuck do we do now?'

'We need to look in Reyes' diary,' I say. 'She might have had some relationship to him. There might be something about Lukas Bengtsson in there.'

'I wonder what he was afraid of,' mumbles Birck. 'Was she going to squeal, do you think? Walk into reception downstairs and tell them that he was paying her for sex now and then?'

'I don't know.'

In the next room, the radio: It's ten o'clock. In two hours, Sweden is introducing border controls. *Panic*, no one says but everyone is thinking.

'The car,' says Birck with a start. 'Fuck me, the car.'

I rewind the recording a bit.

There. A light-coloured Audi arriving. Lights blazing.

'Wait till it's right in front of that street lamp,' says Birck. 'There. What do you make that out as?' He puts his finger on the screen. 'OSK ... The numberplate's filthy isn't it, but I reckon that's an eight rather than a six or a three. OSK 853. Check that.'

The registration OSK 853 sits on a car that has passed its annual roadworthiness tests to date, never been reported stolen, and is still with its original owner. So far, so nice and simple.

The problem is that the owner lives in Varvet, an old no-man's-land down in Småland, and the numberplate in question is attached to a fifteen-year-old Toyota.

And if that weren't enough, this Toyota is apparently blue in colour.

'False plates.' Birck leans back with a nasty grimace and pushes his hands through his hair. 'Fuck. We've got absolutely nothing. What we have is the five-year-old murder of a whore who no one besides us seems to give a shit about. A whore who, according to none other than star witness John Grimberg, may have been the victim of threats. Meanwhile, the world is in meltdown outside our window, with torrents of refugees completely out of control, gangland carve-ups, waves of robbery and theft, and God knows what.' He slowly shakes his head. 'I don't know what we can do about this, Leo.'

He sounds regretful, which surprises me.

'We're on our way to solving a murder,' I say. 'If you go to Morovi, we will lose that chance.'

'It makes no odds,' says Birck.

'It certainly does and you know it.'

'I can't believe that you lied to me. That you're lying to Sam.'

'I'm going to tell her.'

'Are you?'

'Yes.'

I call Morovi, who's in a meeting, and sounds stressed. In the background, someone calls the interior minister and the migration minister, the two men responsible in the eyes of the media and the public for the new border controls in Sweden, 'clowns'.

'I can hear you've got your hands full,' I say. 'But tomorrow, Gabriel and I would like to …'

'You're on a course tomorrow,' Morovi interrupts. 'Don't forget.'

'Am I? Where? What's it about?'

'Am I your mother, Leo?'

'No.'

'Right then.'

The call ends with a click.

24

I'm looking at the scanned pictures of Angelica Reyes' diary, a page for each day of the long year that was 2010.

She doesn't put an awful lot in it: the odd appointment she has to make here and there with her social workers or the housing service, her parents' birthdays, twenty-fifth and thirtieth birthday parties she's been invited to. It really doesn't say much about her, and yet it's only when I actually sit down with it and start flipping through the diary that the rage comes.

On the twelfth of October 2010, it comes to an end. Someone brings it to an end. The diary doesn't record many commitments, but they're there nonetheless. Her mum's birthday was the ninth of December, and Angelica has written *Mum 53*, drawn a little heart, and added, *Bake a cake!*

Those plans come to nothing. It turns white and empty and cold.

She was *a person*.

When I blink, I'm back in Salem, many years younger and a different person to the one I've become, but somehow not. Me and my best friend save a little girl from death. She's got big headphones and terrified eyes, and dreams of becoming an air hostess. Our lives cross that night, only for an instant. In spite of everything, at the time, none of it seemed particularly ominous. Then things go really bad, as they sometimes do for girls from Hallunda and Norsborg.

For many, things turn out alright, while a few slip down into the darkness. Only very few end up like Angelica.

Not Reyes. Now she's Angelica.

I think about the blood, and the stabbing.

The fear she must've felt, the pain. A stranger — *is it* a stranger? — in her own home.

I return to the diary. My rage doesn't blow over, but it sharpens my senses, almost a pleasant sensation.

From the end of September that year, a note in English in the margin: *don't be like the rest of them, darling.*

That could've been a challenge, an aspiration, directed at someone else. Or is it the point where she decides to cut loose? Is *that* what those words signify? Maybe. It might also be the case that the note means nothing.

Sometimes words are just words.

And there's no mention of Lukas Bengtsson, nor a white Audi. Not even Ludwig Sarac.

I wonder where she was planning to go, how the night of the twelfth of October was supposed to end? There's nothing about that. Maybe there was no plan. I think about Jonna Danielsson, who left life on the street behind. It wasn't impossible to escape.

I flip to the ninth of December: *Mum 53. Bake a cake!*

She still had her family. Lukas Bengtsson pushed her so far that she tried to disappear.

25

OSK 853. Audi. White.

I make a note in the margin of my notepad. It's mid-morning on Friday the thirteenth of November, and I'm sitting blinking to stay awake in a lecture theatre at Forensics, along with colleagues from all over Stockholm.

False plates, I add, and *Lukas Bengtsson*.

The course is eight hours long, including breaks for lunch and coffee, and since there are detectives present in the audience, these have been made generous. Apparently, I've been listed as a delegate since September, but I have no recollection of registering. The course is 'Modern Forensics in Digital Arenas — a full-day course for detectives in Stockholm', and is being given by Miranda Shali, the woman informally known within Forensics as 'the Genius'.

She's short and slight, with long, dark hair worn up in a thick bun; she's probably a few years younger than me and has a PhD from Oxford.

The point of the course is to instruct us in how to approach investigations where events occur partly online or in some kind of hardware, such as a computer or a mobile phone.

I write *Lotta Jidhoff, Jorge Grens, Ludwig Sarac* in my pad.

Why is the man at St Göran's/in the Audi after Angelica — and Grim?

Whoever can answer those questions, I think to myself, probably knows why she died and who was holding the weapon.

When the afternoon darkness has fallen outside the lecture theatre's windows and the course is over, I return to the archive room where the files relating to the Angelica Reyes case remain. I find what I'm looking for and quickly make my way back through HQ.

Up in Forensics, the air is dry and cool, and the furniture's old, but in a way that makes you feel reassured rather than hopeless. Dr Miranda Shali's room is right at the end of one of the long corridors. I find her sitting at her desk, filling in a form.

'Yes?' she says, looking up. 'What's this about?'

'Thanks for a good course.'

'Did you learn anything?'

'I think so.' I hold up the memory stick that was found in the wall behind Angelica Reyes' bed. 'I'm wondering about this.'

'What about it?'

'That's what I don't know. Could be nothing.'

She examines the stick, apparently looking for something that you have to be Miranda Shali to find.

'Which case is this?'

'Angelica Reyes.'

Shali's prominent, dark eyebrows slide up her forehead.

'Well I never.' She gives it a last look, before putting it to one side. 'It'll be a few weeks. Cold cases go to the back of the queue.'

'You can't jump the queue?'

'Everyone wants to jump the queue.'

'But …'

'I'll have a look as soon as I can. I expect that will be a few weeks.' She gives me a decisive stare. 'Okay?'

'Okay.'

Shit. I can't help thinking that this is urgent, that someone is in danger.

When I leave the Genius, it's half-past five in the evening on Friday the thirteenth of November. Four hours later, word comes of something going on in Paris.

That's when the storm begins.

26

'Where have you been?' Sam asks when I get in and she rolls over in bed.

In her hands, *The White City*, a thin little book with a discomfiting cover.

'On a course.'

'Was it good?'

'It was useable, yes. You?'

'I've been at work. Then I took my clothes off. Since then I've been waiting for you.'

As she moves to put the book down, I can make out the curve of her breasts through the fabric of her T-shirt. I get undressed and lie down next to Sam, feel her soft skin against mine.

She runs her hand across my chest, before removing her knickers in a supple sweep and then stuffing them in my mouth, holding her hand in place so that I can't spit them out. Her panties are warm, I close my eyes and feel Sam kissing my face, my chin, my neck.

'You need to spend more time at home,' she mumbles, her warm breath and her tongue pushing on my chest.

I try to say something.

'Shhh.' She pushes the panties further into my mouth, and her hand into my boxers where she takes a tight grip on me.

'You're not lying again, are you, Leo?'

For a second, the shame cuts through the lust, makes it wane.

I shake my head.

Sam claws her nails over me, a sharp pain that slowly turns into something else.

She kneels down alongside and looks down at me. Long locks of hair fall across her shoulders and onto the T-shirt that goes down to her belly button. Slowly, she teases her panties from my mouth. Then she straddles me, shifting herself to a comfortable position sitting squarely on my face.

'Like that,' she exhales, her eyes closed. 'Yes, just like that. *There.*'

I try to say something.

'Shhh,' Sam repeats. 'You're not supposed to talk now.' She pushes her fingers through my hair, before grabbing hold of it tightly and grinding her hips against me. 'You're going to be quiet now, gonna stay quiet till I ...'

The words seep out and slip away through the room.

'I need ...' I say, and there must be something in my voice, because Sam lifts herself up a bit, leans on her elbows, and rests her head in her hand.

'What is it? What do you need?'

'I need to ...'

At that very moment, my phone buzzes on the bedside table, a text from Birck.

seen the news?

'What is it?' Sam asks again.

'I don't know, something must've happened.'

I feel for the remote control, and as the bedroom telly flickers into life it's showing special reports from Paris. Eleven o'clock. It's not until dawn that the scale of events become apparent. One hundred and thirty dead, probably more.

A suicide bomber outside Stade de France, shootings in restaurants, a massacre at a concert venue. The attackers are said to have roared *Allahu Akbar.*

The light of dawn is thin, grey, and it intensifies only slowly. Me and Sam stand there sharing a cig on the balcony. I wish that I could tell her about Grim, but I can't.

The day continues with news from Paris: eyewitness reports of those lost, given by those who survived by the skin of their teeth. The perpetrators were Islamist terrorists, and for now they are still at large. They are being hunted by thousands of French police, a hunt that dominates the world's media while the internet is flooded with fear and panic. As if the sheer horror and grief, the violence and the blood and the fire were not enough.

An act of this nature, just a few hours from Sweden, at a time when refugees, many undocumented, are pouring into the country completely unchecked … The people at the Security Police and the Intelligence Units must have their hearts in their mouths.

27

The Monday Meeting is always the worst. All the weekend's shitty events need to be condensed and served up, along with simultaneous attempts to create potential plans of action for the week ahead. Today, there's an elephant in the room that makes it all even more unbearable.

The elephant takes the form of a rumour, seeping down the corridors throughout the morning:

A terrorist suspect may be in Sweden.

He — it is a man — is planning to commit terrorist attacks on Swedish soil. This is the rumour. The Security Police, SEPO, have not yet made the threat public, seemingly keen to avoid hosting a press conference until the government forces them to do so.

The rumour is a bad one, because it's so vague. Good rumours, the ones that gain traction, often have specific details that make them more ominous: a place, a name, a method. These are missing today, but in spite of that fact the angst overwhelms everything else.

Less than three days since the Paris attacks. Everyone is in shock.

Everyone is deployed onto the streets or glued to their computers, under orders to exploit every last contact they might have.

Find him. Arrest him. Neutralise him.

'They have asked me to put all of my employees at their disposal, for the purposes of monitoring Stockholm's Muslim communities,' Morovi tells us as we sit down in her office. 'Everyone is panicking. Even the police are checking over their shoulders out on the streets.' She shakes her head. 'I've put others on that job, but you cannot continue working on the Reyes case. I just want to know what I've put resources into this past week. How did it go?'

That's why we're here. I look at Birck, who looks at me.

'It's going,' he says.

'We're examining a number of technical exhibits,' I continue, explaining about the memory stick and my meeting with Miranda Shali after Friday's training course.

'I told you that course would be useful to you, Leo,' she says.

'It probably won't give us anything,' Birck points out. 'But we're not going to find out for a few weeks, I'm afraid. We're not exactly top priority.'

'If you don't have anything more to tell me when you get the results of Shali's analysis, then you'll have to shelve it. We don't have time for this.' She stands up and signals to me and Birck that we should be going. 'I've got a meeting to go to. I don't fucking do much else these days. In the meantime,' she says in conclusion, while chucking us a pile of newly arrived complaints, 'take your pick, but try and make it something we can clear up, for once. And be ready to get out on the streets if it kicks off.'

Birck grimaces.

'That's just a rumour.'

'For now,' she says.

December is getting closer. People go mad at Christmas time, they say, and the reports we've been handed reflect that, despite it still being over a month to go. Eight cases of threatening behaviour, six of bodily harm of which one is grievous, two of attempted manslaughter, and five robberies — the yield of a single city night.

Birck and I sit down with the assault cases and spend the rest of the day working on them. In police work, real drudgery: checking databases, preliminary interviews, debriefings with the officers present at the scene, and conversations with burnt-out prosecutors. I'd much rather be conducting a few crafty background checks on Ludwig Sarac.

Maybe Sarac has some relationship to the man in the falsely plated Audi that we saw on the tape from Västmannagatan on the second of November. Maybe not, but I don't trust Sarac.

Around half-five in the evening I leave HQ. The headlines on the newsstands are all about Paris. A light drizzle is falling, the kind that soaks you through, getting inside your clothes and making you shiver. On the streets and at bus stops, people are nervously aware of their surroundings, keeping their distance from one another.

These are strange times and I don't blame them, people, not anymore.

28

Police, police, everywhere you look, police. All paranoid, all alert.

He almost got caught, he explains, as he came round the corner onto Tjärhovsgatan and walked straight into two uniformed officers who'd been stationed in the vicinity of the mosque.

'And how are you then?'

One of them patted Grim on the shoulder.

'Good.'

The other, a woman, studied him carefully.

Grim apologised, convinced that the game was up, certain that they were about to ID him and arrest him on the spot. He could see the walls of the remand cell in front of him.

They didn't, though. They stared intently at him for a few seconds, then nodded and turned away. He hurried on, but he could feel their eyes on his back all the way down the street.

'I can't take much more of this.'

'It'll calm down,' I say. 'It'll blow over.'

'Terror doesn't blow over that easily.' He pulls out one of the desk drawers and retrieves a crumpled little envelope. 'Anyway, I found this.'

Inside the envelope is an assortment of identity documents, every bit as fake as they're convincing, in the name of a Patricia

Cruz. I check the pictures to reassure myself that it really is her, and note the dates. A serious-looking Angelica is staring straight down the lens.

'I mean, if you have any doubts that I'm telling the truth.'

'I don't.'

'Gabriel does though.'

'He can speak for himself when he gets here, but quite honestly, what did you expect?'

Grim doesn't answer. He runs his hand through his hair, flattens out a crease in his trousers, and checks where he's got his phone.

'You do know that she was in love with you, right?' I say.

'Angelica?'

'Yes. When she was about twelve or something, after we'd helped her at the bus stop.'

'What makes you think that?'

'A friend of hers said so. You must've made a big impression.'

'I don't think I had anything to do with that. A seventeen-year-old guy tends to make a big impression on little girls.'

'But still.'

Grim smiles.

'Yeah, maybe.'

The sight of his smile stirs a memory, sudden and colourful, and in my head I'm in another time. It's been a long summer, and me and Grim are alone, walking back from the youth centre. Thunder is brewing in the distance and the air is oppressively muggy. Yes, there he is, I can see him in my mind's eye now, my friend with the untameable blond hair and the arch smile, the nimble fingers and the countless *Leo, have ever you thought about* ... The billowing laugh, the seriousness in his face. We're sixteen and seventeen, and walking home through Salem late at night. It feels like heaven is a long way off.

We talk about people we know: she's done this and that, and he got hauled in but the other guy got off, while a third guy called Dani or Danny — *No, Grim, seriously, I know that that's his name, Masha said he was there, but I don't know if he spells his name with an 'i' or a 'y'* — had been on lookout but hadn't dared to actually do anything. How chaos will reign when school starts again; two gangs have been at war since back in July and it simply can't end well. How one of the boys about to start the third grade had apparently been selling smuggled beer from his locker in the corridor next to ours; he still had loads left at the end of term, and he's worried that the beer will have been destroyed over the summer, and worried that he might have to change locker when he starts the new year — which would mean not only losing his business but being exposed.

We laugh. The sky flickers, releases an angry bolt of lightning. The thunder gathers. Side by side, we walk though Salem on one of its narrow pavements, and every now and then the outside of my right hand brushes against Grim's left.

And now, in this room, all these years later, when I stare at my hand I can see the tiny hairs standing on end at the memory.

'I am so incredibly tired,' Grim says, more to himself than to me. 'Of being on the run, of being alone. I've got time left to serve, a ruling based on my psychological condition. But if I'm okay in those terms, let's say the original sentence was incorrect and I should in fact have been sentenced to jail … then what do I do?'

'What do you mean?'

'Do you *want* me banged up?'

That's a crucial question. I think I do. No, no I don't. I don't know.

I stand up from the mattress, head over to the table, and examine the ID cards that never made it to Angelica.

'How many were there, altogether? People you arranged new identities for?'

'Why do you ask?'

'I've never asked you before.'

He thinks about it.

'About a hundred, maybe. After a while, I stopped counting. But not all were successes, some were too tricky. For most of them, though, this sort of thing was enough,' he says with a nod towards the documents on the table. 'Sorting out a new passport, credit cards, things like that. But for others it took more. You had to go in and excise them from records to successfully make them disappear. That takes either friends in the right places, or a long, long time. Let's say I managed it with about eighty of them. About a dozen fucked it up and got caught because they didn't follow my instructions.'

'So seventy, give or take. Seventy people who've committed serious crimes and yet are still at large thanks to you.'

'You mean that I ought to have a guilty conscience?'

'It almost sounded that way just now.'

'You mean that I *should* be banged up.'

'I wonder what your thoughts are on the subject.'

'Most of them would've ended up inside, or in treatment, if they'd lived that long. Presumably a good number would've died as a result of suicide, violence, or an overdose. Either way, they wouldn't have benefited society in any way. On the contrary, they would've cost astronomical sums.

This makes me laugh out loud.

'I ask you about your conscience, and you reply in monetary terms.'

'How do you want me to answer then?'

'I was thinking along the lines of justice and the trauma experienced by their victims, and their victim's relatives. If you care about them at all, that is?'

'Justice?' Grim's eyes darken. 'What do you know about justice? And what kind of a question is that? Whether I care about these people's victims? What do you think? Don't try and make this about you being a better person than I am.'

'I care about what I do, at least, and that my actions have consequences for other people.'

'Do you? Have you told Sam about me, about us? What we're up to here?'

Him mentioning her name stops me in my tracks.

'That's not the same thing.'

'It so is. Of course I care about the consequences of my actions. But what was I supposed to do? I needed to survive. Everyone needs to survive. However much you might think you care about justice and morality, you'll abandon it, put it to one side, if your own freedom is at stake.'

'You were the one who said you were in debt,' I say. 'It was you who started talking about serving your time. I infer that you've started to reconsider what you've done.'

Grim says nothing for a long time. I look at my hand again. The hairs lie flat, the memory gone.

'You haven't found a list then?'

'Eh?'

'A list, I asked for that before. Of her clients.'

'No.'

'And no other lists either?'

'Lists of what? And what's that got to do with this?'

'Nothing,' Grim says. 'Nothing, I just thought it might help.'

There's a knock at the door.

29

Birck closes the door behind him and inspects his surroundings.

'Cosy.'

Grim looks up a number on his phone, dials, and waits.

'It's me. You can come up. Good.' The call ends. 'He's close by.'

Birck walks over to me with Angelica's ID cards in his hand, studying them carefully.

'Fucking hell,' he says, and Grim turns his head.

'What?'

'These are good.'

A list. That's the second time Grim has asked me about a list. There's something he's not telling me.

The door is opened by a bony little sparrow of a man with short dark hair, a sharp beak, deep-set eyes, and thin lips. A few years older than me, he's wearing a worn-out trench coat that reaches down to his knees, and black jeans.

Ludwig Sarac — once part of the pride of Stockholm's police force, the painfully efficient communications division — has a jerky stare and beads of sweat glistening on his top lip.

'I'm whizzing my tits off, to tell you the truth,' he says. 'I had to take way too much just so that I'd dare to come out at all. Fucking bizzies everywhere.'

How he's still alive is a mystery to everyone, given that he's stayed in Stockholm. Two major syndicates have announced a reward for anyone who can bring them Ludwig Sarac, or parts of him in a bag.

'Even in here,' I say.

Ludwig goes stiff and his eyes bore into mine.

'Leo Junker,' he says.

'And this is my colleague, Gabriel.'

'Don't fuck me around, Junker. I'm wired. Makes me unpredictable.'

'At least you're aware,' Birck says as he retrieves a stiff piece of paper from his blazer pocket and unfolds it. 'That's good. Self-insight, sort of thing.'

Ludwig sniggers. He unbuttons his coat and looks at Grim.

'Hardly recognise you these days.'

Grim gives him a hug. I observe them closely, and note that the embrace lasts for a second, maybe two, too long. They'd be able to say something, pass each other a message or instructions. I don't know.

'This man,' Birck says, holding up a series of printed frames of the man from the Västmannagatan surveillance footage. 'Do you recognise him?'

The images are all grainy, with digitally enhanced light and focus, to make his features more visible. He leaves the car, crosses the road, opens the main door. It's not a lot of material, but it's what we've got.

'I recognise him.'

Ludwig takes the printout and examines the images. His nails are filthy.

'Right?' says Birck. 'You're saying that you recognise him. What can you tell us about him?'

'That depends.'

'On what?'

Birck gets the paper back and returns it to his blazer.

'I live in the back of beyond, to tell you the truth. I don't go out.

121

I don't have much to do, don't have the necessary resources, if you know what I mean.'

'You're asking for money?'

Ludwig smiles.

'You've obviously got the money for drugs,' I say.

'I haven't paid for them yet.'

'They can't buy your information, Ludwig,' says Grim.

'Is this the man who visited you about a week ago, asking about our mutual acquaintance here?' Birck perseveres.

Ludwig takes off his coat and sits down on the mattress, all of us closely watching his every move.

'Yes. That was him.'

'What can you tell us about him?' I say.

'To be perfectly honest with you, I already have.'

'Be perfectly honest,' Grim repeats. 'You like that phrase, I remember now.' He takes a step towards Ludwig. 'I don't think you are perfectly honest. I'm fairly sure you know more about him than you let on to me, and I think you kept it to yourself because you know that information has a monetary value.'

'Well yes,' Ludwig laughs. 'Yes, I do know exactly who he is. The question is how much you're prepared to pay to find out.'

'I get it,' Grim says, scowling down at the little man. 'You lied to me.'

Then he jumps on him.

'It was you, wasn't it? It wasn't Lotta, or Jorge. You were the one who contacted him. What do they think I know? Who are *they?*'

'I don't know.'

Birck moves his hand to the holster under his arm, then slowly closes his hand around the P226's handle, holds there.

'Stop lying to me!' Grim roars. 'I hate it when people lie to me.'

Birck puts his free hand on Grim's shoulder.

'John. Calm down.'

To my great surprise, Grim lets go of the little man and stands up. Birck steers him backwards, gently.

'It's funny, someone who's told so many lies having such an aversion to liars.'

Grim doesn't respond. Ludwig is left lying there, panting. Birck lets go of Grim and takes a couple of steps towards Ludwig.

'This is the man we're interested in. If you tell us everything you know about him, then we'll see what we can do in terms of compensation.'

Ludwig's eyes dart around manically.

'Straight up?'

'Straight up.'

Ludwig sits himself up in the lotus position, massages his neck.

'He worked for SGS. His name's Patrik Sköld.'

'SGS?' Birck releases his grip on the firearm's handle. 'You mean the Specialist Gang Squad?'

'He was never my handler, but I know he was an operative there.' Ludwig is slowly writhing where he sits and grimacing. 'That'll be how he knows where I live. I've heard he's with SEPO, but I couldn't tell you. I don't know that much about him, to be perfectly honest.'

'You just said you know exactly who he is,' says Grim.

Ludwig smiles apologetically.

'Tell us what he wanted when he came to see you on Västmannagatan,' I say.

Ludwig looks at Grim and says, 'It was true, what I told you.'

'You said you didn't know him.'

'Sköld told me he knew those who wanted me dead, and threatened to give away my location if I told anyone. I would've been well and truly fucked if I had.' Ludwig's voice sounds tortured, almost pleading. 'That's the truth.'

'Why did you contact me in the first place?' Grim goes on.

'Because I wanted to warn you.'

'Tell us again,' Birck interrupts. 'What happened when Sköld came round. What he asked you, your replies. This is important.'

Ludwig explains that he was just flumping around at home — that's the phrase he uses, and it's one that draws a wince from Birck — on the evening of the second of November, when the doorbell rang. It was about eleven, and standing on the doorstep was Patrik Sköld, former operative with SGS, wanting to know John Grimberg's whereabouts.

The visit was a short one, and once the visitor seemed satisfied with Ludwig's answers — he *really didn't* know where John Grimberg was — Sköld nodded, stood up, and left.

'Honestly, that's it. Nothing else happened. We didn't say anything else.'

'He must've known you were back,' I say to Grim. 'How could he have known that?'

'Did he say anything about that?' Birck asks, staring at Ludwig, who shakes his head.

'Those bastards from SGS were well drilled. They never said a word unnecessarily, back then. They sucked information out of people, but they never let slip anything about themselves. Sköld was the same then.'

We carry on interrogating him: about Patrik Sköld's appearance, whether Ludwig knows who the Audi belongs to, the car's real registration, whether Sköld mentioned any other names besides Grim. Ludwig says he knows nothing, and is becoming increasingly nervous, licking his top lip regularly, grinding his teeth, wringing his hands.

'Angelica Reyes,' I say.

Ludwig raises an eyebrow.

'Yes?'

'What do you know about her?'

'A whore among many out on the streets. One of Djukic's girls. Someone did her in a few years ago.' He turns to Grim. 'You asked about her on the phone.'

124

'Did you say that to Sköld?'

'What? Did I fuck.'

'Don't lie now, Ludwig,' says Grim.

Ludwig sighs deeply.

'Alright. Okay. It might've come up.'

'It might've *come up?*'

'When you called me from St Göran's, I told Sköld about that afterwards. I was dependent on him — him and his colleagues were the ones who could guarantee my safety as an informer, so I didn't dare keep anything from him. He asked me what you wanted, I think, and I told him that you'd asked about her.'

'What did he have to say about that?'

'Nothing,' says Ludwig. 'I swear. If he had, I'd remember, because I'd have contacted you if that'd been the case.' Ludwig buries his face in his hands. 'I'm off my fucking head, to be perfectly honest.'

'Was anyone after Angelica Reyes?' I ask.

Ludwig takes his hands from his face.

'Eh?'

'Had she fallen out with anyone, seen something, heard something, did she know something that made her a threat?'

Ludwig laughs, unsure if maybe that were a joke he just didn't know how to react to, before realising that we were in fact quite serious.

'No,' he says then. 'Not as far as I know. Why, is that what you believe happened?'

'We believe nothing,' Birck mutters.

When Ludwig leaves, he does so with his tail between his legs, mumbling an apology to Grim, who stares long and hard at him before turning away.

Patrik Sköld. SGS. There's an invisible link between him and

Angelica. There's a link to inside HQ. Shit. My thoughts turn to Miro Djukic, the pimp who heard a police radio crackling in the background as he spoke to the evening's third customer, late on the twelfth of October 2010.

'SGS, eh?' Grim says enquiringly.

'This is all starting to get a bit ...' Birck searches for the right word. '... unpleasant.'

30

SGS. The division was established at the beginning of 2008 in response to public pressure on the police force. In 2011, it was wound up. Shortly afterwards, two police researchers, Oskarsson and Banér, conducted an external review of the whole thing.

Somehow that wad of paper landed on my desk — I can't remember how — and that's why I've heard of it. *Combatting Criminal Gangs: Review of Project SGS*, to give the report its full name, was fifty pages long and part of the Linnaeus University Studies in Policing series. On page three, its authors explained the scope of the review, including a statement that's rather telling in terms of the project as a whole:

'During the review, various types of information were requested. Requirements were forwarded to those who had been responsible for SGS, but it emerged that, for the most part, they were unable to meet them. Questions such as what activities officers had actually engaged in, examples of the archetypal gang leaders that the project was designed to deal with, the project's primary goals at various points in time, and supporting paperwork all fell into that category. The task of conducting the review has been further complicated by a lack of cooperation and occasional evasiveness.'

Anyone with a pair of eyes would soon see what that really meant. Oskarsson and Banér didn't have the foggiest about what had gone on at SGS or how it worked, because they weren't allowed to find out anything about it. No one was.

The only thing that was relatively clear was that, whatever it was they'd done, it had worked.

You would have to look elsewhere to find concrete facts. In old case files, mothballed surveillance, SGS' own intelligence database, and successful prosecutions — you could find the odd piece of information.

The original idea for SGS was said to have come from a senior official in the National Police Authority, Carl Hallingström. SGS worked on intelligence-gathering, infiltration, and intervention. Their target was organised crime. They recruited informants such as Ludwig Sarac and Max Lasker, they tailed and bugged people, and they planted weapons and evidence on premises ahead of raids and other operations. They called such tactics 'pre-emptive measures'. They made legends out of officers with a talent for acting, officers they would later offer up as bait as they attempted to infiltrate various syndicates and chapters. SGS adjusted and corrected the records, concealing the true facts and disseminating falsehoods to try to make *their version* plausible even to a trained eye. They succeeded surprisingly often.

Their theatre of operations was basically west of the city, following the metro's Red Line south — towards Skärholmen, Fittja, Alby — and the Blue Line north — Rinkeby, Husby, Akalla. In 2006 and 2007, gang violence was spiralling out of control, so they said, verging on chaos. Everyone was fighting over the same weapons, the same drugs, the same patch. They were motivated by power and pride. All of the old rules had ceased to apply.

Then along came SGS, and they were soon awash with success. Shootings were down, clashes were fewer, and rage subsided as the factions became more cautious.

With the project's victories came plaudits from above, which in turn meant money, and power.

And Patrik Sköld was there.

According to the first search I do of the duty roster on the morning of Tuesday the seventeenth of November, he worked at SGS from the start, March 2008, until December 2010. After that, he took a year's sabbatical, and when he did return in 2012, it was to Drug Squad in Huddinge. And that's where he remains to this day, three years later.

In the accompanying picture, a serious man is staring straight down the lens. Patrik Sköld, born in 1975. Black, curly hair; an oblong face with a day or two's stubble. His features are distinct, his close-set eyes pinch the bridge of his nose, and his lips are thin but curvy, as though constantly curled with disdain.

It's him. It's the man from Västmannagatan.

I go down to the street to smoke a ciggie. Passers-by huddle against the morning's chill winds. I wonder what the fuck to do next, who to talk to. *A Policeman killed Angelica Reyes. Shit.*

To drive straight to Huddinge, walk into Patrik Sköld's office waving the images from Västmannagatan, and demand an explanation isn't a great idea, I do know that much. It might sometimes work for small-time tax dodgers or insurance fraudsters, the type who are terrified of cops because they have a job, wife, and kids to lose if they don't cooperate.

Otherwise it's pointless. Real crooks laugh out loud, while police officers, security guards, and the like just snigger. In police terms, it really is clutching at straws, and they know it. Then it's finished.

I go back in. I meet Morovi in the lift. She's carrying two thick binders and a cup of coffee. I open my mouth to ask her whether she's heard of Patrik Sköld, but she gets in first:

'You know that rumour from SEPO, that says something's about to happen in Sweden?'

'The terror threat, you mean?'

'They even have a picture of the man they're looking for. What they *do not* have is pictures of the ten or so men they suspect are his accomplices. I spoke to SEPO last night.'

'So they're looking for a group?'

'Yes.'

'In Stockholm?'

'It's likely to be carried out here, but in all probability these bastards will be lying low somewhere else until then.' She bites her lip. 'They could've arrived among the refugees. That's what's most alarming.'

The refugees. They arrive in Sweden, and before they make it to the overburdened Migration Agency, a lot of them — *poof* — go up in smoke. Disappear. The border checks won't change that in the slightest.

The lift stops. Morovi's going up another floor. She looks genuinely worried, standing there, pressed against the wall as if by some invisible force.

'Keep your eyes open today,' she says. 'And be careful.'

Ten people. Jesus.

'We'll never find them,' is the last thing she says as the doors close.

31

The TV's still showing extra broadcasts from Paris in the aftermath of Friday's attacks. Part of the terror cell is believed to be hiding out in Brussels. The radio, meanwhile, is reporting on the police checks at the border with Denmark, the pressure on the Migration Agency, Paris again, Brussels — and Sweden. According to the news bulletin, SEPO have declared that the threat level as of today, the seventeenth of November, remains at three on a five-point scale. It is considered high, but unchanged.

Sitting back in my room, I pull out my phone, call Miranda Shali, and listen to the ringing tone. I'm then diverted to Forensics' voicemail.

I don't leave a message.

Patrik Sköld. Who the fuck *is* he? Repeated searches wouldn't look good if they do a random spot check.

My phone rings. At first I hope its Shali, but it isn't.

'Listen,' Birck says in a gravelly voice, 'something occurred to me.'

'Where are you?' I ask. 'Sounds like you've just woken up?'

'A November cold. I'm on my way, but I've got to go to a meeting with the prosecutor about the robbery on Sturegatan. Morovi put me on it. But then it struck me — have you checked Sköld's duty roster?'

'Yes.'

'Me, too,' Birck says. 'I did it yesterday. Strange that the guy goes on sabbatical just two months after Reyes' death. Isn't it?'

'That had occurred to me.'

'It should be possible to run the DNA from the crime scene against our elimination database. He's got to be on it.'

'That had occurred to me, too.'

'Oh right,' he says, irritated. 'And what conclusion did you reach?'

'That we don't have permission, and that obtaining permission would take a very long time, given the level of evidence against Sköld. We've got nothing. We need more, if we're going to do it. And even if we do get permission, against all the odds, the results will take even longer still to come back. That's about it.'

'So we wait.'

'For now, yes.'

'Good. Speak soon. But,' he adds, 'one more thing. What the fuck is going on?'

'What do you mean?'

'The entire city has been occupied by colleagues of ours.'

'SEPO think that a group of ten terrorists are planning an attack in Sweden.'

I can hear him breathing into the mouthpiece.

'Was that ten?'

'Yes.'

'Jesus,' Birck says, and sneezes.

Drearily, the grey day goes on. I get a call from the archive, asking me to clear out the room we continue to occupy despite not having been there for several days.

I'm on the hunt for a five-year-old truth, I think to myself as I organise the crates. The rest of Sweden is hunting terrorists. It's enough to make you doubt your priorities. I flip through some of the documents again, sporadically searching for *Patrik Sköld* as if the name were about to appear on my command. It does not.

On my way back, I pick up the phone and call Sam.

'When do you finish?' I ask.

'In a couple of hours. Why?'

I'm calling to ask her to go home, because the fear is starting to take over. *They're almost never true. But what if …*

'Are you planning to go straight home?'

She laughs at that.

'What's up, Leo?'

'I wanted to hear your voice. Have you got errands to do on your way home?'

'Something's up, isn't it? Has something happened?'

'Don't get the metro or the bus tonight. Walk home instead. I'll explain later.'

This is what makes fear so dangerous. It restricts your freedom to act, makes you paranoid. *That's the whole point:* to plant seeds of insecurity inside you.

At quarter-past nine, SEPO issue a warrant for the arrest of a man suspected of preparing to commit acts of terrorism within Sweden. The news flashes onto the intranet. *In his absence.* That means he's still at large. He could be anywhere. Could strike at any time. Panic reigns.

The next day, the eighteenth of November, SEPO call an afternoon press conference. Journalists' questions pelt the podium like hailstones. One of them concerns whether or not the man is acting alone. The SEPO spokesman dodges.

'Do you have a description of the suspect?' someone asks. 'Do you have a picture?'

'This is the information we have decided to make public at this stage,' comes the official reply.

For the first time in history, the threat level in Sweden is raised from three to four. Everyone on duty is ordered to remain; no one is allowed to go home. Strategically important locations are under heavy surveillance. The intelligence SEPO's acting on suggests that the terrorists will attack 'soft' targets, such as shopping centres, music venues, transport hubs.

Birck and I, having sat in front of the television with our coffees watching the whole spectacle unfold, turn to each other. We've made no progress during the day; he's had to sit with the Sturegatan robbery, while I've been a witness in an assault case at Stockholm District Court.

A few minutes later, our computers bleep in unison as a picture arrives via the intranet. Alongside the image is a short text from SEPO, informing the reader that the photo has been distributed to all personnel.

The picture itself is blurred and grainy. It's a slightly wonky profile view, depicting the man suspected of plotting a terrorist attack in Sweden. It shows a young person, certainly no older than thirty, with a dark beard and a grey or possibly blue-green beanie perched high on his head. He's smiling broadly with his eyes shut — perhaps the photo was taken just as his friend delivered a killer punch line. His teeth look healthy and well cared for.

'Good job you cleared out the archive room yesterday,' says Birck. 'I think we can forget about Angelica Reyes.'

The storm swells to a hurricane.

32

On the morning of the nineteenth of November, two events occur that are both expected — which may or may not have been SEPO's intention; no one knows.

The first is that a picture of the suspect takes up the entire front page of the leading tabloid *Expressen*.

The other is that his name is leaked.

'Fucking hell,' Morovi says as she walks down the corridor towards us, clutching the newspaper.

'If it is him,' I say, 'then at least we've got a few million extra pairs of eyes around the country.'

'Exactly.' Morovi opens the door to her office. 'That's what I'm worried about. What if it isn't him? Or if he's one of ten?'

Not more than a minute later comes the news that the police tip line has collapsed under the volume of calls. Since SEPO haven't specified whether a particular place, such as a certain city or area, faces a higher threat than elsewhere, the country goes crazy. The suspect has been seen in Malmö, Lund, Falkenberg, Jönköping, Uddevalla, Gothenburg, Falsterbo, Örebro, and another dozen or so Swedish towns and cities, from the South Coast to the Northern Border.

'He's a speedy little bugger,' Birck remarks as we rendezvous by his car down in the garage.

'You're crap at sarcasm.'

'I really am not.'

We glide out from underground, onto the streets of Kungsholmen. Our mission is to track down various figures well known to us along the Red Line and wave the picture of the suspect in their faces. We are to ask them if they've had any contact with him. The thinking behind that: Islamist terrorists have, in the past, tended to recruit members among the young, gang-joining men from marginalised urban estates.

'It's not often I feel overqualified,' says Birck, 'but I fucking do now. Wave a picture around. We're not Missing People.'

There just aren't enough officers to cover everything. Everyone has been posted to other duties. Sweden is like a police state; patrols have even been issued with heavy weapons.

'Angelica Reyes,' says Birck. 'John Grimberg. Ludwig Sarac. Patrik Sköld. What a shower.'

We soon find ourselves joining the rear of a great long train of cars.

'Queues?' Birck mumbles and checks his watch. 'Now? What the fuck is going on?'

'People are driving today. They're avoiding public transport.'

Birck turns his head and attempts to change lane.

'What a fucking place,' he mutters.

The police radio crackles. I turn it up. A male voice stating his call sign. He sounds shaken:

'We're a Södermalm unit, posted in to, er, we're standing, we're supposed to be standing underneath the bridge by Central Station,' he manages. 'We're part of the outer ring monitoring the station. But we've just had an incident here, a ...'

'Hello?' says the operator. 'What's happened?'

The man returns.

'I think I just shot John Grimberg.'

PART II

_____

The Whistleblower
Stockholm
December 2015

33

The ghosts.

Ghosts everywhere. Jesus, the streets are *full* of them. Those who walked here before me are waiting in the wings. I'll see them when I get round the next corner.

Not there, *the next one.*

They're here, somewhere. I can feel them. I move at their pace.

Around me, the darkness crackles. The city's neon glitters on the wet tarmac. I am carrying my emptiness inside me. Rain falls.

34

The Audi on Fridhemsgatan isn't parked illegally. The driver has, however, done a poor job of squeezing in between an old Range Rover and a Škoda.

'That's what caught our attention,' Leifby says, adjusting his grip on his umbrella. 'It was parked at an angle, with the front end pointing right out into road.'

'That's right.' Larsson takes a step towards Leifby, attempting to get out of the rain. 'We felt that it could pose a danger to other road users.'

Dan Larsson and Per Leifby are beat officers from Huddinge. They're as lazy as anything and experts in the art of seeing and hearing as little as possible. What they're doing downtown is a mystery — it's not as if there's less going on than in Huddinge.

Leifby steps away from his partner.

'Two of us can't stand under one umbrella.'

'It's my umbrella,' says Larsson, following Leifby.

'It's ours.'

Larsson looks at me, the fresh mustard stain on his uniform almost glowing.

'How much have you had to drink, Junker?'

'I haven't touched a drop.'

'You look a bit rough,' Leifby chimes in agreement.

My ears pricked up when they radioed in details of a badly parked white Audi, but it was only when the radio crackled again that I set off.

'This bugger looks to have false numberplates,' Larsson's nasal dialect could be heard saying. 'OSK 853 is a false reg.'

I only heard it by chance. I was standing next to a patrol car outside HQ, asking whether they could give me a lift home. I was too tired to walk. I hadn't been drinking.

Now the tiredness has been blown away.

OSK 853 is the registration on the vehicle being used by Patrik Sköld.

The car is an Audi A3, 2009 model. It looks fairly well looked-after, as though the owner had the good taste to wash it regularly, thus avoiding any deep scratches to the paintwork.

'Give me one of your torches.'

'Give him yours,' says Leifby.

'I got a new one yesterday.' Larsson puts a guarding hand over the torch on his belt. 'Give him yours instead, it's older.'

'Fuck it,' I say.

'Can't we …'

'No. Leave it alone.'

I pull out my phone and activate its stark, white light. When I turn it towards the driver's side, it dazzles, reflecting off the glass. Despite that, I can just make it out — the police radio mounted inside.

In my head, it makes the sound Miro Djukic heard when speaking to Angelica's third customer on the night of the murder, the twelfth of October 2010.

Our surroundings consist of six- and seven-storey buildings; the hum of Fridhemsplan is like a thick rug. It's evening, the third of December. Everything's cold and ruined, but the windows are lit up with Christmas stars and Advent candlesticks, like remnants of a time when the world was a lighter, warmer place.

Like memories, like ghosts.

'We did a search on the chassis number,' Leifby says, pulling a notepad from his breast pocket. 'The car hasn't been reported stolen. The correct reg is PVV 219. It's registered to a Patrik Sköld, of Stockholm.'

'Where in Stockholm?'

Larsson clears his throat and looks over at his colleague.

'We haven't quite got that far yet.'

'Haven't you been standing here for the last half-hour?'

'Yeah, but ...'

'Yeah, but what?'

Larsson glances at the hotdog stand on the far side of Fridhemsgatan. His slight movement causes the umbrella to tip. Rain drips down Leifby's neck.

'We had to get ourselves something to eat,' Larsson admits.

'We had the car under supervision at all times, though,' Leifby asserts, moving closer to his partner again.

'You went and ate in the middle of your shift, without notifying the station?'

'You called, didn't you?' says Leifby, looking at Larsson.

'I thought you called.'

'You said that *you* were going to.'

Leifby side-eyes Larsson, who shrugs.

'Get out of here,' I say.

'Yes, perhaps we should do that,' Larsson mumbles, before lolloping off alongside his colleague, under the umbrella.

I head a little way away myself, stop on a corner to get my phone out.

'It's here,' I say when the call connects. 'The car from Västmannagatan. There's a police radio in it.'

'OSK 853?' says Birck.

'Patrik Sköld's car,' I confirm. 'The car from Västmannagatan is here. Complete with police radio. Can you … ?'

'I'm in a meeting.'

'Now? It's eleven at night.'

'Ask someone else.'

'Someone else?'

'Yes.'

'Aha. Got ya.'

I hang up without saying another word.

It's been like this for days.

35

The man who pulled the trigger is a Nikola Abrahamsson. Born 1991, grew up in Jakobsberg, in active service for a year and four months when it happened.

According to the report written by his superiors afterwards, based on conversations with those involved, Abrahamsson and his partner, Viveka Cehaic, had been among those posted to the bridge by Central Station to keep the place under surveillance.

Abrahamsson hadn't slept for thirty-six hours, while for Cehaic it was nudging forty. They were ordered to stay on the streets. On the nineteenth of November, three-quarters of the force beat their personal bests for overtime worked.

A man was seen walking towards the bridge, from the direction of City Hall. His head was hunched down between tense shoulders, hands in his pockets. He bore a likeness to a character who'd run into Abrahamsson and Cehaic on Södermalm a day or so before. That might've been why Cehaic recognised him.

'Christ, it's him,' she said, digging an elbow into Abrahamsson's side.

'Who?' said Abrahamsson.

'Police!' Cehaic shouted. 'Stop!'

Cehaic ran towards the man, who turned and hurried back towards City Hall. Abrahamsson was already holding his firearm.

The man was wearing baggy jeans and a thick coat, and had

a hood pulled up over his head. From behind, it could've been anyone.

Abrahamsson fired a warning shot. It whipped through the air with a crack. People around started screaming.

The man disappeared into the shadows under the bridge.

Something flashed. Could've been a firearm, a knife, or a detonator for the bomb vest he might've been wearing under the thick coat.

Abrahamsson took aim and fired towards what he hoped was the man's thigh. The man collapsed there under the bridge. He didn't scream, which was worrying.

'Shit,' Cehaic said once she'd made her way over.

Blood was flowing around the man's head. There was something in his hand. Not a firearm, not a knife, nor a detonator. It was a lighter. On the ground close by, a cigarette, unlit.

In the background, someone screamed.

Abrahamsson's shot forced its way into Grim's skull and came to a stop somewhere above his right ear, sending him into the coma he's been in ever since. It's been two weeks. Grim is in Karolinska Hospital, his condition stable but unchanged. He's guarded around the clock by two constables. I'm there pretty much every day.

Almost nothing is as normal.

Abrahamsson's shot made Birck tell Morovi. There was no other way out, according to him. It felt like a betrayal, and I wanted to punch him, but I didn't. Deep down somewhere, I understood. I still protested though:

'I told you. I gave it to you as it was.'

'Yes, because you didn't have a choice. Because it would've been impossible to carry on hiding it. *That's* what gets me — the fact that you did it for that reason, not because it was what every reasonable person *ought* to do in that situation.'

'Friendship's not always about right and wrong.'

'Friendship,' Birck repeated. 'This is exactly what I'm talking about — this isn't about work for you. You expose both you and me, and Grimberg, to significant risk by acting the way you do. That's why I have to do this.'

In the middle of it all, I laughed.

'You *can't* claim to be doing this for my sake?'

'Partly.'

Then he went, and I was left alone.

I was put on sick leave for five days. That was it, then I had to go back. When I got back to HQ, I was still swaddled in the shock, I think; sudden noises or movements could easily put me off my stride.

Ghosts, apparitions.

Shadows everywhere, shadows after me.

I was summoned to Morovi, who was sitting behind her desk staring at her hands.

'So you wanted to look at Angelica Reyes' murder because John Grimberg asked you to,' she said, without looking up. 'John Grimberg, the escaped inmate from St Göran's. Put away for murder and attempted murder. Your alleged friend. Who tried to kill Sam. How many people know about this?'

'You and Gabriel. And Grim.'

'No one else?'

'No.'

Morovi lifted her gaze. In the room next door, someone turned their radio on, and I could hear music through the walls, muffled and melodic.

I stood there blaming Birck for having grassed. I blamed myself for lying. I blamed Grim for having come back: *this is his own fault, if he'd stayed away it would never ...* Most of all, I blamed Nikola Abrahamsson, and I was scared what I might do to him if we were to meet.

'Why,' she said calmly, without folding her arms across her chest, without so much as adjusting her position, 'didn't you say anything to me?'

'I ...'

'Aiding and abetting. That's the offence you've committed. If you had said something, I would've been able to help you.' Then: 'Are you quite sure that no one else knows?'

'Yes.'

'You need to be completely certain, Leo.'

'I am. And ... sorry. I do apologise for what has ... I didn't know how to ... He is, or rather he was my best friend.'

'No point saying sorry.' She returned to her computer. I could see it in her face, the rage. 'It doesn't mean anything anymore. I just don't believe you.'

I headed for the door.

'Listen, Leo,' her voice came from behind me.

I turned around.

'Yes?'

'Is it true?'

'What?'

'That some officer from the former SGS was after Angelica Reyes?'

I tried to think.

'I think so.'

She nodded sharply. I kept walking.

'Leo?'

'Yes?'

'I've protected you until now. I'm going to keep doing it, because I haven't got the resources to suspend you. But ...'

'Yes?'

'When all this is over, I'll be filing a report.'

36

Yet she's still the one I turn to, standing on that corner watching the Audi, after Birck knocked me back. Morovi knows about the investigation, and she's seen everything we've managed to get hold of. She's the one who has to make the call.

'OSK 853,' Morovi repeats with a yawn. 'Are you sure?'

'I'm sure. It was Larsson and Leifby who saw it.'

'Larsson and Leifby? How the hell …'

'I don't know. The real registration is PVV 219. The car belongs to Patrik Sköld.'

'*The* Patrik Sköld? Where is it?'

'On Fridhemsgatan, but it would be good to know where it heads to after that.'

'Why aren't you calling Gabriel?'

'I did. He said no.'

'What?'

'He told me to call someone else.'

In a marginally softer tone, she tells me:

'You know I haven't got any spare bodies. If you're going to check that car out, you'll have to do it yourself, at least until tomorrow morning.'

She hangs up.

When I blink, lights flash behind my eyelids and I can see Grim in front of me, his empty eyes staring up at the bridge deck above, his rib cage rising and falling unnaturally quickly, almost pulsating, as he gasps for air. Blood is flowing all around him.

Shadows everywhere, apparitions. The streets are full of ghosts. There's also something else about that gunshot that doesn't sit right, something besides anxiety and rage. Something deeper, I don't know what.

OSK 853. PVV 219.

Why would a cop drive around with false plates? On a car that isn't even stolen?

I call Birck again.

'Could you at least do a check on a car for me?'

'No.' He breathes out deeply. 'Leo, I ...'

'It's okay.'

'Are you sure about doing this?' he asks.

'What else am I going to do?'

'Go home. Have a shower. Have something to eat. Save your relationship. Don't lie.' A pause. 'And ring, if anything comes up.'

'Ring if anything comes up?'

'Yes.'

'That's what I'm doing.'

'Sorry,' he says, quietly, then hangs up.

While I stand there, looking over at the other side of the road, I make another call and listen to the rings as I wait.

'Looks like I'll be out tonight,' I say. 'I wanted to say that, in case you ... in case you come home.'

'I understand,' says Sam.

'No, it's not like that. I'm not there.'

'But you're up to something that has to do with him.'

'What makes you say that?'

'Those are the only times you don't come home.'

I want to say something, but I don't know what.

'You're not even there,' I say. 'You're —'

'Bye,' she cuts in, and the line goes dead.

I had to tell her about Grim. I had no choice, and she knew it.

'This is fucked,' she said. 'I haven't got a fucking clue what to say. Can you at least look at me?'

My eyes looked up to meet her stare. It was cold and clear.

'Sorry.'

'And you told me *after* you'd told Gabriel, and after your *boss* found out. You couldn't even tell me first, not until you ... not until you had no choice. That's so incredibly fucking selfish of you, Leo. How the hell can we ...'

Her voice oscillated.

'What?'

Sam's eyes fell onto her hand, which was resting on top of mine. She removed it, folded her arms, and stared out of the kitchen window.

'I don't know. Nothing.'

Then she screamed at me. It culminated in her holding up her hand, the one with four digits. The only trace of the fifth is a discreet scar on her skin.

'Look,' she screamed. 'You're always avoiding it, but *look* at it. Look what he did to me. And you've been lying to me for weeks. Or is it longer than that?' She grabbed a cushion from one of the dining chairs and slung it at me. 'Eh? Lying *again*? I'm so fucking tired of this.'

'Even when I've told you the truth, you don't believe me,' I said in a louder voice, and launched the cushion back at her. Then, louder still: 'Is it any wonder I didn't say anything?'

'But *how* am I supposed to know you've told the truth?' she spat, with tears in her eyes. 'How the fuck I am supposed to know that, after everything?'

I had the urge to throw something against the wall, something hard. A glass or a bowl, something that could smash. Not because I was angry with her, I don't think, but because it hurt so much to be confronted with how badly I'd behaved. I was so frustrated by everything I'd done.

'It's *always* something, Leo. You are *always* hiding something. Don't you get it?'

As quickly as the rage had inflated itself, so it got punctured. Sam was standing in front of me, panting through her half-open mouth. I took the cushion from her hands, pulled out the dining chair, put the cushion back in its place, and sat on it.

'You're right.'

'I …' Sam rounded the table, pulled out the chair opposite me. 'I can't do this. I haven't got it in me.' She slumped in her chair. 'Not again.'

Our eyes met.

'There's nothing more, Sam. This is all of it.'

'Is it really?'

'Yes.'

'I don't know if I believe you.'

That was the last thing she said that night, and I fell asleep restless and anxious, with my face an arm's length from her back and those words echoing around inside my head.

The next morning, I woke up in an empty bed with a text from Sam on my phone.

Staying at Mum's for a few days.

The cat brushed up against my legs, mewing in the silent apartment.

I'd never needed a Serax so badly.

I was chain-smoking all day, and by lunchtime I found myself standing staring at the half-empty whisky bottle in the cupboard. I was seconds away from reaching up and pouring myself a few fingers — fuck knows, maybe a whole glass would've been good

— when it struck me that the last time I'd held it was when Grim was there.

Now he was lying in a coma with a bullet in his head.

I might never be able to talk to him again.

I avoided the bottle. I made no attempt to get hold of any pills.

I laid low.

She still hasn't come back.

'I'm not going to leave you,' she said when we spoke yesterday. 'Not yet. But I … I need some distance right now.'

I said I understood, because I did.

I do.

But these days without Sam are so long, so lonely. The fact that our lives are so deeply intertwined is something I haven't really grasped until now. It scares me.

It's been almost two weeks, and she's still living with her mother. Occasionally, if I've got time, I'll walk past the gallery where she works, just to see her. When I do catch sight of her — a glimpse of her hair or shoulder, or her sweeping past in there — my stomach flutters, and I realise that I love her, before I'm overwhelmed by how great the distance between us has grown, how sad it is, and the fact that it's all my fault.

Then I drag myself away, dejected. A few days will pass before the need to see her grows too strong for me to resist. So I go back there, and the whole thing starts all over again.

I met someone by mistake. That's the truth of it. Two and a half years ago. I shot a colleague dead; his name was Markus Waltersson. I was in Visby at the time, among shadows in the harbour. It was a mistake, but I was the one who made it, just like Abrahamsson. Grim and Waltersson, or me and Abrahamsson — we were all at the wrong place at the wrong time. Chance might be more important than you'd care to admit. It would be simpler if everything did have a meaning, but maybe sometimes it just doesn't. Sometimes things happen as a consequence of events that lead to other events, chain reactions that reach a climax.

I think I understand Waltersson's family — understand his sister, Tove Waltersson — in a way I didn't before. It's weird, impossible to put into words, so I stay quiet. I probably know how Abrahamsson must be feeling, too, I think, if I put my mind to it. But you can't wear two pairs of shoes at once.

There's time. Waltersson died, and that was my fault. I'm living with that, struggling to accept it.

Grim isn't dead, though: he's breathing. My friend's still breathing. I can hear it.

37

Time passes. Midnight comes around, and Friday the fourth of December is off to an unremarkable start. I'm still standing there.

A man comes out of one of the doorways on Fridhemsgatan, points a little fob towards the Audi and makes the headlights flash briefly.

Patrik Sköld opens the driver's door, sits down behind the wheel, and eases out into the traffic, going with its flow.

He disappears, and I can't follow. *If only I'd had a car.* I'm left standing there, wavering. The people of the city are a blurred crowd of backlit figures.

I walk over to the doorway Sköld emerged from, push my face to the glass and look inside. The timer light in the stairwell is still on. On one wall is a list of residents and their flat numbers. I squint to read the names, and recognise one of them the second before the light goes off: *C. Hallingström.*

The man from the National Police Authority. Founder of the Specialist Gang Squad.

There's an invisible connection between SGS, the man in the car, and Angelica. I'm concentrating on that, for now. Sam may have left me, Grim is a hair's breadth from death, and nobody wants anything to do with me. This is one way to keep going.

38

The room is guarded by two police officers. They're standing on the other side of the door and, despite not hearing them, you never forget their presence.

On one side of the room is a large east-facing window. There's a little silver bauble hanging from the blind, as if Karolinska Hospital were keen to remind people that there isn't an awful long time to go until Christmas; that even this long year will ultimately come to an end.

My friend is lying on his back with a substantial bandage around his head. His arms lie limp at his sides; his breathing is in light gasps. He's been in a coma since the nineteenth of November. The bullet remains inside his head, because they couldn't remove it. Another operation, under a specialist surgeon, an expert in the field, is scheduled for the next few days.

'Grim,' I say, and I notice that my own voice sounds unfamiliar, as though it belonged to someone else. 'It's me, Leo. Can you hear me?'

I can't detect any movement or changes in his breathing, no deviation in the monotonous bleeping of the machine. Carefully, I place my hand on top of his, feel his cool skin and the prominent veins.

Nothing. The thought occurs to me that this is just a body. Grim, the person, is not here.

I gently stroke the back of his hand with my thumb.

'Grim. Can you hear me?'

I have to ask, don't really know what else to do. I ask at least once on every visit.

People are saying that Nikola Abrahamsson and Viveka Cehaic are to be censured for what has happened. That he was not legally entitled to act as he did; that she should have been clearer in her communication. Cehaic said *Christ, it's him* and Abrahamsson thought she meant the suspected terrorist.

They are to be *censured*, that's all. I get the urge to hurt somebody when I think about it.

I lift my hand from Grim's.

I've spent a lot of time trawling databases of late. I've done searches and queries that risk landing me in trouble, since I can't point to a current case that I'm involved in. They'll probably find out sooner or later, but I don't have the energy to worry too much about that.

Those searches have delivered a clear result: nothing suggests any connection between the events of the last few weeks, between our investigations into Angelica's murder and Nikola Abrahamsson shooting Grim under that bridge.

On the contrary, I've only found things that suggest that events unfolded broadly as Abrahamsson, Cehaic, and their superiors reported to the Special Investigations Unit, where the prosecutor in charge had dutifully initiated a preliminary investigation.

Two separate events in motion: a world collapsing in Paris, sending aftershocks through Sweden; and then us, investigating a five-year-old murder and making unexpected discoveries. Two different processes, crossing in that instant, that's all.

But, at the same time: there's something not quite right.

It can't be that simple.

What was Grim doing down there, so far from his hideout on Södermalm? Was he meeting someone? If he was, who? He walked out into a Stockholm crawling with police, all desperately tense. There's no way Grim would've ventured out if he didn't need to.

I study his face. It looks peaceful, still and relaxed. The last time we met was in his flat, on the sixteenth of November. Me, Grim, Birck, and Sarac. I've been over that meeting so many times inside my head that the memories have started to dissolve, mixing with other occasions, other days, but I am almost certain: Grim said nothing, neither then nor since, to indicate that he might be downtown just three days later.

Something is missing.

39

On the evening of the nineteenth of November, a man was arrested in Boliden, a village near Skellefteå in north-east Sweden, on suspicion of plotting terrorist attacks. The arrest was not remotely dramatic, given that they were dealing with a radicalised Islamist. The young man offered absolutely no resistance whatsoever.

The prime minister applauded SEPO's efforts, and as soon as the interior minister had found his way to a microphone, he chimed in in agreement. He was smiling, for the first time in days. So was the National Police Chief, and the journalists.

Finally, everyone was on the same page.

The fact that the original information concerned a group, and not a single individual — no one seemed to care about that anymore. Or perhaps it was no longer relevant. No one knew for sure.

What we do know for certain is that the only thing people cared about was that the arrest meant that a concrete and serious threat to the country's security had been averted.

The young man was interrogated by SEPO for three whole days. After that, he was released without charge. It had all been a mistake, a misunderstanding, a miscommunication. A miss, of some kind.

The prime minister, interior minister, and others didn't say much, which was probably fortunate. Not even the racists — those sitting in parliament, or the bog-standard racists out there among the remnants of the welfare state — seemed to know where to direct their frustration.

Me neither. It was the police operation, in which thousands of my uniformed colleagues were given extra weapons and sent onto the streets, that had left my friend in Karolinska with a bullet in his head. Whichever way you look at it, that's indisputable.

Today, the morning of the fourth of December, the former terrorist suspect dominates the front pages once again.

Now back in Boliden, he has invited the entire village round for an Arabian meal, which he intends to cook with the help of other residents at the refugee centre where he currently lives. The young man wants the gathering to be an answer, the papers explain, a way of demonstrating that he came here to live in peace, alongside others.

I read all this sitting in my office at work. When I hear the phone, I'm so consumed by my own thoughts that I've no idea how long it's been ringing for.

'Hello?'

'Is that Leo Junker?'

'It is.'

Despite it still being early, it sounds like Dr Miranda Shali from Forensics has already had her morning espresso. She says she's now had time to look at the memory stick I gave her a few weeks ago.

'It contains images and … I don't suppose you could come up, could you?'

I'm sitting in front of a computer in one of the many rooms that comprise Forensics' IT department. As Miranda Shali moves the mouse, her bracelet scrapes against the tabletop, a gentle, pleasant sound.

'Is this what was on the memory stick, besides the pictures?' I ask and then swig some of the weak coffee I've collected from the machine on my way up.

'Parts of it. I haven't been able to restore it completely.' Clicking away, she opens a collection of image files and flips between them. The subjects of the photos are long and thin.

'Someone put the memory stick into a computer and tried to erase the content. When you do that, though, you leave fragments, or whatever you might call them, behind. That's what I've used to restore these. And don't worry — restoring files that have been destroyed like this wasn't possible five years ago, so it wasn't that they missed anything. They never saw this. This was me and new technology versus an old memory stick.' Shali smiles. 'Me and the new technology won.'

'What is it, then?'

'A sheet of paper.'

'Paper?'

'Or a list, in fact. A PDF containing a list of names. If you look here,' she says, tapping the screen with her index fingernail, 'this long, thin slice is part of the image, a single line in the list. When I've attempted to restore the file, each row has ended up being an image of its own.' She clicks through a series of similar long, thin image files. 'But on the stick, they were all part of the same PDF.'

The row highlighted on Shali's screen:

Avdic, Margit1979AlbyBH5210756288

'Open the next one,' I say.

Cors, Jaako1984KistaOG5210756288

The third follows the same pattern, except that the long combination of digits at the end is slightly different:

Geldin, Linus1980HusbyBH5210754219

'I've managed to restore seven rows,' she continues. 'I've put them together here, along with their position on the original list — I managed to find that, too. Judging by how they're positioned, I'd say that it contained ten times as many rows to begin with.'

I study the page on the screen, a list containing large gaps. Avdic's, Cor's, and Geldin's names sit together, while the other four are scattered from the top to the bottom of the page.

'You hardly need a PhD in nuclear physics to work this list out.' Shali returns to the first row, Margit Avdic. 'Born 1979, lives in Alby, and has gang connections. If I'm not mistaken, she was together with one of the members of the Stockholm chapter of the Brotherhood. This,' she adds, referring to the number at the end, 'is the officer number of her police handler.'

'Handler? You mean she was an informant?'

Shali takes a deep breath.

'That's what the list is. A register of police informants in Greater Stockholm, in around 2010. Lots of them are now uncovered, dead, or out of the picture for various reasons, but several of them are still active today.'

I put down my coffee.

'Fuck me.'

It's pretty much impossible to describe the significance of the list for anyone outside the service, but if it were to leak to the media *now* it would probably lead to several resignations from the National Police Authority's board, all needing to be replaced one by one. In the underworld, people would die. Criminal networks would be shaken up as leading members were revealed to be informants and infiltrators.

Even that pales into insignificance compared to the power the list would've had *then*, in 2010.

A list that Angelica had access to, a list she hid away on a memory stick in a little hole in the wall, behind her bed. A list that someone had tried to erase.

'Can you see when the material was deleted?'

'From what I can see, some changes were made on the twelfth of October, at 23.28. I cannot see what, but some kind of activity took place then.'

'Can you print me a copy?' I ask. 'Not the individual lines, but that composite you made.'

Shali turns away from the computer, pulls out a drawer, and returns with a piece of paper.

'This?'

There's a green Post-it note attached, bearing the words *For Leo*.

'Thanks,' I say, pinching the paper between my fingers. 'Listen, this duty number.' I put my finger alongside *5210756288*. 'It belongs to Patrik Sköld, right?'

'Yes.' Shali bites her bottom lip. 'The guy from SGS. What a place that was.'

'Did you work there? When?'

'Briefly.' Shali checks her watch. 'I never saw that list, but I did hear about it. It has to be the same list. That's why I asked you to come over. Have you got time to hang around for a while? This is … This ought to stay between us, for as long as possible.'

40

SGS needed her help.

She was seconded to them in the summer of 2009, by which time the squad had been operational for a little over a year. Out on the streets, they were winning the war, but in the digital arenas, where a significant amount of gang crime was committed, they were way behind. SGS needed someone who knew about computers.

At that point, Shali was based in the National Police Authority offices, working on a project aimed at expanding crime prevention in high-tech environments. Given that SGS was tied to the NPA, it was hardly surprising that Shali popped up on their radar.

Before long, she was dividing her time fifty-fifty, spending half the time at SGS and the other half with the NPA. At first she enjoyed it, she says, but before long she felt that something wasn't right.

'I remember the atmosphere within SGS. I didn't like it. It was almost a bit like a sect, or whatever. Everyone there had been handpicked and everything was hush-hush and terribly important. Everyone in the unit was perfectly convinced that they'd been chosen by a higher power and that they'd be able to solve Stockholm's crime problem in its entirety, if they were only given the resources and the room to manoeuvre. It reminded me of the stories you'd hear about the Norrmalm Squad back in the

Eighties, except SGS weren't gorillas and bouncers, more like cunning spies.'

'And you remember Patrik Sköld?'

'I remember him,' says Shali. 'He was one of the ones who stuck out a bit.'

'How do you mean?'

'Well ... He was a bit more open. Had a more nuanced outlook on crime and prevention, it seemed to me. Not only that, he was a pleasure to work with. I had no problem with him, unlike how I felt about most of the others. Luckily, I wasn't there more than 50 per cent of the time, so I was never fully indoctrinated. I think it was down to the fact that I was at NPA at the same time that I got to hear about this list.'

Yes, because in early 2010, something happened.

Almost all of the top brass were new at the time, and one of them was ambitious and righteous enough to want to get a grip on the SGS's highly sensitive use of informants.

This board member had just begun to get an idea of the scope of what later that year would become Operation Playa, one of the largest Swedish coke busts in history. It was largely dependent on unconventional operational tactics, entrapment, and informants. Which is probably why the whole thing fucked up completely.

The board member had also read up on parts of the Peter Rätz Affair, an experience that made her fingers turn cold. As so often happened, what had been a serious crisis at HQ was reduced to a play on words — the man's surname being reminiscent of the Swedish word for *justice*.

Everyone laughed, except this one board member, who pointed out that it was a matter of national security and as such deserved to be taken seriously. That was why she wanted a list.

'I overheard her in the corridor up at the National Police Authority,' Shali says. 'It wasn't long before I realised what sort of list we were talking about. People at SGS were fucking furious about it.'

The list was drawn up against their advice and handed over to the woman on the board. Shali knows that much.

'They had no choice, you know. What happened after that, I don't know. Within SGS, they pretended it didn't exist. Imagine if it leaked — that there was a physical list of names in existence. Imagine if the informants and infiltrators found out.'

First of all, everyone down on the streets and out in the housing estates would shut their mouths and keep shtum for good. Second, everyone with an interest in the subject — the factions, the gangs, and presumably the informants themselves — would do whatever they could to get hold of it. It doesn't happen very often, but this would have had consequences that ended up with people getting killed.

Information is power, in the same way that secrets mean money.

'So it was kept very close to their chests. I heard that it was delivered by hand within HQ, passing from one person to another until it reached the woman on the board. No copies, nothing. Her name was Paulsson, by the way. Sadly she's no longer with us — died of heart failure about a year ago. Whether that had anything to do with the list, I don't know, but it wouldn't surprise me.' She gives me a weak smile.

I make a note of the woman's name in my phone.

'But how does a list like that end up in Angelica Reyes' hands?'

'Easy,' Shali says. 'She stole it from someone, someone who, despite the recommendations, had it on them.'

Grim asked me about a list.

I thought that maybe she kept a list of her customers. They sometimes do. That might help you.

He asked about it later, too, I remember: he wondered whether a list of her customers had turned up yet. No, I said.

And no other lists either?

Something like that. I don't remember his exact words.

Once again, he's tricked me.

41

The door to Grim's hideaway is no longer particularly anonymous. Blue and white tape and the NO ENTRY sign mean it attracts a lot of attention.

You can tell that people have been here: it smells different, and the furniture's been moved around. There's something else, too, something that's growing. A void left by Grim. *The silence.*

I wonder what I'll do if he dies. Who'll take care of his funeral. Whether he'd have any kind of estate. What might happen to me.

I open the drawer where the ID documents were last time I was here. They're missing, but I haven't heard any mention of them, which must mean that Grim kept them somewhere else. I wonder where. But perhaps he destroyed them.

In my early days on the force, I used to go with my intuition. I've long since stopped doing that, because people make way for stereotypes, gut feelings. At times though, intuition is all you've got.

My eyes focus on the jumbled elements within the room: the table, the office chair, the mattress, the fridge standing a bit away from the wall, the low ceiling, my own shoes.

Soon I'm standing in the toilet. It's of the old-fashioned sort, one you pull a chain to flush. The floor is covered with sea-blue lino. The pipes that disappear into the wall have turned brown with age or rust, maybe both.

What if he dies?

Slowly, I slump onto the toilet seat, lean back, and close my eyes. I can see Grim there in front of me, lying weak and still in his hospital bed, with the bandages around his head. I can hear the bleeps following his pulse.

I end up sitting like that for a while, not sure how long, before eventually opening my eyes. Everything is still.

There's a vent cover up in the ceiling. It looks untouched.

I wheel the old office chair in. The seat is loose and it spins far too much for me to be able to stand on it without risking falling off. I try to lock it, but the handle has fallen off and I can't locate it. Eventually I think *fuck it*, and clamber on to the wobbly seat and start poking at the vent.

I manage to squeeze my finger and thumb between two of the grille's thin slats and pull. It moves a bit, but not enough, stays put. *They didn't look here.* I pull at it again, and the chair wobbles as I move. I grab the vent cover with both hands and try to rip it off with brute force.

I topple backwards, out of the toilet and onto the floor, followed closely by the chair, and crack my head. Somehow I've still got the filthy vent cover in my hands. My temples are pounding.

Once I get to my feet, I push the chair back into the toilet and gingerly poke a hand into the hole. I grasp at thin air up there, feel with my fingers across the other side of the ceiling through dirt and dust, and I'm struck by the stench of mould.

Nothing. Shit.

Hold on. What's that?

There.

A piece of string, tied to a plastic bag. Inside, a collection of fake IDs and a piece of paper with a telephone number written on it.

I lose my balance again. Fuck.

42

I'd seen the IDs before, all bearing the name Patricia Cruz.

And there's a list. *The* list. Complete: seventy-two informants, along with their handlers' ID numbers.

I spread my fingers across it, a simple piece of A4 that's been folded in two. It's clean and white, slightly worn at the edges.

Since the list is complete, it can't have reached Grim via Miranda Shali. But that's the only conclusion I can manage. Was this the one he was asking about? Did he already have it then? No, he wouldn't have asked in that case. When might he have got hold of it? It must've been right before he was shot. But how? By whom?

I sit on the floor as I read the informants' names. Shali's right that many have been uncovered or killed — Ludwig Sarac is on the list, as is Max Lasker — but a great many are still active, with current ties to the police.

That's it. That has to be it, I think to myself. It's the only thing that fits the pieces of the puzzle.

Angelica has the list. That's the reason someone's out to get her. That's why she ends up dead.

When Grim starts investigating her death from inside St Göran's, Patrik Sköld fears that he either has access to the list already or is in a position to track it down, which makes him a threat. I turn the paper over.

There it is, the phone number. I recognise the handwriting:

Grim's. I pull out my phone and do an internet search on the number — no results. I dial the number and put the phone to my ear, hear the ringing tone down the line.

'Yes, Sköld here.'

'Is that Patrik Sköld?'

'That's right.'

'I'm Leo Junker. We are ... colleagues.'

'Right. And what is it you want?'

'I want to meet you.'

'What for?'

I reflect for a second.

'Because I know you killed Angelica Reyes, but I can't prove it.'

Not terribly discreet. What the hell else am I supposed to do?

Then he says something surprising.

'I think we should meet.'

'You,' says Birck. 'And what do you want?'

I'm standing in the doorway to his office. I contemplate saying that this is about something else, I don't know why.

He avoids me in the corridors; most of the time his door is closed. He doesn't answer my calls — I have to leave a message asking him to get back to me instead. On the few occasions when we meet in the break room or at meetings, we exchange terse, stiff phrases, nothing more.

'I've found something, and I don't know who else to turn to.'

He pats a pile of papers on his desk.

'I've got plenty to be getting on with.'

I take a step into the room and close the door behind me.

'Is everything alright?' I say. 'With us?'

'Why wouldn't it be?'

'You're pissed off.'

'Yes.'

'Because I lied?'

'I've also got a charge of concealing a suspect hanging over me, once this is done with.' He corrects himself: 'If this is ever done with.'

'Sorry. What more can I say?'

Birck stares at me for some time.

'You're not my Grimberg,' he says.

'What does that mean?'

'That I'm not about to let you control me, like he controls you.'

'He doesn't control me.'

'Course he does. I'm pissed off with you, but I'm not stupid. There were two of us. I had a choice. I don't know who I'm most annoyed with, you or myself. And I'm going to try and let go of that.' He sighs. 'What did you want?'

'I'd, er, like some company.'

'Company? For what?'

'Meeting Angelica Reyes' murderer.'

I sit down on the chair this side of his desk, tell him about the complete list I found at Grim's a few hours ago, and about the short telephone call with Patrik Sköld.

How *he* wanted to meet *me*.

'It could be a trap,' says Birck. 'How has Grimberg got Sköld's number? Do they know each other?'

'I don't know.'

I wonder what his intentions are, what Grim got up to those last few days, what he did after our meeting with Ludwig Sarac up until the gunshot under the bridge. It's getting weirder and weirder.

'The list is as good a reason as any for someone to want to kill her,' says Birck. 'That's probably why she was trying to escape.'

'And she must've been trying to escape from someone who's good at finding people who've gone to ground,' I say. 'People like Angelica Reyes are used to keeping out of sight. It points to us being on the right track now, with Sköld.'

    'Yeah, sure. Listen, Leo,' says Birck.

    'Yes?'

    'Don't lie to me again, okay?'

    'I won't.'

    'Good.'

43

Squeezed into the city centre off Olof Palmes Gata is Apelbergs-gatan, a narrow little backstreet that you'd rather avoid. This is where goods deliveries, rubbish trucks, and lorries pull up. It's almost always blocked, and it stinks.

I'm standing with Birck as I suck the last glimmer of life from a cigarette. The bells strike ten, and Friday night descends on Stockholm. Laughter and shouting fill the main streets along with music from the clubs.

Since we don't have any forensic evidence against the man we're meeting here, we've done our utmost to prepare ourselves, but it's hard to know what to expect.

'Nice to have company, anyway,' I venture, mostly for the sake of saying something.

'Hasn't she come home yet?'

'No.'

'Otherwise you wouldn't be standing out here on a Friday night.'

'Is this you being sarcastic?'

He looks at the cigarette, holds out two fingers. I give him the last drag.

'I don't even know anymore.' He pulls down on the smoke. 'Fuck that's good.'

I went past the gallery today. She was there, I saw her. What might be the thing I like most about her, I realised, is the way she's so at ease in the world. She seems to get it. There's no distance between Sam and other people.

I hope she hasn't seen me. I never stay for more than a second; I don't want to attract her or her colleagues' attention or suspicion. I just want to see her, know that she exists.

Birck drops the cigarette butt to the ground. I retrieve another from my inside pocket.

'Are you nervous?' he asks.

It could be a trap.

'No.'

'Can I have one?' he says.

'Are you nervous?'

'Bored.'

We smoke. Sirens wailing nearby, an engine roaring.

Then it's there, a white Audi A3, gliding down Apelbergsgatan. We notice the registration, PVV 219. No false plates now, for some reason. Is it a signal to us? *I've got nothing to hide from you*, something like that?

'Shame we've got no evidence against him,' Birck says, looking mournfully at the cigarette before letting go of it.

The car stops, with the engine ticking over. Birck looks at me, hesitant. *Imagine if he blows us up.* An absurd thought, perhaps, but there's not much you can be sure of these days.

Grim got shot in the head.

Nothing happens. The man stays in the car, waits. We climb into the back seat, Birck directly behind the driver while I can see his face from where I'm sitting. I've got my hand on my firearm.

'I thought you were coming alone,' says Patrik Sköld.

'This is a colleague of mine, Gabriel Birck.'

In the rear-view mirror, I can see his eyes scan Birck's torso, lingering a little on his armpit, the little bulge of his handgun underneath his coat.

The car's interior is warm and smells of leather. The dashboard lighting is soft orange, gently illuminating Sköld's face behind the wheel.

He puts it into first, and we make our way down Apelbergsgatan, out towards Sveavägen.

'How did you get my number?' he asks.

'I found it, written on a piece of paper.'

'You're talking about a piece of paper that belongs to John Grimberg.'

'I didn't know you knew each other.'

'We don't.'

I lean forward in my seat, and Sköld goes stiff for a second as he takes his hand off the gearstick. He soon relaxes, but not before he's revealed just how tense he is.

'I thought you'd met,' I say. 'You and Grimberg.'

'Once. Last spring, at St Göran's. Before he escaped.' Sköld steers the Audi onto Sveavägen. 'This bit of paper we're talking about, with my number on ...'

'Yes?' I say. 'What about it?'

'It was a list, wasn't it?'

'That's correct.'

'Do you know how he got hold of it?'

'No.'

We roll along Sveavägen, that broad thoroughfare as straight as a jetty, on towards the heart of the city.

'Where are we going?' asks Birck.

'I don't know. But inside the car is a good place to talk.'

'That's what we're here for,' says Birck.

'Yes,' Sköld says slowly, one hand on the wheel, the other resting loosely on the gearstick. 'You think that I killed Angelica Reyes.'

'That's correct.'

'I suppose, in a way, I did.'

The phone rang. That's how it started, the evening of the first of November.

One of Patrik Sköld's old contacts from his SGS days had made certain observations earlier that day, and was now getting in touch to share them with him.

During the afternoon, he had seen a man walking through Vitabergsparken on Södermalm. The man wasn't particularly conspicuous, but there was still definitely something familiar about him.

This was a person, the contact's instincts told him, who shouldn't be there. He followed him, not for any great distance, but long enough for something to happen that made him realise who he was looking at.

It all happened in a tobacconist's, and it was the way the man used his hands that did it.

The thing was, he'd seen those hands before: when they'd been busy counting a wedge of notes in a basement. This time they were counting much smaller denominations — the man was buying three packets of cigarettes from a kiosk on Folkungagatan — but the way he used them was exactly the same: handling the notes simply and neatly, assuredly, the way a poker player manoeuvres his cards with his hands. He pinched off two fifty notes between his ring and little fingers while the rest of his hand was busy producing three twenties. It was this detail that was so unusual.

And it wasn't just the hands, the contact added to reassure a somewhat sceptical Patrik Sköld. The man was John Grimberg. A bit overweight, maybe, and with a different hair colour. But it was John fucking Grimberg, sure enough.

The contact had called in the hope of getting compensation of some kind. That was why he'd rung Sköld, and not — for example — the detectives within Stockholm Police who were actually in charge of investigating John Grimberg's disappearance.

Sköld had not been overly convinced, but as he hung up, he did so with a certain sense of foreboding. It could be that his contact was making the wrong conclusions, but it was also possible that he wasn't. That would mean they had an escaped inmate on the streets of Stockholm, one armed with dangerous information and a desire to get to the truth of the murder of Angelica Reyes.

'How do you know he wanted to do that?' I interrupt. 'And what information are you referring to?'

We approach Stureplan and the dense buzz of passing traffic. He drives us out onto Birger Jarlsgatan, towards Strandvägen and the waterfront.

'I met him, as I said, during the time he was at St Göran's. An old SGS informant, Ludwig Sarac, had had a call from him. I'm guessing you know who Sarac is.'

'Yes,' says Birck.

'Grimberg had made various attempts at enquiries into the Angelica murder, including contacting Sarac, who knew everything about everybody back then. I tried to persuade Grimberg to leave well alone. During my visit, it became apparent that he knew about the list — the one that you presumably have with you. He knew that Reyes had got hold of it and used it, he suspected this was connected to her death. I asked him what he wanted the list for, if we were even going to admit that it existed, which I never did. He said he was going to use it as a tool.'

'A tool?' asks Birck.

'Yes.'

'To do what with?' I say.

'To get what he wanted, to be able to exert pressure in order to improve his own situation. Or rather, to put it plainly — to get free.'

'Did he *say* that to you?' I insist.

'"I need that list so I can start again." That's what he said. About eighteen months later, I'm guessing, he'd had enough of being on the run and wanted to come back, but not without a certain ...' Sköld ponders the right word. 'Advantage.'

I look at my hands.

'You're lying,' I say. 'Trying to wriggle out of this.'

'No.'

It doesn't sound like the Grim I've met lately. He's changed.

People don't change. They adapt.

Someone said that to me once, in another time, another life. A darkness gathers inside my chest, heavy and deep. I have felt it before.

The darkness inside me is the feeling of betrayal.

After hearing that a resurrected John Grimberg might possibly have returned to Stockholm, Patrik Sköld got in touch with Ludwig Sarac to find out more. He knew that Sarac had been dumped by the force and spent his time stewing in an apartment near Odenplan, so one evening he paid a little home visit, as he calls it.

Sarac didn't know where Grimberg was, and while he didn't rule out Grimberg being back in Stockholm, he did think it was unlikely.

'At least now you know where he is,' Birck grunts. 'You and the rest of Sweden.'

'I've seen the headlines,' Sköld replies. 'I hope he makes it.'

'Do you?' I say, something burning inside my chest.

'Yes?' Sköld looks puzzled. 'Yes, of course.'

We glide along Strandvägen. The tall, beautiful buildings stretch towards the sky. The waters of Lake Mälaren glitter. In the distance, you can make out the arching silhouette of the bridge over to Djurgården. I adjust myself in the seat. Sköld stiffens up again — his eyes flash back and forth in the rear-view.

There's something about him. Something vulnerable and afraid.

'This car,' I say. 'I've seen it before, with false plates.'

'That's my paranoia. Certain duties are best carried out under a false flag.'

'And yet you answer with your full name when someone calls,' I say.

'There are very few people who know about that number.'

'Was this the car you were using around the time of the murder of Angelica Reyes?' Birck interjects.

'My car has nothing to do with her murder.'

Between the seats, I can just see the police radio. The one that crackled in Miro Djukic's, the pimp's, ear, as he spoke to the third customer that evening, on the twelfth of October 2010. It has to be. The pieces all fit.

'Is this your car?'

'It is now, yes. It used to belong to SGS, a duty vehicle. If you look through the reports you're sure to find a white Audi A3 with registration OSK 853 in a few places. The false plates are from the SGS days. We would often operate that way.' He sniggers. 'Elegant, eh? Guardians of the law and all that.'

Elegant. I stare out into the darkness.

'There are two — no, three things I don't get,' I say. 'First of all, how did Angelica Reyes get hold of the list of informants and what did she want with it. Second, you said that in a way you were the one that killed her.'

'And the third?'

'Your intentions. What it is you're up to, what you've been up to since 2010.'

The resulting silence is tense, heavy. I peer over at Birck, who raises an eyebrow.

'The thin blue line,' Sköld says eventually.

'The thin blue line?' Birck leans in. 'What about it?'

'You might well ask.' Sköld shifts down. We reach the lights by the bridge. 'But that's probably what this is all about.'

44

The phrase 'thin blue line' has its origins in the British police. Its use has spread from there to, among others, the American and Canadian forces, where the phrase is used officially. In many other countries, including Sweden, its use by the police is more informal. It has also become a commemorative emblem for killed or injured colleagues — people talk of how *the thin blue line was breached last night*. Swedish police, primarily those on patrol duties, sometimes wear the symbol as an armband or as part of the uniform's trim.

The emblem takes the form of a flag with a black field. A bright blue horizontal line makes it look like the flag is divided into three parts: a black top, a black bottom, and a thin blue middle.

The black at the top represents civil society, the general public. Those who obey the law, who go to work or to school every day, who care about their nearest and dearest, pay their taxes, and start families, thus securing society's continued existence.

The black at the bottom, meanwhile, symbolises the criminal underworld, where bandits, robbers, and desperate gangs from forgotten estates rule a lawless, greedy realm.

All that separates them — as society's specially chosen protectors, stopping violence and anarchy from spreading into every corner — is the police. Standing in the middle, like a barricade. A front line. Maintaining social order, cohesion, safety, and security.

We are the thin blue line. Between order and chaos, life and death.

'It's a nice idea,' says Sköld. 'The problem with high ideals is that they often turn to shit when put into practice. Now don't get me wrong. Swedish Police isn't a bad organisation — on the contrary. It's outstanding. In spite of the strains we're under now, we still manage to prevent and investigate crime. That's fantastic, really. The vast majority of police are decent people, working in departments under perfectly good leadership. It's not that. In certain parts of the organisation though, things can go wrong, even when you're trying to get it right. That's what it was like at SGS. In order to get on top of organised crime and protect the public, we had to use some risky methods. Informants, infiltrators, telephone tapping on the edge of what's legal, bugging rooms — definitely on the far side of that line — and so on.'

We wait for him to continue. The white Audi is soon enveloped by the Djurgården night. I get the feeling he's already lied, Patrik Sköld, but I can't put my finger on when.

'That list,' he goes on, 'you know that it consisted of the names of SGS's informants.'

'Yes,' says Birck.

'And you know that its compilation was ordered by NPA in the aftermath of the Rätz scandal, in conjunction with Operation Playa.'

'By Inger Johanne Paulsson. Yes, we know. But what does Angelica Reyes have to do with any of this?'

'The list ended up in her hands.'

'Ended up?' says Birck. 'Bit vague. How?'

'Through someone who paid for her services. Either this person leaked it to her, or she stole it. I'm inclined to believe the latter.'

Paid for her services. It sounds so formal, almost clinical, despite what it's actually about: sex in exchange for money.

From the back seat, I've got a decent view of Patrik Sköld's face, or parts of it: one ear, his cheek, the corner of one eye, his nose. He's well groomed, a man who normally likes to take good care of his appearance. Right now, though, he looks stressed.

'Someone at SGS paid Angelica Reyes for sex,' Birck says, unconvinced.

'I shouldn't be saying this. And I can hear that you don't believe it, but yes. That's what happened.'

I lean back in my seat. This is no surprise. On the contrary, this is the chain of events that seems most plausible. But still, *the risk*.

'And she used it.'

'She did.'

'How?'

'How would you, if you were in her situation, how would you use a list like that? What's the first thing you'd ask yourself?'

I peer out through the window. The tree-lined streets of Djurgården look like a ramshackle wall from in here. Everything's blurred; the lights glow warmly.

'How much is it worth.'

'Exactly.'

'She was extorting money from someone at SGS,' I say. 'The same person she was selling sex to, who either gave her the list or the chance to steal it.'

Sköld lowers his speed as we roll up behind a lorry. It's filthy and it turns off by Skansen open-air museum.

'Yes.'

'And this person at SGS killed her for it,' says Birck.

Sköld squirms in the driver's seat.

'Do you have any evidence whatsoever for this?' I ask.

Sköld doesn't respond.

'Why should we believe you?' Birck attempts. 'It all sounds to me like an excellent explanation for a guilty party trying to slip the noose.'

'Well it isn't.'

'So who did it, if it wasn't you?'

'I cannot answer that.'

'Why not?'

Sköld scrabbles around to find the words.

'The truth is … that I don't know. But given that I was at SGS at the time of the murder, and given what I've told you, it would be a bit strange if I didn't have an *inkling*. That's not enough, though, the stakes are far too high. This is about *police officers*. Whatever else, it must not get out that I was the one who blew the whistle on it.'

'It doesn't have to,' says Birck. 'If you tell the truth, then it isn't going to.'

Sköld's eyes flash in the rear-view mirror, meeting Birck's for a second.

'It always does,' he says. 'It always gets out. Believe me.'

Before long, we've done a circuit of the island. Downtown Stockholm and Södermalm shine out from across the water, an aura of light surrounding them. My friend is in hospital, lying in a coma with a bullet in his head. It's a surreal thought. What if I never get to speak to him again?

What if he's been stringing me along the whole time?

People don't change. They adapt. What if that's true?

'Let's say we believe you,' I say. 'SGS has been disbanded. Why are you so concerned the fact it was you might get out?'

'I'm forty, I've been a policeman for fifteen years. I've never been able to imagine doing anything else. This is the only thing I can do, the only thing I'm good at. Ten years ago, I had a family, I was married, my daughter came along, and I was happy. Then the marriage broke down and I started drinking a bit too much. I lost contact with my little girl — today she probably doesn't even know whether her dad's alive or not. That's every bit as awful as it sounds. The only thing that kept me from sinking completely was my job. I've got another twenty-five years, maybe more, left in the force. Or rather,' he corrects himself, 'I *want to* have twenty-five years left. Critics, the ones who call things into question and start asking about things, are regarded as potential whistleblowers. They get muzzled, one way or another. You know all this. Only last month, a colleague reported our boss for misconduct. Soon enough, there was a rumour doing the rounds that this colleague was mentally ill. It was just plucked out of thin air, but somehow it took root. It all led to a psychiatric assessment and him losing his firearm.'

That's a lot more humiliating than it sounds. *Castration* isn't the right word, but it is the first thing that springs to mind.

Birck adjusts himself in his seat, and with some exertion manages to fold one leg over the other. The legroom inside the little Audi is less than generous. Sköld listens carefully to Birck's movements, you can tell.

'I was to be moved out. It was going to be done discreetly, of course, nice and calmly. I haven't ...'

He doesn't finish the sentence.

'What?' I say.

'There are eyes on me already. My record is not quite squeaky clean.'

'What does that mean?'

'It was down in Södertälje, on an SGS operation. A raid. I was still drinking a fair bit, but I'd really pulled myself together. And I was good, that's why I got sent there in the first place. I ended up committing a serious narcotics offence, something I had to do to save the raid, but that's probably not what it looks like if you're not familiar with the background. I think they've already noticed that I'm sort of moving around a bit. That I'm asking a few more questions than I ought to be.'

We head back to the centre. The city gleams. I follow the lights with my eyes, unsure whether I'm looking for something or not.

'Why are you telling us this?' I ask.

'Because you called,' is all Sköld says. 'Because, at the end of the day, I don't want you to think it was me that did it. I don't even know who pulled the trigger.'

'You don't?'

'I did not kill Angelica Reyes,' says Sköld.

'We're not entirely convinced about that.'

'But you don't have a single piece of evidence. Or do you?'

'So there is evidence,' says Birck.

'Rhetorical question.'

Birck looks at me.

'An employee of the very unit within the force that's home to the keenest proponents of the ideology behind the thin blue line goes to whores.'

Sköld laughs.

'People become disillusioned for less, don't they?'

'And yet you want to stay in the force,' says Birck.

'I don't know what I'd do otherwise. For me, it was a vocation. The police force we have has a lot of systemic flaws, but it's better than nothing.'

Before long, he stops the car close to the square in Östermalm. He says there's more, that there's something he wants to show us, but there are certain measures we need to take first.

'There's still one thing I don't understand,' I say. 'Your motive. Visiting Grimberg at St Göran's, looking for him now, meeting us, and so on. What is it you're after?'

'That's the tricky thing about people's motives,' Sköld draws out his sentence, 'isn't it? That they change, over time. I think … I was shaken up when I heard about Reyes' murder, then, in 2010. I mean, we all heard about it, I'm sure you did, too. Sounded messy. As I started to realise that there were probably things in the Reyes case with links back to HQ, I tried to protect ourselves, first and foremost.'

'How did you come to realise that?'

'I know this is frustrating, but I can't really say just yet.' He clears his throat. 'That's why I visited Grimberg at St Göran's. I wanted to leave it alone. But then, I don't know, it could've been something to do with him, or maybe it was just me getting sick of the lot of it, maybe because I'm not twenty-five anymore. The Angelica murder was messy, I knew that, but after my meeting with Grimberg I felt a mess myself. I was busy doing something that was wrong. That's when I started to ponder where my loyalties actually lay. In fact, I'm probably still doing that now. Part of me wanted to see the whole thing blow up. I don't *know* anything. The Angelica murder is a puzzle, or a maze. There are lots of pieces missing, probably always will be, so I don't have any more than indicators and careful guesswork. And I'm far too … As I said, this job is all I've got. I can't lose it, certainly not by guessing about things. And that is what'll happen if it turns out I've turned my back on my force. My own *section*, in fact.'

'So you're going to let us do it.'

'I tracked down Sarac,' Sköld goes on, 'to find Grimberg. That's true. But not to hurt him or to threaten him, just to see what he knew. He might know something I don't. At that point, I didn't know that you two had also started working on the case.'

'So you want to tell us what you know, or what you *think*, but you don't want it getting out that it came from you. Easy. We can arrange that.'

'I'm going to need a bit of time to think, too.'

'About what?'

'Can we meet after the weekend — Monday? Monday evening?'

Neither Birck nor I are particularly inclined to say yes, but something tells me we don't really have much of a choice.

Birck and I climb out of the car. He looks dubious. Doesn't look good, a narcotics offence. Regardless of the surrounding situation, it's not unthinkable that someone who was prepared to commit such a serious offence on duty might also be prepared to commit an even more serious crime to protect his old unit.

As Sköld disappears into the night, it could be Angelica's murderer getting away.

'In that case, why would he tell us so much?' I say when Birck points that out.

'To trick us into trusting him.'

'Yes,' I say. 'Yeah, maybe.'

A nasty wind sweeps across Nybrogatan, and the night continues in that vein — nasty, and dark.

I head home. The place is empty tonight, again. I shuffle restlessly on the spot as Kit brushes around my feet. Since Sam left, I've made the effort to take care of him, make sure he eats and drinks. Most of the time, he sticks close to me or lies down on the rug in the hall, waiting for Sam to come back.

I drink coffee, to keep myself off the booze. The cat falls asleep on the rug. *Sam.* The pain of missing her is almost physical, a pain in my chest about level with my heart.

i need you, I text her at about five. There's hours left before dawn arrives and I write, *i love you. come home?*

45

Morning is unfurling, and I head out. Need to get away from here. The streets, empty and open as they are, are easier to cope with. I head towards Solna and the hospital, where something's happened.

One of the nurses emerges from Grim's room and shoves past the two officers posted to guard my friend around the clock, saying that he's going to get a doctor.

'What's happened?' I ask.

'Who are you?' the nurse asks me, but then moves on without waiting for me to reply.

The two cops, serious and upright, look quizzical.

The door creaks open a bit. I take two steps into the room and I can hear a low groan coming from the bed.

Grim is no longer in a coma.

He's lying perfectly still. His mouth is moving but there's no sound. The bandage around his head covers his eyes and would be obscuring his vision, if indeed he has his eyes open.

'Grim. It's me.'

The low moaning, like a muffled wail, resumes.

'It's me,' I repeat. 'Leo. The doctor's on the way. They're coming.'

I study the array of tubes and machines, unsure whether he's only still alive thanks to them. I hope not.

Grim's hand looks for mine and grasps it.

'Grim. Can you hear me?'

'Uh-huh,' he hisses and gives my hand a short, gentle squeeze, almost like a tug.

Like a confirmation.

'Are you in pain?'

Nothing at first. Then he squeezes my hand again.

'No?' I say tentatively. 'You're not in pain. Is that what you mean?'

'Uh-huh.'

Another squeeze. He's scared. I can sense it in his touch.

I tell him that its Saturday the fifth of September, that he's in Karolinska Hospital with a bandage around his head. It covers his eyes. I tell him that he isn't blind.

I can feel the lines across the palm of his hand. Our skin, the two thin membranes meeting, is all that separates us from each other.

Scared? Who wouldn't be?

'What were you doing on Kungsholmen? You were approaching on foot from the direction of City Hall,' I attempt. 'What had you been doing there?'

'You,' he forces out, and I don't know what he means by it.

'Me?'

'Live there.'

'What's that got to do with it?'

'I …' He hesitates. 'Safe.'

'It makes you feel safe to be around where I live?'

'Uh-huh.'

I don't know why that means so much, but it does.

'There's something I need to ask you. It's important.' I lower my voice. 'I've got the list. In your flat, I found it in the toilet. Do you know which one I mean?'

Seconds of silence. Then his hand squeezes mine.

'When did you get hold of it? From who?'

No answer.

'Grim. When did you get hold of it? Was it …' I hesitate. 'Was this what it was all about? Is it what you were after? The Angelica murder, our meetings, was that …' I stumble, not sure how to express the feeling. 'Was that it? You mustn't lie to me now, Grim. You have to tell me the truth.'

I look at him, the parts of his face not covered by the bandage — his chin and mouth, one ear, his jawbone and cheeks, his nose. Not one muscle is tense, I think to myself. Maybe he just can't.

A tug on my hand. Once. *That was it.*

'You knew it existed and you planned to use it. I was supposed to help you find it. Am I right?'

A slight hesitation at first, I can feel it despite him not moving a muscle. Something, I don't know what, is flowing between us.

'Uh-huh,' he grunts.

'That was it?' I ask, for confirmation. 'And the person you were going to contact about it was Patrik Sköld.'

'Yes.'

I try and think my way through to the next question, but everything is moving so slowly.

'How did you find out about the list?'

The name, short and weak, slips into the room:

'Angelica.'

'She told you about it.'

He smiles gently.

'Course she did.'

'Who had she got it from? How had she managed to get hold of it?'

He attempts to say something else, I can see his mouth moving but can't hear any words. I get up from my chair and lean over him, so that my ear can sense Grim's warm breath escaping.

'Not sure,' he whispers.

'But you have a hunch.'

'Not sure,' he repeats. 'Sorry.'

'For what?'

'Everything.'

He has betrayed me. I have betrayed others, by trusting him time and time again.

We are two of a kind.

We do exactly the same thing — he does it to me, I do it to Sam. I'm no better than him. Maybe we deserve each other.

Everything is a circle. I collapse into the chair again.

'Why?' I ask.

Grim opens his mouth but nothing comes out. He gives my hand two quick squeezes: he doesn't understand.

'Why did you try and trick me?' I elaborate. 'Did you really think I was going to give you the list if I found it first?' The question comes out again, angrier, I'm not in control of it: 'Why did you trick me?'

'I ...' His tongue finds its way out between his lips, moistens them slowly. 'Because I never learn.'

That's the last thing he says to me that morning.

The door opens. At last, the doctor's here.

46

I see us sometimes, in my mind's eye.

It'll be summer one day, maybe the next one, or the one after that, and the sun will be shining white and warm over Norr Mälarstrand. I see us there, yes, there we are, arriving at the waterfront terrace from different directions.

Grim's hair is sun-bleached and unruly. He's wearing sunglasses, which he takes off when he sees me, then he gives me that big smile, the one that for a second always makes him look seventeen again. As I embrace him, I can smell his hair and the softener in his clothes, the heavy scent of sunscreen and sweat. That's how I imagine him.

We order some beers and sit smoking at one of the tables, laughing at the past, and from the bar's speakers Peggy Lee sings *time is so old and love so brief.* Wounds heal, distance in geography and lifestyles can be bridged, you can get yourself through anything.

Death is a long way off. We speak about it frankly and openly, the way you can when you feel secure. We talk about how close we've come to it, not once but several times, we both recall — at the same instant, as those with a shared past do — something that happened to us in Salem.

It's about the girl, the one who was standing waiting for a bus one night. The one who later lost her life, tragically; but on that particular night in Salem, after having her life saved by two strangers, death was a long way off for that girl, too.

We talk about her, Angelica. Grim asks if I really think she was in love with him. I say I don't know, that he would know better than I would. But maybe. Probably. He's easy to fall in love with, I can imagine, and she was a girl with a sense of adventure. He's living with someone now, I don't know who, and working somewhere, and we might not get together that regularly — that's often the way in the middle part of your life — but when we do, those meetings mean a lot to me.

Love is pure gold and time a thief, Peggy Lee sings and we toast something banal, and we laugh again and I think how it was winter for so long, that those years without Grim were so lonely, and how the summer that surrounds us has finally arrived.

In my imagination, we speak about the solution, me and Grim, as though it's already happened. *The solution to the Angelica murder,* we say, but never in any more concrete terms than that. That's where the illusion disintegrates; a crack or a tear appears in the dream's backdrop, and the light of reality breaks on through.

This, me and him on a terrace in the sunshine, is never going to happen. We're too far away from each other. Everything's too messy, too complicated, too raw.

The solution to the Angelica murder. What is the solution?

Perhaps it's Patrik Sköld. I can see the weapon in his hand, and the motive that drove him to it. But he was partly telling the truth; his suspicions about Grim's motives have been proved right. Part of me wishes I'd never asked, that I'd never heard his explanation.

Because I never learn.

Maybe we'll never get any closer to each other.

47

'Are we agreed on this?'

It's Morovi asking the question, Monday morning. She often does that, says *we* and *our* when she means *you* and *your*. Apparently, it's something to do with leadership, using a certain form of words to indicate that her understanding is based on ours.

Both me and Birck answer yes. We're agreed.

The meeting has been going on for less than fifteen minutes, which has proved to be sufficient to present all the latest developments in the Angelica Reyes case. Morovi seems surprisingly unmoved. She moves her fingers down the list of informants.

'Someone at SGS is supposed to have taken Angelica's life because she gained access to this list by selling sex to them. She is then alleged to have used it to extort money, and then been threatened with death by this person, so she goes on to contact John fucking Grimberg to help her disappear. The perpetrator beats her to it, kills her, and retrieves the list. Or so he thinks. The murderer, being familiar with our methods since he is, at least technically, one of us, carries out the crime in such a way that it could easily be mistaken for a classic case of man kills woman in fit of rage. That's the theory.'

'More or less,' Birck replies.

'And we don't know who?'

'We're meeting Patrik Sköld again tonight. It could be him. Or else he knows who it is.'

'And we're agreed on this,' she says.

'Yes?' says Birck, confused.

'Good. I'm going to ask again, since what we're about to do amounts to nothing less than shooting our own force in the foot, revealing a group of highly successful officers as potential criminals, including a prostitute-visiting murderer, costing the justice system several million kronor and starting a media campaign against our own HQ the likes of which has never been seen before.'

'Yes?' Birck says weakly.

'And this is all because of a five-year-old murder of a prostitute, a crime we might get to prosecute, but where the suspect, if we were to find one, is likely to walk free. Chances are I'll get sacked, and what might happen to you I have no idea, but it probably won't be much fun. *So,*' she concludes, 'I want to be *perfectly sure* that we are in agreement.'

Birck clears his throat.

'Are you trying to get us to drop it?'

She shakes her head, and lowers her voice.

'Investigate SGS,' she says to me. 'Find something *conclusive.* Who was there, when, what they did, and so on, focusing on the time around the murder. And not a word to anyone. Goes for you, too,' she adds, staring at Birck. 'You're working on this now. Off you go.'

i'll probably come home tomorrow

Sam leaves it at that. A warmth spreads through my chest, means I don't hear Birck's question.

'What did you say?'

'I asked you what you were thinking about.'

'Aha. Patrik Sköld.'

'Me, too.' Birck looks with disdain at the bit of paper in his hands, a duty roster from SGS. 'We should've arrested him.'

good, I text Sam, attach a picture of Kit. *we miss you*. Then I put my phone away.

'For what?'

'I don't know, but we should've done *something*. Now he's had an entire weekend to tidy things up. Or disappear — we don't even know if he's still in Stockholm, or the country. I'd much rather have had him locked up.'

'But on what grounds? We've got nothing. Calm down.'

'I will.' He sighs, lets go of the piece of paper. Something is hanging back in his voice. 'I was thinking, you mentioned that you'd been to see Grim.'

'Yes?'

'I've heard at HQ that he's conscious, apparently. Did he say anything? Was he … Was Sköld right?'

I can hardly bring myself to say it.

'He was trying to get hold of the list.'

'So you were a useful idiot. How does that feel?'

'How does it *feel?*'

'Yeah … or however you might put it.'

'He's my friend. How do you think it feels?'

'You need some new friends,' Birck mutters. 'Shall we keep going?'

'Yes, please.'

We examine printouts of duty rosters and staff records. We do have access to them, but it's not straightforward. That's why it's taken so long. Our efforts so far have led us to one, not particularly helpful, conclusion.

During its short existence, between 2008 and 2011, SGS was a powerful place.

With a staff of more than thirty to call on, most of them operatives and men, even if the proportion of women eventually climbed to a little more than a quarter. On top of that came the countless informants and informal colleagues constantly used by the unit. They had premises here at HQ and out at a local station in Huddinge. The number of cars being used by SGS seems to fluctuate between five and ten, depending on which records you consult. Some of the vehicles, including a white Audi A3 registration PVV 219, are listed as operative equipment — that is to say, classified — and as such not recorded in all documentation.

In October 2010, thirty-one people — twenty-three men and eight women — were working within SGS. A few days before Angelica's murder, much of the unit's manpower had been deployed on a large-scale smuggling bust. The documents show that five people — four men and one woman — can be immediately excluded from our inquiry. They were in Gothenburg at the time, since that's where the smuggling was taking place, even if the goods themselves were ultimately intended for Stockholm.

'That leaves twenty-six people,' says Birck. 'And of them, I would probably dare to suggest that we can rule out another six. Three, for example, are in court, giving testimonies in the trial of those accused of shooting up a restaurant in Husby, two were at a conference in Chicago, and one was on holiday.'

'So we have a list of twenty possible suspects,' I say.

'Of whom, five have strictly administrative roles,' Birck adds. 'Can computer geeks and desk jockeys kill someone like Reyes?'

'I would think so.'

'But would you put money on it being one of them?'

'The opposite more like.'

'Exactly,' Birck says, his eyes fixed on his computer screen. 'So get rid of them for now. Then we've got fifteen. Not bad, really. More than half the names on the list have dropped off.'

I study it.

'Four of them are women. Do we rule them out? Considering the third-customer thing, I'm thinking. That's a man of course.'

'And the question of incitement?'

'You mean that one of the women might have hired a guy to kill another woman?'

'Alright,' says Birck. 'I hear you. I'll adjust the list.'

Eleven candidates is still too many. Both he and I know that. To rule out others will take closer investigations and we've yet to talk about how we're going to undertake them. Birck is eyeing the piles of paper on his desk with obvious displeasure.

'Duty rosters, equipment lists, and staff records don't cut it. We need more.'

'I know.'

He pulls a paper and pen towards himself, starts writing something down. I quickly disappear into my own thoughts. Useful idiot. That's what I am. That is what I've been.

'I was thinking ...' says Birck.

'Yes?'

'Now you know Grimberg's motives about the Angelica murder, does that change anything for you?'

'You mean do I want to say, *fuck it*, and go home?'

'Sort of thing.'

I pause for thought.

'Yes, partly.'

'But?'

'That would be a selfish thing to do. The correct course of action from a policing point of view, on the other hand, would be to try to make some progress, given the new information.'

'So you're trying to do it again, only better,' Birck says with a crooked smile.

'Something like that.'

Birck hands over the piece of paper, a list of fifteen names. Eleven men, four women, name and current age. No faces yet: we still haven't searched for any pictures.

'If we're right, then it was one of these.'

(Sandra Amiri, 36)

Josef Anyuru, 40

(Olivia Berggren, 34)

Marcus Bylander, 45

Mohammed Fattah, 36

Hernan Fernandez, 47

Jesper Hansson, 37

Karl Jansson, 51

Tobias Lundin, 44

(Miriam Redar, 38)

Lehel Reljanovic, 35

Patrik Sköld, 40

Jon Wester, 51

(Ann-Sofie Österdahl, 53)

Somewhere among them, a murderer.

48

I call him in vain, hoping to hear his voice.

Grim's asleep, the nurse informs me, as he has been for most of the day. He's extremely tired. He's got another X-ray coming up and he needs to rest up before that and the planned operation. They need to get the bullet out.

It sounds dangerous. When we end the call, I'm nervous.

During the afternoon, Birck and I augment the list of fifteen names with new information about them, as and when we find it: their specific responsibilities at SGS, how long they served, and who their immediate superior was.

We make few telephone calls and send as concise emails as possible. We're investigating our colleagues. It feels almost like investigating ourselves, and it doesn't feel right. There's always the risk that someone might react. Someone might see us, might already be watching us from a distance.

The list of candidates gets shorter.

Josef Anyuru, 40, Operative in the field A, 2009–2011. Immediate superior: Karl Jansson.
Mohammed Fattah, 36, Handler, 2008–2011. Immediate superior: Jon Wester.

Hernan Fernandez, 47, Handler, 2008–2010. Immediate superior: Jon Wester.

Karl Jansson, 51, Group Leader, operative unit A, 2010–2011.

Tobias Lundin, 44, Operative in the field B, 2008–2010. Immediate superior: Ann-Sofie Österdahl.

Lehel Reljanovic, 35, Operative in the field B, 2009–2010. Immediate superior: Ann-Sofie Österdahl.

Patrik Sköld, 40, Operative in the field A, 2008–2010. Immediate superior: Karl Jansson.

Jon Wester, 51, Director of Operations, 2008–2011.

Eight remaining names. Of them, five are still in the force, those who have left being Mohammed Fattah, Karl Jansson, and Jon Wester. Fattah works for the armed forces, Jansson seems to have retrained as a social worker — a fairly common career development — and Jon Wester works for the private security sector, another not uncommon destination for those who've tired of policing and are looking for a more lucrative alternative.

'So what are we going to do?' I say.

'We're going to meet Sköld tonight.' Birck is scrolling through a document on screen. 'We'll start with him.'

The hours pass slowly. Tomorrow, Sam's coming home.

I don't know what to expect.

I call Karolinska again. No answer.

Birck draws a ring around Patrik Sköld's name on the list, and adds a question mark alongside.

49

It's evening, Monday the seventh of December. Cold, raw air out there, no snow.

Patrik Sköld lives on the second floor of Surbrunnsgatan 62, just north of the City Library and the green open space of Observatorielunden. The journey there I spend in the passenger seat, with the list of SGS staff in one hand and the list of informants in the other. I don't know what it is I'm looking for.

Birck runs an amber light, out onto Sveavägen. A horn beeps behind us. Birck ignores it.

'What are you thinking about?' he asks instead.

'Me being a useful idiot.'

'We've all been there, at some point,' he says consolingly.

We wait by the entrance to Surbrunnsgatan 62, shivering in the icy wind, hoping that someone arrives or leaves soon. It's best to avoid the intercom, best to be cautious. Someone has daubed the words *I'll love you with all the madness in my soul* on the wall of the building opposite, in jerky, uneven letters.

The door clicks and is pushed open from the inside by a young man. We smile at him. He doesn't smile back. Two flights of stairs later, we're outside Sköld's door — a reinforced modern one. It's thick, and it doesn't allow any noise to pass through from the other side. Birck knocks. We wait. Nothing.

Birck places his hand on the door handle, attempts to open it. It's locked, and he knocks again, harder this time.

Nothing.

'Oh dear,' he says quietly. 'This doesn't bode terribly well.'

I retrieve my phone from my pocket, find the number, and call. Birck looks puzzled.

'Switched off.'

'Try again. Could be the network.'

I ring again. It takes a second before the automatic click cuts in.

'No, it's switched off.'

Fuck. He's done one.

Birck sinks to a crouching position, opens the letterbox, and attempts to peer through it.

'Trainers on the hall rug, bit of junk mail. Nothing else. It's dark in there, though, so you can't see much.' He stands up. 'Fuck. We *had* him. We were sitting in his fucking car. We let that bastard get away. What the hell do we do now?'

We call the locksmith. It's the only way.

'Christ's sake,' Birck says while we're waiting. 'We got too close. He disappeared, from right under our noses. Shit, I knew we should've been tougher. We should've brought him in.'

'Yeah. We should've.'

Fucking hell. *Fucking hell.*

Birck turns to the door.

'Do you think it's a door you can kick in?'

'It's reinforced. You'll get a pain in your foot, not much else. Wait for the locksmith, he'll be here soon enough.'

There's no way to contain our frustration. We watched Sköld drive off. *We stood there watching him drive away.*

The locksmith arrives, and in the ten minutes he spends working on the lock he doesn't say much. Birck asks to borrow a couple of pairs of latex gloves from the packet poking out of his bag. The locksmith grunts in reply.

When he thinks he's finished, he pushes the handle down to check that the job is indeed done. He then stands up, removes his gloves, informs us he'll send the invoice as usual, and adds a mumbled remark about us using his services during office hours from now on.

The door to Patrik Sköld's apartment is ajar. We pull on the gloves.

There's a light on in there somewhere, further in. We step over the trainers and the leaflets on the floor. There are a few winter clothes hanging on the rail in the hall, but mostly just empty coathangers, as though he'd just left. *Bad. Shit. How the hell are we going to explain this to Morovi?* I pull out my phone to put out a search call.

Birck tries a light switch. The hall is illuminated. Beyond it, a living room that leads onto a bedroom, and in the far right-hand corner, the kitchen. The home is sparsely furnished, with high ceilings; the floor is old and creaky. The clothes are neatly ordered, the bed made. On the table in front of the living room sofa, there's a copy of one of the National Police Authority's reports alongside a book, Frederick Forsyth's *The Devil's Alternative*.

'Mm hmm,' Birck says, irritably, looks around before heading into the kitchen and switching on the light, then recoiling. 'Jesus, Leo. Close the door.'

There's a little table at one end of the kitchen, and two chairs. That's where he's sitting, leant back yet still slumped, surrounded by a red shawl of blood. His firearm is lying on the floor, and on the wall a metre or so behind Patrik Sköld is a smear of blood and brain debris. It smells.

Sköld's face is pale, his eyes open, staring. His mouth has been scorched by the muzzle flash. A nauseating sight.

'Watch where you put your feet,' I hear Birck say.

That's when I notice, not before.

He's wearing his uniform.

50

There's a laptop on the desk, its screen dark. Directly in front of Sköld are two pieces of paper. I pick up one of them.

It's a document stating that Patrik Sköld, ID number and officer number given, is hereby suspended from duty with immediate effect. The background to this is the compelling evidence of a serious narcotics offence in 2009, which took place during a live investigation with Södertälje Police. During the inquiry, it also emerged that Sköld has been guilty of forgery on a number of occasions.

Taken together, the allegations are so serious in nature that Sköld's position as a police officer must be called into question, and the disciplinary committee unanimously approved his suspension. For more detailed descriptions of the case, the document refers to the appendices.

'Forgery?' Birck studies the document over my shoulder. 'They mean the false plates on that car.'

'I guess so.'

Serious narcotics offence, Södertälje Police. That must've been the case he mentioned to us.

'He's got the sack,' Birck says.

'It says, "suspended".'

'Haven't you worked for Internal Affairs? You know what suspended means. He's finished.' He pauses. 'It's Monday today.

We met him a few days back.'

'Yes?'

He examines the piece of paper again.

'The disciplinary committee reached its verdict in an unreasonably short time. They must've had this prepared well before.'

'Or else Sköld's been being watched for longer than he let on. That's almost how it sounded. Didn't he say something about having eyes on him?'

'Yes, he did. The question is, whose?'

Birck picks up the other piece of paper. It's a note. Handwritten.

They got me, and the abyss opened up beneath me.
I've got nothing else, and I can't take any more.
I hope it doesn't make too much of a mess.
P.S.

Then in the bottom corner, added later — you can tell not just from its position but also from the handwriting. It's sharper, hastier; he'd probably made up his mind and was getting impatient, wanted to act:

I never came any closer than this. I found the file on his computer in
winter 2010. I had a bad feeling about it and I opened it.
That's how it started, for me.
I don't know if it was him or whether someone did it for him.
Destroy this note.

Then there's a password.

That's it.

I look at Birck, who's looking at Patrik Sköld sitting there on the chair.

'Do you still think it was him?'

'I don't know.' He crouches down and studies the dead police-man. 'I'd say it was a fairly typical suicide. Wouldn't you agree?'

'Yes.'

'But,' he goes on, 'you do wonder whether he actually did this himself, or if it's supposed to look like that.'

Birck's eyes slide from the soot in Sköld's mouth, to the position of the weapon, to the splatter on the wall. He moves around slightly, examining Sköld's body.

'Staged suicide?' I say. 'Doubtful.'

'Yes, but a perpetrator who knows how things *should* look to fit a particular story can probably dupe most people.'

'We should call someone,' I say.

'Soon.'

He turns on the computer. The fan whirrs into life, humming gently as he enters the password.

The screen displays a neat desktop. The wallpaper is the police heraldic emblem — a shield beneath a royal crown, laid across two laurel branches, each complete with a broad axe. I've never liked it. It looks threatening, almost violent.

There's only one window open, the media player with a video clip ready to play. The first frame is waiting, frozen. The scene is indoors, inside an apartment, and I know which one.

The camera wobbles as Angelica adjusts its position, presumably on one of the small shelves in the kitchenette. The unmade bed comes into view. She looks like she's concentrating. There's a clock on the wall behind the bed, and it's quarter-to nine in the evening. Outside the flat's windows it's dark, you can just about tell. What day are we looking at? Not the day of the murder, anyway: the objects on the little bedside table are not the same.

Once she's finished, Angelica stops in the centre of the shot, looks into the camera before allowing herself a weak smile.

'I've got the list. Give me the money. You know what'll happen if you don't.'

She gives him a playful wave goodbye, before reaching for the camera and pressing a button.

The screen goes black for a second.

The wall clock now shows a few minutes past nine. The gloom in there makes the colours grey-blue. Angelica takes a few steps backwards, having just set the tape rolling again. She turns to the mirror and runs a hand through her hair. The dress she's wearing only reaches as far as her thighs, accentuating her hips.

The sensation of seeing Angelica moving, hearing her voice: ghostly. Like temporarily stepping over to the other side.

There's a knock at the door. Angelica disappears out of shot. Muffled sounds, no discernible words.

She returns. A man walks into the edge of the shot. His hands are visible, you can see them unbuttoning the shirt he's wearing. Angelica is counting some money with her back to him. The dress has a deep-cut back, showing off her sharp shoulder blades.

Then she places the notes on the bedside table. The man's shirt falls to the floor.

'Here,' he says.

'Wouldn't you rather do it on the bed?'

For a split-second, Angelica's eyes dart towards the kitchenette.

'No, here.'

'I don't want to do it standing up,' she protests. 'It hurts.'

'Who's paying who?'

She gives him a smile, but it's a hostile one, you can almost feel it. She takes his hand and tries to pull him towards her, into the shot.

She doesn't manage it. She's too nervous for it to seem natural. The man remains out of view, you can hear him:

'What are you playing at?'

'I've been working all day,' she says. 'I'd really like to lie down.'

'Working all day,' the man repeats with something approaching revulsion. 'Sexy.'

His voice has no accent; it's bland, devoid of distinguishing characteristics. It could belong to absolutely any man, perhaps even Grim.

She makes no further attempts, presumably worried that he might get suspicious. He suspects nothing so far, or does he? You don't know. He's the one who pulls her towards him. He forces her to her knees. All you can see is the sole of one of Angelica's feet. A slathering noise accompanies the man's heavy grunts.

'Oh fucking hell,' says Birck

'I don't know why you're messing about,' the man says gruffly. Something rustles. Two five-hundred kronor notes sail nonchalantly to the floor. He lets go of her; she's gasping for breath. Then it starts again.

This is no longer paid-for sex we're watching, but an assault.

Angelica is gagging, you can hear it. He lets her go. She catches her breath. They go again.

'Fucking hell,' Birck says again. 'I can't watch this, it's making me feel sick.'

He says this standing alongside a policeman who's shot his own head off. I don't bring that up. He still forces himself to go on watching, as do I. A split-second will do it, if the man bends over or takes a step to one side. That's all we need — him stepping into the shot. We're close now.

He stops Angelica, and gets her onto her feet. What he's just done seems to have drained her of energy, made her body weak. He pushes her against the wall. They're completely out of sight. You can hear the man putting on a condom, then his body slapping against hers, her whimpering every now and then. That's all that's happening, until she pants and moans, asks him to do it harder, faster.

Her mask is convincing — well used, presumably. You could

almost believe she was sincere.

When he does empty himself, he does so without a sound, silently. He moves away, takes two steps backwards. He groans as he pulls off the condom and you can hear him putting his clothes back on.

'Can you open the window?' Angelica asks. 'It's got so warm in here.'

To do that, he has to pass the camera lens. It's her last chance. She lies down on the bed and stretches out, looking at him.

The man doesn't answer. He gets dressed.

Watching a defeat.

Then it happens.

He walks past the camera, its eye capturing him on his way to and from the window. It happens quickly, just a few seconds.

Once the door has slammed shut behind him, Angelica smiles broadly, before she turns over and starts looking for something behind the bed. That little hole in the wall? She pulls out a joint and grabs the lighter from the bedside table. Her body relaxes and drifts off.

It looks nice.

She's about to nod off but suddenly remembers something and turns towards the kitchenette, stares straight into the camera. Without saying anything, she stands up and walks forward slowly, hand outstretched.

The camera jerks the instant before the clip ends.

Birck leans over the screen, clicking away until the technical details of the video are displayed.

'The file was created on the eleventh of September 2010.'

'A month before the murder. We need to call someone.'

Birck rewinds the clip back to the start so he can hear her say it again.

'I've got the list. Give me the money. You know what'll happen if you don't.'

He stops the film.

'There we have it. Then the subject of the extortion arrives.'

'Yes,' I say. 'You saw who it was.'

'Yes.'

I don't know if it was him or whether someone did it for him.

The man in the clip is Jon Wester. The man in charge of SGS.

Fuck.

51

Anja Morovi lives on the third floor of a lovely old building on Torsgatan. The apartment is in darkness, except in here, where a ceiling lamp casts a warm, soft glow on the living-room furniture. Morovi is wearing a white towelling robe. Her hair's all over the place, her cheeks are rosy, and her stare is clear and alert.

She didn't sound overly pleased about a visit on the phone. Since Birck insisted, she agreed to hear the explanation, and when he said *Patrik Sköld is dead* she went quiet, before ordering us round here. Now her eyes glide past the bedroom door. It had been ajar when we arrived, and before she'd had the chance to close it I heard light snoring inside. Neither Birck nor myself have made any comment.

'What a trio,' she says. 'A policeman who killed himself, or possibly was murdered, and had been sacked, a murdered prostitute keen to disappear, and a high-ranking police officer who is paying for sex. Not only that, it's all on film. You know how to keep your boss awake at night.' She strains not to raise her voice. 'It's a fucking disgrace.'

I feel uneasy. There's something about all of this, about Angelica and Grim and SGS and Sköld's dead body and his empty staring eyes, *the thin blue line* and *Jon Wester, Jesus,* that makes you lose your footing.

'Sköld was framed for the drug offences,' she says, speculatively.

215

'According to him, he wasn't completely innocent,' Birck says.

'We haven't looked into that case, but I should think that's about right. They probably used it against him when they realised that he'd been speaking out of turn.

'Why, though, did he choose that way out? He could easily have leaked the lot of it to the media, stormed into NPA, or ...' Morovi's thoughts drift away. 'Or pointed his weapon at Jon Wester instead of turning it on himself.'

'He did actually seem composed when we saw him,' Birck agrees. 'But there was still definitely something ... vulnerable about him. The flat was ... It was a lonely person's home.' He turns towards me. 'Wouldn't you say?'

'I don't know. But being that disillusioned with the force, yet still wanting to stay, and then getting shut out like that ... I can imagine that it felt the way he described it.'

The abyss opened up beneath him.

Morovi raises an eyebrow.

'I do hope you're not talking about yourself and your own imminent suspension now.'

'Don't worry. I'm too much of a coward to take my own life.'

'Good.' She nods over at the computer. 'Put the film on. And pass me those headphones from the table over there.'

She watches two minutes of it, her face expressionless as she observes the events on screen.

'When do you get to see him?' she asks.

Birck spools forward. We see the man walk through the shot. This time, no longer obsessed with the man's identity, other things become noticeable: he seems hunted. Something — a demon, or desperation — is driving him on.

Morovi stops the tape and pulls off her headphones.

'Fuck.' She stares at an invisible spot somewhere in between me and Birck. '*Jon Wester*. Fuck.' She takes a deep breath. 'This investigation,' she continues, 'or whatever we're supposed to call what it is you're up to, is no longer a secret within HQ. I had an unwelcome visit before I left work today.'

The visitor was a man from the National Police Authority, Carl Hallingström. He had recently had lunch with a good friend of his, one of the female archivists. Hallingström had asked how things were down there, to which the archivist had replied that for the most part things were pretty calm, but with busy periods. She happened to mention that two men from Violent Crime had occupied one of the rooms a while back, before abruptly abandoning their work.

'Yes, it was Junker and Birck,' the archivist had explained.

Since Hallingström had heard about Junker and Birck — Jesus, who hadn't — he obviously had to ask what case they'd been working on.

She knew, of course.

'It was about the Angelica murder.'

'The Angelica murder? Why? There's at least a dozen unsolved murders in Stockholm, none of which are more than a year old, and all with decidedly better starting points. Why work the five-year-old murder of a whore in the city centre?'

Needless to say, the archivist hadn't been able to answer that question.

That was why he was sitting there, puzzled, in front of Morovi. Hallingström wanted, bluntly, to know what Junker and Birck were playing at.

'By the way, isn't the Reyes case about to be handed over?'

'Yes, it is,' Morovi replied, 'which is precisely why I've asked them to take a look at it. Make sure everything is in order before the handover, that all the minutes and exhibits are in the right places and nothing that should've been done during the investigation has been left undone.'

If Junker and Birck found anything worth chasing up, they had her permission to do so.

'And how did that go?' Hallingström enquired drily.

'They have conducted some supplementary interviews, attempted to get a few details confirmed,' Morovi replied. 'That's all. But,' she added politely, 'how come NPA has deigned to concern itself with what my officers are getting up to?'

He was the curious type, Hallingström. The kind whose lives are powered by their doubts and not their convictions, as some wise person once expressed it. Among the tasks on his desk following the restructuring was the Stockholm region's administrative handling of cold cases. Which resources should be allocated where, and when, how much, and so on. He'd reacted to the fact that Junker and Birck seemed to be spending vast amounts of time out in the field.

Hallingström simply wanted to hear which directives Morovi had given them and the amount of resources their execution had involved.

'And now you know,' Morovi said coolly.

'Well then,' Hallingström concluded, and after a polite farewell he was on his way out — but then stopped in the doorway.

'You haven't by any chance had recent dealings with a certain Patrik Sköld?'

'Patrik Sköld? No, I haven't. The name's familiar, though. Is he at HQ?'

'No, he isn't, and, you know what — forget it,' said the man from NPA, and left.

Morovi adjusts the bathrobe around her thigh.

If you listen carefully, you can still hear the snoring from the bedroom.

'Recently,' says Birck.

'Eh?'

'This Hallingström said that he'd recently had lunch with one of the archivists. He wasn't more specific than that?'

'No. My guess would be that you've had him, or one of his foot soldiers, on your tail since last week.'

'I think that Sköld went to see Hallingström,' I say. 'When I spotted Sköld's car, the Audi, on Fridhemsgatan, I later saw him coming out of a building where one of the residents was a C. Hallingström.'

'Hmm.' Birck frowns. 'Wonder what they chatted about.'

'But I still don't really see what the problem is,' I say. 'We haven't actually broken any rules.'

'The problem,' Morovi says, exhaling heavily before she continues, 'is that, at the time, Hallingström was on the board that was responsible for SGS. Officially, he was Jon Wester's boss.'

'And unofficially?'

'Yes ...' Morovi folds her arms across her chest. 'Unofficially, he seems to have been there to protect Wester.'

'What does that mean?'

'He helped make sure that SGS got the resources that Wester said were necessary. Any criticism directed at Wester, Hallingström would be there to defend him. He realised that Wester was good, and would be a key figure in delivering SGS strong results. And SGS got a great record when it came to convictions. They were efficient, unsurprisingly given the methods they deployed, but then not too many people knew about that. Being efficient goes a long way, it makes us look good. So SGS and Wester were protected, not least by Hallingström, although he was far from alone.'

'I don't get why SGS was disbanded, if it was so successful,' I say.

Morovi smiles a crooked smile.

'It was soon after the Angelica murder. Is that what you're getting at?'

'The thought had occurred to me.'

'Formally, it was because SGS was a pilot project. It was never intended to be a permanent unit; rather, elements of their operations were to be integrated into other units and divisions. If you look at the form of words used by NPA, it's quite apparent. But informally …' She shakes her head again. 'Who knows. The use of informants and infiltrators had recently been in the eye of a media storm. The Rätz Affair was still fresh, Operation Playa was well on its way to a full-blown disaster. I think the list that Inger Johanne Paulsson demanded was important, too — looking at it, you realised just how much of SGS's activity was completely dependent on informants, and the scale of the risks they needed to take. And,' she adds, 'this is the police we're talking about. I've seen fully functioning divisions and units scrapped or reorganised because the boss isn't enjoying his job anymore and fancies doing something different. It's much easier than you think to sabotage things within the force. Whatever you do, don't do management.'

She laughs, then realises what she's doing and glances over at the bedroom door.

'So you don't think that SGS was broken up because of Angelica Reyes' death?' I say.

'I don't know what to think about so many things nowadays,' she mutters. 'What I do know is that we need to finish this off. A dead officer who might have killed himself and not only that but used his own weapon to do so. Jesus. You sent people in, I take it?'

'Plenty,' says Birck. 'All good. We took the letter and the computer. I lied and said that both contained personal information.'

Strictly speaking, not even a lie.

'Good,' Morovi says. Then, more contemplatively, '2008 to 2011, isn't most of the material from back then digitised now?'

'Our stuff is, anyway,' I say.

'SGS's, too, I should think,' says Morovi, 'even if their most sensitive activities were never committed to paper. The most important documents were probably omitted, or destroyed when it was wound up.'

She looks at us with a weird expression, almost like a different face. She looks greedy.

'Dig, then. Earn your wages. Make sure you find something concrete tying Jon Wester to Angelica Reyes' murder, if it is him. Thus far, you can only prove a sex purchase that falls under the statute of limitations. The rest of it is all circumstantial. Get hold of something else. Quickly,' she adds, 'and without speaking to those concerned. Don't do any strange overtime, and be sure not to miss any meetings. Do it during working hours, and look out for Hallingström and his tentacles. Don't forget, there are eyes on you.'

I look at Birck. He looks like I feel. It's been a long, long night and it's far from over yet. I'm so happy that Sam's coming home tomorrow.

'I don't think it's possible,' Birck ventures. 'Not without speaking to ...'

'You're probably right,' Morovi says, climbing out of the armchair and adjusting her robe. 'But since I'm your boss, I can tell you that I don't give a shit what you think. Just do it.'

52

I don't go home that night. It's as if Patrik Sköld's dead face is stuck inside of me, I don't know what to do with myself. I end up heading down to Karolinska to sit with Grim.

They're operating on him first thing tomorrow, I'm informed, and the preparations for that are already underway. He's in a deep sleep.

I sit down on the chair next to his bed, study his face.

All of this, I think to myself, started with you. Birck asked me today whether knowing about the real reasons for your actions changed anything. I dodged the question a bit. I didn't want to show that I was unsure, but I am. I'm hunting a murderer for you. *For you.* So fucked up.

I agreed to investigate the details around the Reyes case because I thought you were in danger. I did it to help you. *Protect you*, if that makes it sound better.

And you made a useful idiot of me. I hate feeling stupid, thick, duped. It's so humiliating, do you understand that?

The betrayal seems ancient, almost pre-historic. As though it happened before, in another time, in another life.

It's twenty-to three in the morning, on Tuesday the eighth of December, and I'm busy telling myself that tomorrow everything will be okay.

You're having an operation. You're going to get better. You're going to make it, you always do. Not even a bullet in the head can finish you off forever. *Maybe you're immortal.* You're going to get better, and you'll be charged, then assessed by the court. A minor psychiatric assessment will be carried out, and you'll be found sane, no secure treatment this time. A period in prison will follow — you might get five years, six at the most — and you'll behave yourself, of course, you know it's worth pretending. Once you've done two-thirds of your time, you'll be a free man again.

Maybe everything will be different then. We'll meet down on Norr Mälarstrand. I'll be waiting at a table on the waterfront terrace …

I realise that I don't even know what you're dreaming about, beyond all this. You've never said what you want to work with, not even in Salem in the days when me and you were everything. Others wanted to be footballers, artists, firemen, pilots, lawyers. Some idiot even wanted to be a cop, but not you. Right?

You never said anything.

I've never asked you either. Maybe you knew even then that your path was going to be different? *No, that's wrong. That's hindsight.* It's so easy to spot them now, the signs, they're so easily read with the answer sheet in hand. At the time, they were hard to interpret, if there even were any.

Your breathing, hearing its rhythm, makes me calm. Do you know that? Do you realise that you, despite everything, have a calming effect on me? *How fucked up is that?*

You could almost fall asleep here.

I'm yanked from the blackness by a movement inside the room. The clock on the wall shows quarter-to six. My eyes are stinging, and my body is aching from sitting in the chair for so long. My neck hurts.

Propped up against the wall is a man who looks like he's going to fall down at any second. He's wearing unwashed clothes: black jeans, and a T-shirt that hugs his chest and shoulders tightly. His dark-black hair is on end, and his eyes are shiny and erratic, his skin so pale that the stubble across his chin and jaw looks almost blue.

'Didn't mean to wake you up,' he says quietly.

'Have you been there long?'

'Just got here. Shall I go?'

I don't know what to say. What's he doing here?

'It's you,' he goes on. 'You're the one they're always talking about.'

'Talking about?'

'You're the one who comes a lot. The nurses often talk about you. You're his friend.'

Friend. Sounds weird when someone else says it.

'My name is Leo.'

'I know.'

'And yours is Nikola.'

Nikola Abrahamsson. The man who shot my friend in the head.

He slides slowly to the floor and sits down with his back to the wall. It's barely a movement at all, more like a drawn-out slump.

'I usually come at around this time. There's never anyone else here then. I think they feel sorry for me. Fucked up, eh? They feel sorry for the one who pulled the trigger.'

'Has he said anything to you?' I ask. 'When you've been here, I mean.'

'No, I heard he'd woken up, but ...'

I haul myself out of the chair. My back crunches and my legs tingle.

'Have you sat on that thing?'

Abrahamsson shakes his head. I stretch.

'Don't fall asleep on it.'

That's not a joke, not something light-hearted to defuse the situation. I don't know myself why I said it.

'I don't sleep anymore,' says Abrahamsson.

I walk round the bed and slump onto the floor next to him. It's not as uncomfortable as it looks.

The latest I've heard about Abrahamsson is that he's still suspended because the investigation into the shooting is ongoing.

'I met a suspended colleague earlier,' I say.

'Did you?'

'He'd blown his own head off.'

'That's why I drink.'

Up close, the stench of alcohol emanating from his pores is unmistakeable.

'Whisky, is it?'

'Bourbon. I like the softness.'

A new silence, less charged than the one before.

'I haven't been a policeman that long,' he mumbles. 'Maybe I won't be doing it for much longer, either. So I don't know. But there's something about this job. Something fucked up. Isn't there?'

'Yes.' I hesitate. 'Is the version of events in the report correct?'

'Yes. It is.'

I hadn't planned to ask him. He looks down at his hands.

'We were standing on our spot. He walked into view. We watched him from there. In that tunnel, or viaduct or whatever you call it, something flashed. And so on. I aimed low, but he must've moved or something, maybe he dropped his lighter and bent down to pick it up? Maybe he crouched down when I fired the warning shot. I don't know. No one else saw either, apparently. Not that particular detail.'

We can hear each other breathing, and Grim in front of us.

'I'm not saying this as an excuse, or even an explanation, but … everything that day felt so unreal. There was a terrorist in our

225

midst. He was about to strike at Medborgarplatsen or Central Station, maybe the Galleria. It wasn't a matter of if but *when* and *where*. Preventing it, saving lives, was *my* responsibility. Ours. All these people, bodies ... it's a crazy burden to put on anybody.'

I say nothing.

'Do you hate me?' he asks.

I had convinced myself that if I ever met him, I'd be compelled to violence, that my body would demand it. It would be unavoidable, and, according to old-fashioned morals, justifiable. An eye for an eye is an awful maxim, and its appeal is always greatest for those closest to the victim.

But hate him?

A year or so ago, I would've. I was different then. I think about Markus Waltersson, and his sister. I see him dying before my eyes.

'Not yet,' is the only thing I can say that doesn't feel like a lie.

Then I get to my feet and leave the room.

53

HQ, Tuesday morning. The buzz in the corridor, a machine spluttering into life as it fills another cup with coffee, a toilet flushing, ancient fluorescent tubes humming on the ceiling in the first few seconds after you flick the switch. Sleep deprivation has made my hearing more sensitive and the sounds sharp and threatening.

The rumour is already circulating. *A police officer killed himself last night. With his own weapon, left a right mess. It was down to private stuff, apparently, but that doesn't make it any less gory. No, they're not done yet, the technicians are still there.*

Sam's coming back today. I should've gone home last night, should've tidied up. Should've given the cat some food.

Birck arrives at my door with a water bottle in his hand, closes it behind him before slumping into the empty chair opposite me. He looks to have had about the same amount of sleep as I have. Not only that, he smells bad. I don't think this has ever happened before. Feels almost pleasant.

'I've just been sitting down, trying to think,' he says. 'Unfortunately, it was on a barstool.'

His eyelids flicker, and he crosses his legs.

'What were you thinking about?' I ask.

'Reyes. Sköld. Wester and SGS.'

'Did you get anywhere?'

'No.' Birck unscrews the cap from the bottle. 'But maybe I am, gradually. In the meantime …'

He smiles joylessly and gulps down some water.

'Yes,' I say. 'In the meantime, we'll get on with it.'

'What's up with you, by the way? You look like you've slept less than I have.'

'I met Nikola Abrahamsson.'

It takes a second for Birck to work out who I'm talking about.

'How did that go?'

'Well, I suppose.' I hesitate. 'Grim's operation is today, and Sam's coming home.'

'Is she?'

'I hope so.'

'Good,' he says. 'That's good. Bit much, though, right?'

'Yes.'

Birck continues drinking water but asks no more questions. Instead, we get to work. First Jon Wester, the man whose harried face was captured by Reyes' camera a month before the murder.

There are eyes on us. Everything we're doing is being watched, by someone. Somebody in IT has been instructed, or persuaded, to monitor what we're doing behind our computer screens. Unfortunately, that's precisely where we're going to have to do our work. Much of the material survives only in electronic form. We proceed with caution.

'What year was he born?' I ask.

'1964,' Birck says, blinking wearily at the screen. 'Childhood in Södertälje, joins the cadets in 1987, patrolling our streets by 1990. He's twenty-six at that point, and he continues his training alongside work. After three years, he ends up with the Drug

Squad, before moving on to a special group closely modelled on the successful Huddinge Group.' Birck squints. 'Strange. But I think I've heard about that.'

'Where does he end up after that?'

'No fucking idea.'

He clicks and clicks some more.

'Haven't you got the other database open there somewhere?' I ask.

'No. I can see that he leaves Central in 2006 for Solna. Then ...' More clicking. 'Yes, here we go. In 2007, he's recruited by NPA to establish what will become SGS. With Carl Hallingström, among others. He remains there until the Squad is disbanded in the first half of 2011, which would seem to be the last trace of the guy within the force.'

He then abandons his earlier career path, and, following a two-month break, Wester establishes his own consultancy business in August 2011. Since then he has acted as an advisor and project manager within the private security industry: G4S, Securitas, Lansec Security, Falck — all are or have been Jon Wester's clients. He lives on Timotejgatan on Södermalm, not far from Skanstull.

The public never get to know his face during his time as a cop; he never cuts through the media noise that way. He's often mentioned in connection with the Squad's latest raid or arrest — sometimes a quote might appear, a picture very rarely.

Via Lansec Security's homepage, we manage to source a photo of Wester taken at the beginning of the year. At a conference, shaking hands with somebody. Smiling.

Jon Wester is a man with certain appeal, an angular face, its form accentuated by his shaven head, where only a shadow of stubble covers his scalp. He's wearing a black blazer in the picture, over a light-blue shirt with the top button undone. His black-rimmed geometric glasses look expensive.

'He looks nice, don't you think?' I say.

'Göran Lindberg looked perfectly charming in pictures, too.'

As the day progresses, an updated version of the rumour begins to circulate: *It was down to a suspension. Apparently, the guy had been in SGS*. Details sketchy.

'Do you think it was him?' says Birck. 'In her apartment, on the night of the murder. Do you think that was Wester?'

'At the very least, he's been there before,' I say, as I study Jon Wester's face, trying to imagine him with a knife in his hand, stabbing Angelica Reyes to death.

In the clip, Wester seems driven by lust or power, maybe both, or perhaps they're actually one and the same, yet he seemed in control, cold. Would he take such a risk? If necessary. I remember Patrik Sköld's words, *I don't know if it was him or whether someone did it for him*, and try to work out which scenario is the more likely. Impossible. You can't deduce that much from looking at someone's face.

'I think someone did it for him.'

'Me, too,' says Birck. 'Sköld?'

'He's dead, though.'

'Exactly. There's no better way of getting off.'

'In that case, why would he act the way he did?' I say.

'Whistleblowing, you mean?'

'Yes, for example.'

'That could be it. He blew the whistle, then regretted doing so when he realised what a storm he'd unleashed. Could see only one way out.'

That stops me in my tracks. It hadn't even occurred to me.

'I don't know,' Birck continues. 'It'll become clear, if time is on our side. Shall we keep going?'

SGS was launched on the first of January 2008, with Jon Wester in operational charge.

The first prosecutions began in April that same year. Firearms offences, drug offences, threatening behaviour. SGS-led investigations. They worked, resulting in guilty verdicts. The perpetrators were young men from deprived urban estates, and an analysis of their links revealed that all had strategic positions within Stockholm's criminal networks.

Right from the outset, SGS attacked crucial nodes. They knew who they were looking for, thanks to their informants.

'Impressive,' Birck declares.

We decide to skirt around the actual case files to begin with. They've been sanitised, they're clean. The keys could well be elsewhere, in other materials: meeting notes, bulletins, agendas. Those documents could contain something left behind unintentionally.

'Their vehicle fleet,' says Birck. 'There must be lists, user records. If we assume that it is the murderer who calls Miro Djukic — the third customer — a police radio was heard in the background during their conversation. If we can trust his account, I mean, but he'd know that sound, so I think we can. I can't see any reason for him to lie, either. It could be the car that Sköld had, as we thought, but it might be one of the other SGS cars? I hadn't thought of that before, had you?'

'No,' I say.

'There you go. Whichever car it was, if we can tie it to the scene, and put someone behind the wheel, then the case is basically done and dusted.'

'You make it sound so easy.'

'It is, though. In theory, it's almost banal in its simplicity. It's in reality that it all turns to shit.'

54

An operation targeting a suspected arms smuggler on the Fittja estate is preceded by weeks of careful planning. It's spring 2009, and this is one of over a hundred cases that year.

They lay groundwork for recruiting informants, sift through surveillance notes, train and rehearse raids, produce sociograms plotting the city's criminal networks. The prostitutes are there, around the edges, including Angelica, who features as a user and the final link in a supply chain that SGS are deciphering step by step. She's one of those to obtain items from the shipment, which according to SGS has its origins in Thailand.

In the intranet archive, the documents are not in any kind of order, one from 2008 next to one from 2011, a memo explaining extra surveillance activity in Husby followed by meeting notes detailing administrative resources.

'They never bothered to sort them when it was disbanded. When they got to the archive, they just scanned the lot and got on with their lives,' says Birck. 'Hardly something you can blame them for?'

The archive has no search function; you have to go through each document manually. I sit there for most of the day getting nowhere.

The choice of words in these documents is often revealing. During meetings, recruitment is discussed and phrases like *freethinking* and *our cause* keep cropping up. *We're looking for someone who supports our cause. Preferably not a freethinking type.* Even when SGS is subject to criticism or when the group's relationship with the wider world is discussed, the vocabulary is striking. *The criticism comes from the other side.*

The other side.

The thin blue line is a thread, woven through everything. They're convinced that they are a force for good, making society a better place.

And they are a force for good. There's no doubt about it, but you do have to remind yourself of that. The number of potential victims of crime who've been spared violence or threats of violence, who have not had to endure break-ins to their homes or cars, the number of parents who haven't had to worry about what might happen to their kids on the way home from school — before long, you're talking about an awful lot of people.

The documents start to form an image of the past. I go outside for a cigarette, return to the present. I think about Patrik Sköld's dead face, the blood on the wall behind him. A thin blue line, giving way. I wonder how the blood spattered after the shot under the bridge, whether Grim's blood hit the ground or the wall. I haven't checked.

Sköld. I need to concentrate. Sköld left Fridhemsplan on the third of December. I saw him. I think he went to Hallingström and told him that he wasn't going to keep quiet anymore. That he believed Wester was involved in the murder of Angelica Reyes. That's what he wanted to say to us the whole time. That's why he was suspended.

Perhaps that made Wester keep a close eye on him, directly or indirectly. Wester hasn't been a serving officer for several years, but the likes of him often have lackeys prepared to run their errands.

In which case, Sköld was probably being followed when we met up with him on Apelbergsgatan the following evening.

Is that how we ended up being watched?

When I get back inside, Birck is sitting there flipping through a list of some kind. He seems less than impressed. I tell him what I'm thinking.

'Probably,' he says when I go quiet. 'But can it be proved?'

'What do you reckon?'

'When I got in today,' Birck says, 'I was certain that some bastard had been here during the night and had a snoop around. This case, all this secrecy, is making me paranoid.'

I know exactly what he means. I pull the notes he's been looking at towards me.

'What's this?'

'The section's vehicles. Not all of them, but the ones I've managed to link to them so far. Some of them appear to be their own duty vehicles, others they seem to borrow or just use occasionally.'

'And?'

'Nothing, thus far.'

That would've been too much to hope for.

'What bothers me most,' I say. 'Is that I don't even know what I'm supposed to be looking for. Which bits are pulling us in the right direction, and which ones are dead ends. There doesn't seem to be anything linking Wester with Angelica.'

'That'll come,' he says. 'When we're getting close to something, we'll notice.'

'What do you mean?'

'I'm thinking about Patrik Sköld.' Birck, now apparently full of beans again, returns to the list of vehicles. 'When we're getting close to something hot, then they're going to try and stop us.'

On the table, there's a photo of Angelica. An old one, which can't have been taken much more than a year after me and Grim met her at the bus stop. I study the picture, and the words she wrote in the margin of her diary suddenly come back to me, *don't be like the rest of them, darling.* Without really knowing why, I feel a burning sensation in my eyes.

55

The electric Advent candle in the window is on. I see it shining above me from the pavement; that's how I know that she's back.

I've made my way home quickly. From a distance, I'm sure it must've looked like I was in a hurry. But when I catch sight of the candlestick shining warm and clear and I know she's waiting up there, I feel the need to go slower.

I don't know why. Am I scared?

In the hall, Sam's bag, open but not unpacked. She's on the sofa, with a mug of coffee in her hands, watching an old *Gilmore Girls* on TV.

'Hi,' I say.

I am scared.

Sam stares at me for a long time.

'You need a shave.'

She puts the mug down. I sit down next to her. She touches me, rests her head on my shoulder.

'I know you've been outside the gallery,' she mumbles into my shirt.

'Sorry. I wanted to … see you.'

'I know.' She takes a deep breath and puts, finally, her hand on mine. 'But I'm home now.'

Later, much later, it feels — but can't be since the same *Gilmore Girls* episode is still playing, she turns towards me in bed and says:

'If you lie to me again, I will leave you.'

Then she doesn't say any more.

The next morning, we have breakfast early, listen to the news. We've got some time before we have to separate for the day, and we spend it moving candlesticks around. It feels so natural, somehow.

We discuss where they should be, whether we want a Christmas tree, if we should get the box of decorations from the basement. The mundaneness makes me feel safe. She's in her dressing gown, standing there with an illuminated Christmas star in one hand and a mug of steaming coffee in the other.

'That's a good spot, isn't it?' she says, admiring the star that's now hanging in the kitchen window. 'Lovely there.'

'I thought it was nice by the balcony, where I'd put it.'

'We only go out there to smoke.'

'So?'

She mutters and shakes her head at me.

We put it up in the bedroom, where we both agree it doesn't really fit in but at least we agree.

'This is what relationships are about,' Sam says. 'Compromise. No one's happy.'

Then she laughs. So do I.

'You mustn't go thinking everything's okay,' she says, buttoning her shirt in front of the mirror, ready for a day's work.

'I don't. But we have to be able to talk to each other.'

'Exactly.' She looks at me for ages. 'What's up?'

'What do you mean?'

'There's something on your mind.'

I look at my phone. I should've heard something by now. *We have to be able to talk to each other.*

'They operated on Grim yesterday.'

'I understand.'

'But I still haven't heard anything. I don't even know what happened.'

'Ring the hospital then.'

'I will.'

Sam stops in front of the mirror.

'You're scared.'

'It's weird, talking to you about it.'

'About being scared?'

'No, about him.'

When she's finished buttoning her shirt, she adjusts the collar, inspects the results in the mirror and pats down a crease on her arm.

'I get that,' she says. 'But you'll have to learn.'

'Doesn't it feel weird for you, hearing it?'

'What's the alternative, though? For you to not talk about him with me at all? He is your friend. Of course I don't like it, considering what he did to me.'

He is my friend. It's weird to hear someone else saying it, even when she says it. I need to tell Grim, I think to myself, that I don't blame him for trying to get hold of the list. *It's true, I don't.* He must've been desperate, exhausted from being on the run. If I'd been in his situation, would I have done the same? Maybe.

I'm going to tell him that today.

'Sorry,' I say. 'I'm sorry for …'

She takes my face in her hands and pushes her lips against mine.

'You said it. That's good. But if you lie to me again, I'm off.'

'I won't.'

The clock is ticking behind us in the kitchen, and I can hear it at first, but then it fades out because as she keeps kissing me something happens.

Everything's singing.

56

The call from Karolinska is logged in my phone at fourteen minutes past eleven in the morning, and the person on the other end, the consultant, delivers his message concisely.

This morning, the ninth of December at five past eleven, John Grimberg was pronounced dead.

At that point, his heart had been lying still for over an hour, after complications resulting from an acute surgical procedure they had been forced to undertake to deal with the repeated blood clots caused by yesterday's operation. *His life could not be saved.* The consultant's words.

I count — five past eleven, minus an hour — and work out that my friend must have taken his last breath on the operating table at about the same time as I was in the apartment on Alströmergatan telling Sam that I was scared.

It's the ninth of December. Everything was singing. Just now.

Now everything is silent.

PART III

What You Know about Me
Stockholm
December 2015 and March 2016

57

No stars in the Stockholm night, but that's the only thing.

The clock is ticking, traffic lights change, buses sweep down the road, and music pounds away inside the clubs. Passing by on the pavement, you can smell the cigarette smoke and perfume, hear people's laughter.

I am a long way away from them. I'm walking like someone who doesn't want to be seen.

No stars, but that's the only thing, they were shining down on the city yesterday and now they're gone. In the world, nothing else has changed. My friend has left it, with no concrete trace, one second he was lying there in his hospital bed, the next ...

Nothing.

The bleeping of the heart-rate monitors echoes in my ears. Sound that comes from someone still alive. It has stopped.

I walk across Kungsholmen to Karlberg station, catch the last commuter train south, towards Salem. The floor of the carriage is sticky from spilt booze. In one corner, a few red-nosed men and women are nodding off. Somewhere just before Rönninge, a handful of kids hop on, mid-party. It's Wednesday, but that sort of thing doesn't make as much difference as you'd think. One kid is playing music on his phone — Rihanna, *shine bright like a diamond* — and as the train weaves its way into Rönninge it stops abruptly, making another kid fall over.

The rest laugh and help him to his feet. I watch them with interest.

We were like them once. Remember? Me and you, we were just like them once.

I walk the streets of Salem, pass the bus stop where me and Grim met a young Angelica Reyes. I see our old street, the housing blocks of the Triad reaching upwards towards the dark sky. I pace past what was once the entrance to Grim's, and around the edges of the place where I grew up, just as I used to all those days and nights when I didn't have anywhere to go but didn't want to go home either.

I wasn't alone then, not even during those long years without Grim, or while he was at St Göran's. He was around, somewhere out there in the world, and I knew it.

And now?

By the water tower, where we first met, I stand and stare at its heavy silhouette, just aware of a dark matt firmament beyond. I remember a shot that whined through the air, and there he was. Sitting up there with an air rifle, shooting at birds. That's how we met. I was curious and I climbed up myself. I was sixteen. When we looked at each other, something happened, electric almost. Suddenly there was a before and an after, a time before I met Grim and everything that happened afterwards.

Everything that happened.

It wasn't supposed to end like this. There should've been a time for us. There really should. A chance to be together again, on equal terms. And then one of us went and died alone on an operating table.

It wasn't supposed to end like this.

I'm lying on my back on the cold earth. The moisture is seeping through my clothes. I can't work out how long it's been since I stepped off the train.

Everything's so lonely now.

But he can't really be gone? It must be an illusion; he's going to appear at any moment, out from between the trees, onto the gravel. He's going to lie down next to me and ask me what I'm playing at.

I wait. Is he coming?

It can't just end like this, surely?

I lie there for ages. *Love is a spark*. He's not coming.

58

We go to the church. It's the feast of Santa Lucia and I'm sitting there with Sam, in a rare moment of tranquillity. All my emotions are new, as though I'm experiencing them for the first time. This moment terrifies me, anyway; I feel weightless, as if the only thing keeping me on the ground is Sam's hand inside mine. I've almost stopped eating. I can't really explain why, it just ... occurred. I don't feel any hunger, none. Why would I eat? *His life could not be saved.*

I go to HQ every morning, in spite of everything. No one says I should go home. They don't say anything.

On Monday the fourteenth of December, it's been five days since John Grimberg died.

On that day, two strange things happen.

The first is a phone call from a man whose number I don't recognise. He represents the undertakers appointed to deal with John Grimberg's death.

'And why are you calling me?'

'I spoke to the hospital staff. You seem to have been his only visitor, so ...'

'I understand,' I say, even though he never does finish that sentence.

'I was thinking … as far as I can see, John Grimberg left almost no personal possessions, and the few he did form part of an ongoing …'

I don't like the man from the undertakers. Grim might be dead, but that shouldn't prevent us from speaking in complete sentences.

'Yes,' I manage.

Apparently, the funeral will take place in Salem Church on the twenty-second of December, at twelve o'clock.

'Thanks then,' I say.

The twenty-second of December, twelve o'clock.

Something that cannot be fixed is broken. I'm crying, suddenly it's here, I can't stop. Sitting there, phone in hand in my office, I fall. Burning, tearing inside my chest. Something in there wants to get out.

That's the first thing.

The second thing that happens does so shortly after I've pulled myself together, and concerns the Reyes case.

Something, says Birck, has happened.

59

'Something's happened.' Birck's standing in the doorway with his phone in his hand. 'How's it going? Shall I come back later?'

'What's happened?'

'It's Jonna Danielsson.'

'What about her?'

Birck says she's waiting in reception. Apparently, she wants to talk to me about something. The receptionist did try to get hold of me, but I didn't answer, so she called Birck instead.

'But it's you she wants to talk to.'

'About what?'

'She won't say. Why didn't you answer anyway?'

'I was busy,' I mumble, but my face is hot, my eyes feel swollen, and I wonder how I must look.

'You really should eat something,' Birck says before he goes. 'Drink something, at least. Shall I get you a glass of water?'

Like a child, I think to myself. That's how they regard me now, helpless. Maybe that's just as well.

'Yes, please.'

'And Danielsson?'

I stare at my desktop phone, then pick up the receiver and ring down to reception, ask them to let the visitor in.

After that, my decidedly unsteady legs carry me to the bathroom, and I wash my face. When I get back to my desk, there's a glass of water waiting for me and I drink from it greedily.

Jonna Danielsson shifts position in her chair.

'Can't be done,' I say.

'What?'

'Sitting comfortably in that chair.'

'Aha. Right, maybe I should give up trying.'

She smiles an uncertain smile. Then she puts her hands in her lap and starts chewing on her bottom lip.

'It was … Well, it's about this John Grimberg.'

'What about him?'

'When was it we met last time?' she says. 'Out in Norsborg.'

'November, I think. Why do you ask? What about John Grimberg?'

'I read in the paper that he died recently. But just after we met, you and me, I saw him.'

She looks at me as if she's trying to see what importance I attach to the information.

I can't do this. Not now.

'Did you?'

'He came to my place.'

It was pretty weird. She had just got back from a seminar and had barely locked the door when the doorbell rang through the hall.

Through the peephole, she studied the man waiting outside. She saw that he was standing in plain sight, with a friendly expression and his hands at his sides, making no attempts to hide them. She could tell that he, somehow, must've worked out that she was the type who expected to inspect her visitors first. That made her curious, so she let him in.

He said his name was John and that he'd been a friend of

249

Angelica's. She realised then who he was, and instantly felt uneasy, not least because he was so polite and personable.

'That was the guy you'd asked me about a day or two before,' she says. 'I realised that then.'

She took a step backwards and asked him to leave.

He told her that he wanted to talk to her about Angelica.

'What for?'

The man called John thought that maybe Angelica had something that other people wanted to get at.

'He asked me,' she says, 'whether I'd got anything from Angelica, or if I had anything that used to belong to her. I said, "No, like what?"'

'I was stunned, of course, and upset. Along comes someone — just like you did, but you're a cop — along comes someone, five years after the death of my best friend, ripping it all open again. I said that to him.'

He apologised.

'If it turns out,' he concluded, 'that you do find something amongst your stuff, or happen to hear anything about Angelica, please contact me. Especially if it's something about a list.'

'A list? What kind of list?'

'I can't really explain. But,' he added, 'if you find it, don't go to the police.'

That's what he said.

Jonna studies my reaction. I nod. *We are familiar with this. Go on.*

'I got his number before he left. I must admit I was a bit shaken up for the rest of the day. I've been there before, right, I know that world. I'm not easily scared. And I know the police, too, I know how you work. Do you know how many cops I met?'

'While you were …'

'Yes.'

'More than I'd like to think, I suppose.'

'Must've been at least one a week while I was doing that. And you always knew they were cops, you've got a certain way. You couldn't put it into words, but you just always knew.'

'I understand. I think.'

I imagine Grim's visit. Him standing outside the door, introducing himself, then shaking her hand.

'Was that it?' I ask, and it feels like there's a cord around my neck.

'Not quite,' she says, looking uncertain once more.

You see, after he'd left, something occurred to her.

60

Angelica stayed over at Jonna's the night before someone took her life. They'd been working at opposite ends of town on the eleventh of October before they met up at Slussen and then went to a mutual friend's place in Skärholmen. They'd stayed there, drinking, until well into the night. Instead of travelling back into town and John Ericssonsgatan, Angelica slept at Jonna's in Norsborg, mainly because that was the closest bed but also because Angelica had some clothes to pick up from there.

They arrived at about half-three, and at nine a.m. Angelica's fast, sprightly footsteps could be heard from the hall, the door slamming as she left.

Angelica had rinsed away the tiredness and the hangover with tablets. She usually did.

And she'd forgotten the clothes that she was supposed to pick up, Jonna noted when she dragged herself out of bed an hour or so later and spotted them lying in a bag in the hall.

'I forgot them myself,' she says. 'When me and Angelica were meeting for lunch, which we'd arranged the day before. I had a punter, so I was heading straight home after lunch, so I had to sort myself out, and of course it was all last minute. I was hungover and dopey as fuck, so when I rushed out the door I forgot the bag of clothes.'

Jonna didn't realise until she was sitting at a table in the restaurant and spotted Angelica, who was late, walking past the window. Angelica asked if Jonna had seen her diary.

'No?'

'Are you sure?' Angelica asked. 'I know I had it at yours yesterday.'

Of course Jonna wasn't sure: she'd had no idea it might be in the flat, so she hadn't looked for it.

Jonna said she could drop the clothes round later; she was going to go home for a shower and a change of clothes after her last customer anyway, so she could also have a look for the diary and bring it if it did turn up.

'Great,' said Angelica. 'That would be great. There's something I have to tell you, too.'

'What's that?'

'We'll talk tonight.'

Jonna didn't give it a second thought, Angelica was like that sometimes. Angelica described the diary's appearance, and that was the end of it.

'But,' Jonna says, 'that's not really what happened in the end. I got home later than I'd hoped, and I was really fucking stressed because I'd gone overtime with the punter. I got in the door, jumped in the shower, and then a quick change. I grabbed the bag of clothes as I left. Then, standing in the doorway, I remembered what she'd said about the diary. I had a very quick look, but I couldn't see it. *Shit*, I thought to myself, *I'll have to look for it later, that's if it's even at my place.* She could've left it somewhere else. Now, I loved Angelica so much, but she was always so dippy and distracted. So yeah, I took the bag of clothes and caught the metro. If the diary was at mine I'd find it and I'd be able to give it to her the next day, no big deal, I thought. And then I got there about midnight. You know the rest.'

Her best friend on the bed, all that blood. The darkness outside and a detective, Levin, arriving at John Ericssonsgatan in the rainy

October night. An investigation with good prospects rumbling into action.

Yes, we know the rest.

'Do you know what it was she was going to tell you?'

'No. That was just something she mentioned in passing. I guess that … No, I don't know.'

Her best friend was going to tell her something. That she was going to run away? Perhaps Angelica Reyes wasn't planning to set off without saying farewell to her friend.

'But the diary,' I say.

Yes, the diary. It was days before she thought about it — must've been the shock. That's what happens: you forget. It wasn't until the Saturday after the murder that she thought about it, and even then only because it was right in front of her.

She was watching some brain-dead comedy show on TV — just to do something. The TV was on a little shelf, next to a dry pot plant. *Should water that*, she thought to herself, and that's when she saw it. In front of the plant was a little blue diary. It hardly stuck out. Maybe the fact it took Jonna so long to find it wasn't just down to her state of mind after the murder; it might also have had something to do with the diary itself. It sort of blended in with its surroundings.

It was one of those diaries with a little cord to keep it shut. She opened it and flicked through. The pages didn't contain much at all: there were days at a time where Angelica hadn't made any entries. She wrote in her appointments, when she needed to call the benefits agency, and, occasionally, reminders about bills: rent, electricity, mobile phone. The odd party.

As she's talking, Jonna picks her bag off the floor, pushes her hand into it, and fumbles around before placing the diary on the table between us.

'I called the police, of course,' she says. 'Rang the same day, went and handed it in the following Monday.'

'We know,' I say. 'The whole thing was scanned into the files. I've read every page.'

A plain-clothes officer on reception, whose name she doesn't remember, took the diary. It was probably Aronsson — his name's on the docket.

Jonna asked for it to be returned to her afterwards. It was, over a year later, when the investigation had hit a dead end. She had to go down to HQ to sign for it.

It was handed over in a sealed plastic bag, along with the document where all forensic examinations on the exhibit are logged. Since it hadn't been at the crime scene around the time of the murder, it had barely been looked at, except to try to map out the last weeks of her life. There hadn't really been time for anything else.

'I got it back,' says Jonna, 'and put it in my wardrobe. That's where it was for five years.'

'Until ...'

'Until after he'd been round, Grimberg. After he left, I started thinking about it and I got it out. I sat and flipped through it in front of the telly. That was when I found it.'

'Found what?'

'The list.'

The diary had a pocket. And if you didn't know it was there, you'd never spot it.

'Look here,' she says, turning to the last page. 'See that?'

An empty, white page, a bit stiffer than the others. It's the inside of the cover.

'No.'

She bends the back page until it clicks.

'How about now?'

There's a little slit visible inside the cover. Someone's used a knife to carve a little pocket.

'It was in here,' she says.

I take the diary and run my fingers across the slit.

Jonna explains how she removed the piece of paper that had been in there, a folded A4 sheet. She looked down the list and thought she recognised a few names.

'I guess you knew about it back then, 2010,' she says. 'Since you kept hold of the diary for so long, I mean. Didn't you?'

'We know about it.'

'At first I thought it was a list of customers,' she continues. 'That for some reason she was writing down the names of those she met. But then I noticed that there were women on there, too, added to the fact that I knew some of the names, including this Ludwig Sarac. I knew that he'd been working for you but was then exposed. Then I got thinking about what Grimberg had said, that it would be about cops.' She looks at the floor. 'I didn't know what to believe. And I'm not really in the habit of trusting the police.'

'So you gave it to him.'

'That's who I called, yes.'

And so he came back and got the list off her. His face lit up when he saw it, so she knew it meant a lot to him. He thanked her profusely — that's the word she uses — and asked her not to talk to anyone else about this. *Could get her in trouble*, he said, and she believed him.

What was she going to do? She'd been there before, knew what they were capable of.

'They,' I say. 'You mean …'

'I mean you. Cops. I know the kind of shit you've got up to before. As I said, I used to meet a lot of you. I got told things.'

'And yet you're here now,' I say.

'I suppose … I don't know, I just wanted to tell you what little I do know. I heard he died recently, Grimberg, and I thought … better late than never. I hope,' she adds, like a question. 'But I wanted to talk to you.'

I picture Grim's face. I like the way she described it, that my friend's face lit up at the sight of the list.

So that's how he got hold of it.

At that moment, I break down.

This comes as a surprise to her, I realise that but I have to leave the room.

I crumple onto the toilet seat, put my head between my knees, breathe. I don't know what's happening. It's just happening. I shouldn't be here.

From November, shortly after his return, a note in my pad. It's about them: *ask him about J.D.*

That's all that's there. I meant Grim, but didn't dare to write his name, not even an initial, in case someone were to see and ask. I must've suspected a possible link between them, but that question got lost among all the others, in the chaos.

It's too late now. Lots of things are too late. And unnecessary, it turns out. I found out, but not from him. Maybe he did want to tell me, near the end, but couldn't.

I think about Patrik Sköld — you could say the same thing about him. He wanted to tell us but ran out of time, *the abyss opened up beneath him.*

I convince myself that that's what happened with Grim, too. He would've told me, eventually, he *wanted* to tell me, but he didn't get the chance.

That isn't particularly likely. It's what I tell myself nonetheless.

Jonna is still sitting there. Dizziness is gathering in the distance, but I push it away, exerting myself to walk without leaning against the wall. It works, until I go to sit down on my chair. That's when everything starts swaying and I have to grab hold of the armrest to keep myself upright.

'Are you okay?'

I pull the diary towards me.

'I had to … thanks for telling us about this. It may be useful later. Was there anything else?'

'You look … it looks like you've just been …'

'I'm okay.'

'If you say so.'

A weird silence follows.

'Do you know who did it, by the way?'

'Who killed Angelica?'

'If you do, I want to know. She was my best friend.'

I really shouldn't be saying anything. Yet the two of us have got something in common, I realise. We have both had someone taken from us, lost them before time. There are certain things you have to do to stop yourself disintegrating from inside.

'We think we know what happened. Right now, we're trying to prove it.'

'I would really like to know how it goes.'

'If we succeed, I'm sure you'll notice.'

Jonna looks at the diary in my hands.

'Was that why she died? I mean, the list that was in there.'

'Maybe.'

'You knew him, didn't you?'

'Who?'

'Grimberg. You were friends.'

'Yes.'

'Close friends?'

'In a way.'

'I'm sorry for your loss. I know how it feels. Do you cry?'

'It does happen.'

'Good.' Jonna stands up and gets ready to leave. 'It's the only thing that works.'

61

She's gone, and I'm left sitting holding the diary. The smell of her clothes, a fabric softener, hangs in the air. It's a pleasant smell. I flip to the last page of the diary and prod the slit on the inside of the cover, before I put my hand in my inside pocket and retrieve the list I found at Grim's. This is where I keep it. I don't know what else to do.

This little piece of paper has travelled a long way. From someone — Jon Wester? — to Angelica Reyes, to Jonna Danielsson, to Grim — who jotted down Patrik Sköld's phone number on it — to me.

It's folded in two. I gently ease it into the little slit in the cover. Then I close the cover, turn the thing back to front and upside down.

No difference. The paper is thin, you can't see it. When I open the diary again, I run my fingers over the inside back cover. Since it's stiff, you can't tell that there's something inside it. And unless you bend the cover like Jonna Danielsson did, you wouldn't even see the slit.

It could be true.

We stored this for over a year; I remember the notes from our run-through down in the archive. We received it in October 2010. Jonna Danielsson got it back in January 2012. A single rudimentary forensic test was carried out on its cover, looking for blood or DNA. Nothing there, of course.

Its inside was never examined quite so carefully. If there was anything of interest in there, it should've emerged during the scanning process — that's the assumption they were probably working under. Perfectly understandable.

The person doing the scanning, Aronsson, was probably standing restlessly in between turning pages and waiting for the scanner to do its thing before he turned the page. Then more waiting, next page, more waiting. It was, in itself, a meaningless exercise that must have taken hours. Chances are, he was pretty chuffed to have reached the last page and to be able to move on to the next thing in life.

A knock at the door. Birck opens it and steps in.

'What did she want?'

I give him a tired smile and hold the diary up in front of him.

'Examine this for me, would you? Come back when you've found it.'

Birck, looking puzzled, takes the diary from my hand.

'Found what?'

'You'll find out.'

'Is this a joke?'

'This is an experiment.'

'I hate experiments,' Birck mutters, closing the door behind him.

About an hour passes, not more, and when he does come back he's annoyed. He went through every single page in the diary, he says, without finding anything.

'So you didn't find it?'

'Oh, I did, but not before I'd wasted an hour. Couldn't you have just told me?'

'I wanted to see if it was possible to miss it.'

'This doesn't get us any closer to our man.' Birck points at the list, before he passes it to me. 'You take it.'

He had it in his hands, I think to myself. Grim was looking for that list for so long, and in the end he found it. His face lit up. I take the list off Birck and put it in my pocket.

Three days later, the breakthrough comes.

62

I saw someone today. Our eyes met for a moment, not long, in fact more like a second than a moment. He reminded me of someone, had the same smile as the man who, a month ago, was Sweden's most wanted man, suspected of conspiracy to commit terrorism on Swedish soil.

The evenings and the nights are disorientating. I wake from a dream and sit up dizzily. I know that I need to return to Salem. I have to go back.

It's happened before. I've never told anyone, but many years ago, when things between me and Grim first cracked and I wasn't living in Salem anymore, something similar happened. It got so bad that I was there several nights a week. I took the bus, because it was so late the trains had stopped running, and got off in Salem. Then I would walk the streets where we used to hang out, stopping to look at the buildings where our friends once lived.

I didn't really know what I was doing, or why. I just knew that I needed to do it.

Every night, I would end up by the water tower. On one occasion, I climbed it and sat on the edge. But once I was up there, I didn't really know what to do; from a distance, it probably would've looked like I was waiting for someone. Maybe I was.

Sitting up the tower, I watched the sun expanding over the horizon, bleeding red. Then I understood.

Something went wrong here, a long time ago, and I came back to try to make things right. That must be it.

But it can't be done, I thought. The dead are gone forever, the disappeared are lost. You have to learn to live with that.

With that insight, if you can call it that, I climbed back down to the ground. A curse had been broken, and I stopped going back.

I think about the man who looked like the suspected terrorist. Maybe it was him. I wonder where he is.

Grim. They thought he was someone else — that's why he got shot. Grim, the man who spent twenty years of his life trying to be someone he wasn't, to live in the shadows under false identities, the man who put caution and discretion, and above all his own security, first — shot dead on the street in central Stockholm because the shooter feared that he was someone else.

Such a mundane fate.

63

The seventeenth of December, the day of the breakthrough.

We've dug deeper into SGS. The digital archives have become old basement vaults. Files, working materials, and documents fill boxes that are stacked along the stone walls. That's what it feels like — walking into old rooms. You open the boxes one at a time, give the contents a cursory inspection. The thin blue line shines all the brighter in the darkness. The outside world is shut out. It's nice, you can almost forget.

From March 2009, documents detailing a comprehensive operation. The Black Cobras are attempting to gain a foothold on Stockholm's problem estates, recruiting from those who took part in the riots and fires in Rinkeby and Tensta the year before. SGS attempt to disrupt the recruitment, and succeed in slowing but not stopping it.

Jon Wester is in the field. From his car, he has long conversations with young men in the southern districts: Skärholmen, Rågsved, Hagsätra. He rolls up alongside them, *appears*, persuades them to get in the passenger seat, after which they drive through Stockholm. It's information he's after: Who has spoken to whom and when? What about? He shows them pictures of known Black Cobra members. *Have any of these men approached you? If it does happen, here's what you need to do: ring this number, that's right, and then ...*

The car's registration number is recorded only once in the documentation: MCC 860. Wester wanted to get reimbursed for fuel he paid for, so the number was recorded. Maybe SGS have been careless by allowing that information to remain in the archive. This is the first time we've been able to tie Wester to a specific car.

A completely separate incident report, dating from the twenty-third of July 2010, less than three months before the murder, is also interesting. It describes events in Grimsta, one of the estates on the north side, where a woman is believed to have sold sex to the leader of the local criminal network. This woman, a then twenty-five-year-old Lisa Vargas, is part of Miro Djukic's pimping operation, has Chilean roots, and lives in a rented flat in Hagsätra. She is a person of interest, the SGS operative later explains in his report, because of indications it may be possible to recruit her as an informant.

What those indications might be are not stated, and it looks as though no recruitment took place. Her name is not mentioned again.

I do a multi-field search on Lisa Vargas. The databases rustle through criminal records, general surveillance records, charge sheets, and so on. Everything points to her still being alive, and still living at the same address. She has a turbulent past, having had repeated contact with the Prostitution Unit and Stockholm Drug Squad, but she seems not to have had any contact with the law since 2012. In the surveillance records, there's still a note explaining her links to the gangster in Grimsta, from July 2010. *No further meetings confirmed*, it says, and then, *former potential SGS case (07-2010, edited 02-2011)*.

There's also information from the Prostitution Unit, again dated 2010. Lisa Vargas wants to report a man, a customer, whose name she doesn't know, for sexual assault. According to the official record, Vargas is *high as a kite* at the time, which might explain why she convinces herself that something might come of it, and dares to come forward.

The man in question is a policeman, she claims. The officer from Prostitution Unit writes that Vargas says she caught a glimpse of the man's badge in his wallet as he went to pay, but not enough to be able to read the man's name.

She is shown pictures of known punters, some of whom are or have been serving officers. She recognises many of the men in the photos, several have been customers, but none are the man who assaulted her. The Unit do what they can, but fail to get anywhere. Vargas takes it badly. *He was strangling me*, she apparently says, loud and upset, before screaming, *I could've fucking died*, and leaving.

That's July 2010. The case was mothballed six months later.

Vargas appears in the Reyes files, I remember that. An old entry in the surveillance records lists her as one of Angelica's acquaintances.

I head to Birck. He's sitting with a pile of papers in his hands, reading diligently.

'I've found something weird,' I say.

'So have I,' says Birck.

64

Birck explains that, according to the archives, one SGS car behaves a little strangely around the time of Angelica Reyes' murder.

It was used in the preceding days and immediately afterwards, but on the twelfth of October 2010 it seems to have remained stationary.

Birck says *seems*, because there's no record of it being used then. SGS have used the car regularly, but have also been careful to register the usage of all their vehicles, presumably because they used them so much in their operations. Cars can be admissible in court, as documentation.

'It could be that the car simply was stationary that day,' Birck rounds off. 'It wouldn't have been the only one — two more of their cars went unused, too.'

'What car is it?'

'A Toyota Auris, 2009 edition. Registration MCC 860.'

The same registration. I sit down. The days and the hours, the meetings in Birck's room, everything melts together.

I hand him the printed copy of the report on the Black Cobras from 2009, in which the same car is mentioned.

'It was being used by Jon Wester, at least in 2009.'

Birck looks at the printout with a vaguely uninterested expression.

'It was also used by five others, including Patrik Sköld.' Birck puts down the paper. 'That's what I've got. A car that probably was parked up all day. Hardly a breakthrough. In fact, it isn't even *weird*, at all — it simply wasn't used. What have you got?'

'A person we should go and talk to straightaway,' I say. 'If she wants to.'

She doesn't. When we arrive at the apartment block in Hagsätra and ring the bell, Lisa Vargas opens the door with a child — a girl of two or three — in her arms.

'I've got nothing to say to you.' She goes to close the door, and we make no attempt to prevent her, we're not that daft, but then halfway through closing it she stops. 'I've quit. I'm clean. I keep out of trouble. I'm married to an economist. I've even got fucking kids. What is this about?'

Birck smiles at the child, an unusual occurrence.

'What's your name?'

The girl doesn't respond. She has her mother's mouth and cheekbones, but her eyes come from someone else. She pushes her face into her mother's shoulder. Birck stops smiling and turns to Lisa.

'We need your help.'

'What's this about?' she repeats.

'Angelica Reyes.'

Something happens to the woman's face. She looks determined.

Lisa takes a step backwards, lets us in. She puts down the kid, who wraps herself round one leg and refuses to look at us. Lisa points a remote at the TV in the living room and when it flashes on she bends down to whisper something to her daughter, who goes over and flops onto the floor with her eyes on the screen.

It's three in the afternoon. We're in a two-bedroom flat with low ceilings and small windows. It'll soon be dusk, you can feel it in the air. On a chest in the hall, there are photographs of a happy family. Her husband is handsome, well dressed, and smiling towards the camera in almost every shot. She shows us into the kitchen.

'My husband will be home in an hour,' she says, as if that means something.

'We can be discreet,' Birck says. 'Does he not know that you used to, um …'

'Oh yes,' she cuts in. 'But we don't get to spend a lot of time together, so we have to make the most of it. We live hectic lives.'

Lisa folds her arms. She's wearing a muted green cardigan, with a blouse of some kind underneath. A heavy necklace with a long chain rests below her chest.

'I understand,' says Birck. 'We won't hang around. Are you working, or … ?'

'Studying.'

We stay standing up. My colleague leans against the doorframe. You can hear the TV, kids singing a song with a neat little melody. I think I recognise it.

'How did you know Angelica?' I ask.

'My parents knew hers. They came to Sweden from Chile at about the same time. So we knew of each other, or whatever, but we didn't hang out until years later, when we were about twenty and met up in town.'

'Were you close?'

'No. I think we …' Her eyes drop and she stares at her folded arms. 'It was always a little bit weird, looking at Angelica. We had shared history, in so many ways. It was like looking at myself, seeing what could've happened to me. Whether she felt the same way, I couldn't say. Anyway, I kept my distance a little bit, because thinking about her was almost like thinking about me. But what's happened now?' she goes on. 'Have you arrested someone?'

'Not yet.'

'We'd like to talk to you about a complaint you made,' says Birck. 'Do you know which one we're talking about?'

'I've only ever done that once,' says Lisa, 'and I regret it.'

65

'I hardly found out anything about him. I know Angelica met him after I had, I heard Miro talking about it.'

'Miro Djukic?'

'Yes. After that complaint, when I refused to see him, Miro sent him to her instead. And I don't know what he was like with her, but Jesus that guy had problems.'

'What kind?'

'Do we have to do this now?'

'The more you can talk, the faster this will be, and the quicker you'll be able to get rid of us.'

She walks out into the hallway to check the girl's still sitting by the TV.

'Everything okay, darling?' she asks. 'Turn it up a bit if you like. You know how to do it, don't you?'

She waits while her daughter fiddles with the remote.

The noise swells like a wave until it gets so loud that a roaring, grating din is all you can hear.

'Not that much,' Lisa shouts shrilly and rushes to the living room.

'What kind of problems,' Birck repeats once she returns to the kitchen, 'did this man have?'

'It's weird talking about it. But if you really want to know, he was the type — maybe I'm prejudiced — that is either far too fond of his mother, or absolutely hates her. If you know what I mean.'

'Not really,' admits Birck.

'As I was saying, I didn't know much about him. Not even what he did for a living, until that last time when I realised he must've been a cop. I'd had my suspicions, a lot of the time you can sort of feel it, but it was only then that I really realised.'

She pauses, maybe trying to work out how that's gone down with us, which side we're on. Hardly surprising.

'How did you come to realise that?' Birck asks.

'I saw a bit of his badge sticking out as he was paying. Unfortunately, I didn't see his name, or his ID number. Now of course he could have had someone else's badge, but I can't really think why he would? And right then, I didn't want to know any more about it. But in that business, or whatever you want to call it, you know … Being able to read people is a survival strategy. It's crucial — if you're no good at it, you won't be around for long. After two meetings, three at the most, you know your punter.'

'I can imagine,' I say. 'What did you find out about him?'

'I'm not one to start moralising. I mean, look at me.' She does actually laugh. Then she lowers her voice. 'I'm not in a position to do anything about it without, you know, throwing stones in a glass house. But he had problems. With sex, I mean. Wanking several times a day.'

'How do you know that?'

'He told me, as an excuse. You should've seen him ejaculate. It was hardly streaming out of him. Wanking that often, I'm sure a lot of people do, that's not what I'm talking about. There was more to it. If it hadn't been so risky for him, then he'd have been surfing porn and having phone sex, too.'

'How do you know he wasn't?'

'I asked him. And the other thing was that he always got so low afterwards. Anxiety or something, I don't know. Sounds like a great shag, eh?'

'Absolutely.'

'Basically, he'd always behaved like a pig, been a bit too rough, that sort of thing. But then he tried to strangle me. That was, in some way, the turning point for me. I knew that reporting it wasn't going to make any difference, but I still wanted to do it, like I was putting down a marker for myself. After that, I started slowly trying to put my life back in order. It wasn't easy, but I got there.'

'Were you ...' Birck says before changing his mind. 'Was there ever a police officer trying to get you onside? Who wanted you to start reporting information,' he clarifies.

'They never said as much to me, but I heard that they were planning to, yes.' She laughs. 'My guess is they dropped that plan when I went to the Prostitution Unit and told them that some bastard cop had tried to strangle me. You don't really want people like that as informants, do you?'

You. There it is again.

'I don't suppose they did, no,' says Birck.

'Did you ever find out who it was?' I ask. 'The man, the customer who tried to strangle you?'

She shakes her head.

'No, I put it all behind me after that, I didn't even want to think about those years. Jesus, what a load of shit.'

I pull out my phone and show her a photograph of Jon Wester.

'Was it him?'

Lisa looks stunned.

'What the fuck do you think you're playing at?'

'Was it him?' I try again, not really understanding what's going on.

'You appear out of nowhere, asking about Angelica. It's so fucking callous of you to do that, you reopen so many wounds with all your questions — are you aware of that? Not only that, you shove a picture in my fucking face, a picture of the man who tried to strangle me. What the fuck are you doing? Have you known all along or what?'

'No, no,' says Birck. 'Sorry, I apologise. It's only now we've begun to understand. And we still don't understand everything. That's why we're here.'

She stares at Birck, then at me.

'Who is that?' she asks.

'He used to be a policeman,' I say.

'You mean he's not anymore?'

'No.'

'Did he get sacked?'

'No.'

She laughs.

'Course he didn't. Bastards like him never do.' She returns to studying the image. 'He tried to strangle me because I refused to obey him. It happened once, but I could tell from the start that he was capable of that sort of thing. There was just something about him, I can't explain it.'

'What was he trying to get you to do?' says Birck.

'I can't even remember. Some stupid shit, I was supposed to get dressed up or do something. He offered me more money, but I said no, I didn't want to. There was no particular reason, I think I was just high and contrary. I used to get that way,' she adds, shaking her head. 'Anyway, that's when he put his hands around my throat. He let go after a while, but Jesus I was terrified. I hated cops at the time — still do as a matter of fact — but then it was … Whatever, because I'd worked out that he was a cop I thought, no, fuck that, he's not going to get away with it.' She rolls her eyes. 'I'm sure I was high when I had that thought, too. It was pointless.'

'And what about Angelica, she met with him after you?'

'Yes, she took over. Or however you put it.'

'Do you know how often they met?'

'No, but he used to come every couple of weeks. It might've

been a bit longer between me and Angelica, if he was being careful. I think he needed to find a girl he felt he could trust.'

So the beginning of August, maybe. That would be two months before the murder. A month before Angelica Reyes captures Wester on tape, a month before the extortion attempts begin. That could be right: He stops seeing Vargas in July. He finds Angelica at the beginning of August. They start meeting regularly, once every other week. By their third or fourth meeting, Angelica has worked out who he is. A plan takes shape, and she puts it into action. None of that breaks the timeline.

'We are going to go,' says Birck. 'Thank you. One more question, though, there's something I don't understand.'

'Okay?'

'The risks he was taking. Why did he come to you?'

'You mean why wasn't he seeing one of those exclusive escort girls?'

'Yes,' Birck says, unsure. 'That's if you're going to pay for sex in the first place in his position.'

'If you knew what positions of power some of my punters had. There aren't many escorts, or at least there weren't back then. The few there are have power and influence. They have friends in high places. The rest of us ...' Lisa laughs. 'Well ... who's going to believe a smack-whore? Obviously it's preferable to come to us. Just look at Angelica. Someone killed her. That was five years ago and whoever did it got away.'

66

'Another piece of the puzzle,' says Birck. 'That's all.'

We head back to the city centre. The southern estates, Rågsved and Högdalen and Bandhagen, swish past. Thursday's light is fading.

'And as of now,' he goes on, 'we can't prove anything more than payment for sex, which now falls under the statute of limitations anyway. But still, Jesus ... the risks he must've taken.'

'Remember Göran Lindberg.'

Göran Lindberg, the lawyer from Uppsala, Police Academy chancellor, later chief superintendent, and perhaps a future National Police Chief. In January 2010, he was arrested at a petrol station in Falun, on his way to meet a fourteen-year-old girl he'd made contact with via a telephone chat line. They found a bag in his car, containing leashes, straps, a gag ball, a whip, and Viagra tablets.

That was the tip of the iceberg. In November 2010, little more than a month after Angelica's murder, he was convicted of aggravated rape, rape, assault, procuring, and attempting to pay for sex.

Everyone knows that there are more Lindbergs out there — police are no better than anyone else at reining in their sexual desires, or need for power, or whatever.

It's Thursday the seventeenth of December, a week before

Christmas. Five days until Grim's funeral. On the way back into town, the rain arrives.

Then, suddenly, it happens. Birck's phone rings.

'What's that noise?' he asks.

'It's your mobile.'

'Shit, that's right, I changed the ringtone.' He pushes his hand into his inside pocket, searching for the phone. 'That trainee we have, you know, she swapped rooms. She used to sit down by your room but now she's in the room next to me. She has the same ringtone as me, so whenever it rings I hear it through the wall and I think it's mine. It was driving me mad, so I changed to another tone. Now I don't realise when my phone's ringing, so now *that* drives me mad instead. Where the fuck is it? Aha.' He fumbles his way into his trouser pocket and pulls out his phone. 'Hello?'

The wiper blades drum rhythmically across the windscreen. Grim's words come back to me, *because I never learn.*

Five days till the funeral. *A final farewell, rest in peace, the memories remain.*

From this point on, I'm alone with them, our memories, and that might be the hardest part. The memories you once shared, that you now have to carry alone — and despite lots of them being bright and warm, a thick, dark mist converges around them. Memories are easy to carry if there are two of you, but so heavy if you're carrying them alone.

'Cancelled?' Birck says down the phone. 'Are you sure? Fucking hell. Can you send it to me then? Yes, we're coming in.'

Birck hangs up. We glide up onto the bridge where Grim was shot, now smothered by the heavy traffic.

'What was that about?'

It was, it turns out, about a parking ticket. As part of the process of identifying SGS's vehicles, Birck contacted the beat officers and asked one of the old foxes to do a search on MCC 860 in their databases. He asked him to pay particular attention to October

2010, but that was all. The man doing the search found nothing, but was the meticulous type.

'Fortunately,' says Birck, 'he took the registration number, then went and double-checked manually, in the archive.'

And so he found something. A parking ticket from the twelfth of October 2010.

Well, actually, no, he corrected himself. A *cancelled* parking ticket. It was only now, on the phone, that the man noticed the word *cancelled* had been added at the bottom.

We stand in Birck's room examining it.

The ticket was printed half an hour before midnight, on the twelfth of October 2010. It's not clear when it was cancelled, but because the details never migrated to the central system, it probably wasn't long afterwards. It all surrounds a car parked illegally next to Kungsholmen's fire station, on a little branch of Kronobergsgatan.

I know where that is: it's an unobtrusive little dead end about five minutes' walk away from Angelica's home on John Ericssonsgatan. One side is lined with a huge brick wall, the other with the trees and shrubs of Kronoberg Park.

'Hey,' I say, pointing at the issuing officers' names.

Birck stares at the ticket.

'For fuck's sake.' He takes a deep breath. 'Bring them in. Get them in here *now*.'

67

Within half an hour, they're sitting in front of me. That might sound pretty efficient, given that the task was to bring in two officers from out in Huddinge. Yet it could actually have happened a lot more quickly.

The reason was as follows.

Earlier today, Dan Larsson and Per Leifby had found themselves at Forensics in Solna — what they were doing there, no one knows, and no one bothered to ask. Larsson stood sipping a can of Fanta while Leifby browsed through a motoring magazine. At that point, the National Police Chief himself, the top dog, there in the flesh, walked past. His suit was immaculate but his face betrayed stress in some form, which was obvious to a sensitive soul like Leifby. Which is why he swatted his magazine at his colleague's arm, spilling some soft drink onto Larsson's uniform.

'Oh fucking hell,' Larsson said in his thick Småland accent. 'I told you it's just been washed.'

'Dan, it's him.'

'Who?'

'It's the NPC. Listen.' Leifby had raised his voice, causing the National Police Chief to stop by the door. The man looked confused. 'Do you want a lift?' asked Leifby.

Larsson brushed the liquid from his uniform and straightened himself out. The NPC gave them one of his normal vacant smiles, and asked where the gents were heading.

'We'll go where the boss is going,' Leifby said, and when the NPC raised a surprised eyebrow in Larsson's direction, he quickly reassured him that the back seat was of course at his disposal.

The NPC was going to Kungsholmen. Leifby drove, looking almost entranced, while Larsson attempted to ask as many sycophantic questions as possible. The NPC's replies were short; he was busy with something on his phone. When they arrived at HQ, he thanked them for the lift, called Per 'Dan' and Dan 'Per', and didn't make eye contact.

'He's got his hands full, that one,' said Larsson.

'Oh yes,' said Leifby. 'I don't bloody doubt it.'

They needed to get some coffee inside them. Partly because they needed to debrief after their first meeting with the NPC. Partly because it was so tiring to traipse around the city fighting crime left, right, and centre, and for this money? They should've mentioned that, by the way. That'd have to wait for their next meeting, that would.

The canteen in HQ was almost empty at this point, which was good. They could sit there having their meeting until their shift was basically done.

They had ten minutes to go and were just about to make their way back onto the streets again — how much shit could happen in the time that was left — when a man who'd left the canteen a while ago came back and called out their names.

It was a charge sergeant, Stockholm Police. He'd been down for a coffee and seen the pair of prize idiots sitting there in a corner. When he got back to his room, he heard that Violent Crime were looking for that very twosome.

By this point, people were already getting annoyed.

Larsson and Leifby had been sought, quite naturally, via

their local station in Huddinge. No one knew where they were, but someone had heard them talking about going to Solna. The receptionist there had seen Larsson, Leifby, and the NPC himself heading out the door. They were going, as she understood it, to give him a lift back into town, which ought to mean that they were in the vicinity of, or indeed inside, HQ itself. At the source of the inquiry, funnily enough.

But in the meantime, no one saw the funny side.

'Does anyone know where these fucking idiots are?' the charge sergeant's superior steamed, in the middle of the open plan office with the phone in his hand. 'Apparently, they're in the building, and they need to go to the Violent Crime Unit immediately.'

The charge sergeant sighed. He couldn't very well keep it to himself. He was a good old honest policeman, and whatever it was might actually be important.

So he stood up from his chair and said that he thought he'd seen them a little while ago. Presumably, given the two they were talking about, the 'idiots' would still be there.

When, finally, they amble into my room, Larsson is carrying a sandwich, Leifby a rolled-up magazine. They look confused but hopeful.

'Sit yourselves down.'

The two officers each sit down on a chair.

'What's this all about?' Leifby asks. 'We haven't really got time for this.'

'No, we've got a job to do,' Larsson adds, staring at his sandwich.

'You can eat that in here,' says Birck.

'It's about this.' I give Leifby the parking ticket. 'Do you remember it?'

He looks like a dog being shown a dishcloth — just as clueless and equally as interested.

'2010,' he reads aloud. 'MCC 860. You know what, that one's slipped my mind.'

'It's from the night of the twelfth of October 2010,' Birck attempts. 'You pulled up a Toyota at the edge of Kronoberg Park.'

'Yes, I remember that,' says Larsson, who is now leaning against his partner to get a better view. 'It's funny you know, that was my Mum's sixtieth, that day. I got off at two, slept a few hours, then it was off to Vetlanda for her party. So I do remember, for that reason. And because he was who he was.'

'Oh shit, yes.' Leifby looks shaken. 'That was that time.'

'Because he was who he was?' I repeat.

'Start from the beginning,' Birck says instead. 'The twelfth of October 2010. Start there.'

68

Yes, it concerned the twelfth of October 2010, and for reasons every bit as unclear as the ones that had taken them to Solna earlier today, the duo had, on that night, stationed themselves on a Kungsholmen backstreet.

They came on at six and stopped at a hotdog stand to refuel. Once there, they noted that the owner was using a larger area of the pavement than his permit allowed. This was tricky, they couldn't have that, but if the owner was to be so friendly as to provide law enforcement with two specials with gherkin relish then they'd be able to turn a blind eye to the infraction, this time.

This encounter wasn't mentioned in the duo's handover, a few hours later. The stand's owner, however, contacted the police to report the reprehensible behaviour the two officers had displayed. They were rude and even casually racist, and as if that wasn't enough, they attempted to blackmail their way to some food.

'Besides, I operate within the boundaries on my permit, with plenty of room to spare,' the owner added.

That night, the twelfth of October, Larsson and Leifby found themselves in the heart of Stockholm, roughly fifteen kilometres from Huddinge, where they should've been. Larsson had worked it all out; he was driving down to Vetlanda the next morning and was very keen to have a quiet shift so he didn't get worn out. The city centre was crawling with squad cars and foot patrols, so the chances of him and Leifby being closest to any possible incidents was minimal, and if it came down to it they could just move on.

Which is what they did. As evening turned to night, they were starting to get bored, and Larsson's sugar cravings were making themselves felt. They rolled up onto Drottningholmsvägen and stopped at a late-night kiosk. Larsson went in and bought two cinnamon buns for himself and two cups of coffee, one for himself and one for his tight-fisted partner.

Not long afterwards, about eleven, something happened. They were crawling down Kronobergsgatan when they spotted the car in front suddenly veer off to the left, up the little backstreet.

'Well,' Larsson said, putting down the first, half-eaten bun. 'Look at that.'

They continued past the turning. The driver had parked up and was now making his way on foot. He moved quickly and purposefully, following Kronobergsgatan down to Hantverkargatan before heading east towards City Hall. Larsson and Leifby weren't daft enough to follow him, deciding instead to stay put.

'That bastard,' said Leifby. 'We'll have that.'

The car had no permit and was badly parked. Admittedly, the nearby fire station didn't use that route when responding to calls, but it still didn't look good. They decided to do their bit for safety and security, and occupied a position further down the street, cunningly obscured from view by the branches of Kronoberg Park.

Larsson finished his first cinnamon bun, and drank some coffee. He was keeping an eye on the car; Leifby the immediate environs.

'Aren't you going to eat the other one?' Leifby said, glancing at the paper bag.

'I think I'll save it a bit,' said Larsson.

Time passed. Fifteen minutes, half an hour. He took a bite of the second bun.

'Shall we do a search on the car maybe?' Leifby suggested, having got the parking ticket all ready to save time when the moment came to deploy it. 'So we know who we're dealing with.'

'I'm going to finish this first,' mumbled Larsson, who was fully occupied with the bun and the coffee, being careful not to spill anything on his uniform.

Leifby rolled his eyes.

They never got that far. The car's driver returned.

By now, it was approximately twenty-to twelve, and there was no doubt that this was the same person. He was wearing jeans and boots, a heavy coat that reached his hips, and a rucksack slung over one shoulder.

'Look at that,' said Leifby. 'Let's get him. Fire it up.'

With a shuddering start, bloody blues and twos on and everything, Larsson and Leifby's vehicle roared towards the man who'd just blipped the badly parked car, opened the driver's door, and placed his rucksack on the passenger seat.

That's when he heard them. He was, needless to say, surprised — what would you expect when two cunning cops like these strike — but at that point something unexpected occurred.

He left the car and ran across the street, up the slope, and in among the trees and bushes of Kronoberg Park. Larsson and Leifby scrambled after him, and Leifby, easily the faster of the two, caught up with him after less than a hundred metres, forcing him to the ground, face down in the cold grass.

'What the hell do you think you're doing?' Leifby snarled, his knee pushed hard between the man's shoulder blades as he fumbled to open his handcuffs.

'Police,' the man hissed, struggling to talk. 'I'm a police officer.'

'Yeah, right,' said Leifby.

Flanked by his breathless partner, who had finally managed to catch up with them, he hauled the crook to his feet. The tumble must've drawn blood somewhere because the collar of the polo shirt peeking out underneath the man's jacket, Larsson noted, was bloody.

'It's true. I am a policeman.'

'Come off it.'

'Listen to me, for fuck's sake, I am. I'm here on duty.'

They ignored him, of course. Larsson and Leifby had seen it all before. Back at the car, they still needed to fill in the remainder of the parking ticket. While Larsson got back in the warm of the patrol car to carry out a records check, Leifby and the man stayed next to his car — a Toyota, registration MCC 860.

'My name is Jon Wester,' the man said. 'I work for SGS.'

Despite the handcuffs, and with a little help from Leifby, he managed to pull out his badge. As Leifby inspected it, he heard Larsson's nasal tones emerge from their vehicle.

'Listen, MCC 860. It's a police vehicle.'

He approached Leifby and the man with the search results in his hand. Larsson was as white as a sheet.

The badge looked, as far as Leifby could discern, authentic, and the man in the picture was undoubtedly identical to the man standing in front of them.

Jon Wester. SGS's Director of Operations. Wasn't he well connected with someone up in the NPA?

'We do apologise,' Leifby said as he unlocked the handcuffs, his fingers starting to tremble.

'We didn't know,' Larsson reiterated. 'If we had known, then …'

'Don't worry about it,' Wester replied.

'We'll tear up the parking fine of course,' Larsson went on.

'Are you alright?'

Leifby studied Wester anxiously. The blood on the collar made him uneasy; he was looking for a wound or a scratch on the man's face, but, confusingly, couldn't find one. The blood on the polo shirt was already starting to dry.

287

'Do you want us to drive you in, so someone can have a look at you?'

'No need,' answered Wester.

'But you're bleeding.'

'It's nothing to worry about.'

With those words, he climbed into his car and drove off. Like the patrol officers, he seemed keen to forget about the whole thing. Which was big of him, Leifby thought. He knew that even the best can get it wrong.

Sitting in their own car, the two stayed silent as they tried to determine what the consequences of the scene they'd just caused might be.

Leifby located the parking ticket, finally managed to find his pen, and annulled the fine, thus clearing Jon Wester of any wrongdoing, at least on that front. After all, he was a cop, on a mission. It must've been a risky one, Leifby thought to himself, given the blood. As the two officers left Kungsholmen, the rain arrived.

69

Sitting in the chair, Leifby clears his throat and crosses his legs. Larsson has finished his roll and is busy brushing the crumbs off his uniform.

I show them a picture of Jon Wester.

'Is this him?'

'We've told you it was Wester,' Larsson says, discomfited, as though he's embarrassed at being reminded of the incident. 'I know what he looks like.'

Birck has opened Patrik Sköld's computer. He's searching for the point in the video from Reyes' apartment where Wester goes to open the window, passing the camera lens as he does so. Once he finds it, he shows them the screen.

'Who is this?'

Leifby puts down his motoring magazine and squints at the display. Larsson leans in.

'Well, it looks like the same person,' he drawls.

'Looks like?'

Larsson seems confused.

'Eh?'

'You said it "looks like" the same person. How sure are you?'

'You can see that it's him,' Larsson says, turning to his colleague, who has stopped squinting and now folds his arms instead.

'Yes, it is him. What's this all about?'

'The man on this tape is the same man that you met on the evening of the twelfth of October 2010?'

'Yes,' Leifby declares.

'Jon Wester.'

'Yes.'

I put Sköld's computer to one side, pick up my own, and pull up a map of Kronoberg Park.

'Can you show me where the tackle took place? Here's where you and the Toyota were parked, according to the parking ticket. Here's Kronoberg.'

Larsson hesitates.

'But what's this about?' he protests. 'This is over five years ago.'

'Show us.'

'Well …' Leifby looks sheepishly at the map. 'He made it a bit into the park, I think, but not that far. I'm a lot quicker than Dan, but it didn't take very long for him to catch up with us.'

'You're not *that* fast,' Larsson says icily.

'Somewhere over here,' Leifby says, putting an index finger on the map, then moving it around in a little circle.

'Thanks,' says Birck. 'That was everything. You can go.'

Larsson looks astonished.

'That was it?'

'We were double-checking the detail, but thank you. We're lucky to have such dutiful colleagues.'

Leifby looks at Larsson, who looks at Leifby. They shrug and get up, before walking out looking thoroughly disheartened and very much as though they hope to avoid any further such encounters for a very long time.

Beneath the tiredness, a wave of adrenaline is growing. The spot Leifby circled with his finger is pretty well exactly the spot where Angelica's mobile phone was found shortly after the murder.

You can see it all: Wester has it on him. But then why not in his rucksack? Maybe he remembered it at the last minute, just as he was about to leave. *Oh shit yeah, her phone.* Yes, maybe.

He's got it on him. Leifby grapples him from behind, and the phone falls out of his pocket, down into the muddy grass of Kronoberg Park. Where it remains.

Birck studies the map of the park.

'Well blow me. I need to think.'

'Me, too. But if we leave it too long then they might stop us.'

'We need the nod from Morovi. It's six o'clock, I bet she's gone home.' He turns to me. 'Tomorrow?'

'Tomorrow it is.'

Birck hovers in the doorway.

'Listen, I ... I've been thinking.'

'What about?'

'That thing Morovi said a while back, about the consequences of this thing. This risks going right to the very top. A senior officer visiting whores, one who, thanks to this, we can place very close to the crime scene at the time of the murder. You saw SGS's results. They achieved a lot. We all do the best we can. The very fact that we manage to catch crooks at all is a miracle, but we sometimes do, even though we're on our knees. This force is under great strain as it is, what with restructuring, the refugee crisis, terrorism, the union's demands ...'

The sentence seeps out into the room, left unfinished. The police force is an animal, shot and wounded, a great colossus struggling just to keep breathing.

'SGS is disbanded,' I say. 'Wester isn't even with the force anymore. Sköld is dead. What are they going to do?'

'It's not just about that, and you know it. It's about the public's perception of us. Who we are, what we do. Which side we're on. Don't you remember what it was like in the aftermath of the Lindberg shit? I was thinking ... taking that into account, do you still want to try and do this?'

'Yes.'

'Good. Me, too.'

I gather up my things, grab my coat and leave the room along with Birck. It's going to be so good to get home. It's been a long day.

'Leo, Gabriel,' I hear a familiar voice in the corridor and I turn around.

Morovi hasn't gone home. She's here, heading straight for us with a stiff expression on her stony face. Walking alongside her is a man who I recognise immediately.

It's the man from the NPA, Carl Hallingström.

70

Stuck.

We're stuck. I haven't a fucking clue what they might have come up with, but we're stuck. That much is obvious.

Hallingström is a little eel of a man, with a proper handshake but a moist sheen to his eyes, which are constantly darting back and forth, and he's forever licking his lips. He's like a parody of himself, but there's nothing funny about the situation.

We're back in my room. Birck is leaning against one of the bookcases with a sarcastic smile on his face, I don't know what to make of that. Morovi is also standing up, but propped against the door, as though she'd most like to get out of here and not have to witness this. I'm sitting in my chair while Hallingström has placed his peculiar frame into one of the chairs opposite. He's struggling to find a comfortable position. The wood creaks.

'What's this about?' I say.

'It's about …' Hallingström folds one leg over the other, places his clasped hands around his knee. 'Anja, can't you explain? These are your personnel, after all.'

That isn't really a question.

'My understanding is that we've been the subject of a random spot check in the last few days. The searches Violent Crime Unit have made in the record of convictions were examined, and the inspectors reacted to yours.'

'Among others,' Hallingström points out, raising a bony index finger. 'Not just yours.'

'A *random* spot check,' Birck repeats. 'I see.'

'You don't seem surprised,' Hallingström says with his back to him.

'I can't say that I am, no.'

'So you knew you were operating outside the rules.'

'We suspected that you would say so, if nothing else.'

Hallingström turns to face Birck and raises a bushy eyebrow.

'What is that supposed to mean?'

'You know what that means.'

'No, I do not.'

'Which,' I interrupt, 'searches, more specifically, does this concern?'

'I'm glad you asked.' Hallingström pulls a list from his blazer pocket. 'The following.'

Lisa Vargas, Jonna Danielsson, Ludwig Sarac, and Miro Djukic are the first names he mentions, but it's not about them. They've been flagged for further investigation by the inspector, but we can link them with Angelica's murder. On this, they've got nothing.

It's about a series of searches in November, mostly mine, about Nikola Abrahamsson and Viveka Cehaic.

I suspected that it might not have been chance that saw Grim get shot. I was looking for a connection between them and the Angelica murder, but never found one. I knew I'd end up in deep water with those searches. I knew as much, but I did it anyway.

'Nikola Abrahamsson and Viveka Cehaic operated within the rules, the investigation will show, I'm convinced of that,' Hallingström says coolly. 'Regardless of their conclusions, I find it impossible to see why *you* got involved, as a police officer. It is unacceptable, despite your relationship to this Grimberg, which has only recently been brought to my attention. Perhaps the most alarming search, however, is one you have both conducted, concerning a Huddinge policeman, the now deceased Patrik Sköld.' Hallingström looks up from his list. 'Performing searches like that about a colleague. A *deceased* colleague. People in this building have been suspended for less. This is exceptionally serious, in my opinion.'

It is exceptional. Not the search, which, under the circumstances, was perfectly justifiable. Not only that, Sköld was alive when we did it. What is truly exceptional is Hallingström's stupidity. Or is this an act?

'You exposed Sköld to his colleagues in Södertälje,' Birck says, determined. 'He talked to us and you broke him, destroyed his credibility by framing him for narcotics offences. You were the one who caused him to take his own life.'

'Nonsense.' Hallingström doesn't even turn around. Instead, he folds the paper and places it on the desk between us. 'Naturally, you will be formally interviewed, and given the chance to give your account of events. You will remain in service, but on administrative duties only until a decision is made. It shouldn't take longer than a month or so. I'm sure you understand, but I still want to make quite clear that you are not authorised to conduct surveillance or participate in practical investigation.'

In a month's time, we will no longer be authorised to work on the Reyes case. Hallingström knows this, which might be why he's straining not to smile.

'We will appeal,' I say.

'I thought you might. But it doesn't actually change anything in practical terms. Until both versions have been collated and assessed, you are restricted to administrative duties. That's a routine safeguard.'

'So, like records searches, for example,' says Birck.

'I fail to understand why you are attempting to make light of this,' Hallingström says. 'This is regrettable, very regrettable. But I must take the measures that discipline ...'

'How much money did Angelica Reyes extort from Jon Wester?'

'Leo,' Morovi snaps and takes a step forward.

'Before she was killed,' I continue. 'Before Wester got desperate and realised that he was losing his grip. How much money are we talking about, fifty thousand? A hundred?'

'Leo,' Morovi repeats.

'What was toughest for Wester — being blackmailed for fucking whores or managing to misplace the list of informants?'

'Or was it the old rock and a hard place?' Birck chips in.

Hallingström purses his lips.

'I would say that we have luck on our side,' he says drily, 'in terms of random checks of record searches. Officers who come out with that kind of nonsense could certainly do with a break from active investigative duties.'

He stands up and gets ready to go.

I pull out a desk drawer and lift out Sköld's computer.

I unlock it and show him the still frame showing Jon Wester about to leave Angelica Reyes' apartment.

'You know that he was paying her for sex,' I say. 'And that she wasn't the first. I *know* that you're familiar with all this. He must have been protected.'

Hallingström stares at the screen.

He turns to Morovi.

'Would you be so kind as to take care of the paperwork here, I need to get going. There's another meeting I have to attend before I can go home.'

'Is it with Wester?' I ask.

'Leo.' Morovi opens the door for Hallingström. 'That's enough.'

I turn to my boss.

'Why are you protecting him?'

'See you next time,' Hallingström says without a smile, then adjusts his shirt collar underneath his blazer before heading out into the corridor.

71

'Why am I protecting him?'

Morovi's the one asking the question. She's closed the door behind Hallingström and is leaning against the wall again, eyes closed as she massages her own temples.

'Jesus, Leo,' she goes on, 'you're getting paranoid.' Morovi opens her eyes. 'What've you got?'

'I think he knows,' I say, and look over at Birck. 'Hallingström knows.'

'Yes,' Birck agrees. 'He's probably on his way to see Wester as we speak.'

'Hello.' Morovi raises her voice. 'Have you got Wester?'

'What difference would that make?' Birck looks at me. 'Our hands our tied. We can't do a fucking thing.'

Morovi runs her hand through her hair and repeats:

'Have you *got* him?'

'Yes,' says Birck. 'We've got him.'

'Go on.'

'First of all, as background, and as circumstantial evidence, we have recorded instances of Wester buying sex, more than once. Reyes, of course, but Lisa Vargas, too. In Vargas' case, we also have an alleged assault. That isn't particularly pertinent to the Angelica murder, but it still means something. It shows that he visits, or used to visit, whores, and that he can, or could, turn violent. Secondly, we have a documented relationship between Angelica Reyes and Jon Wester. We know, broadly speaking, what it was based on. She sold him sex, got hold of the list of informants, and then used it to milk him for cash. She threatened to expose him if he didn't pay. There's our motive. We've also got a timeline that fits, from their first meeting up until her death.'

'Thirdly,' I cut in, 'we have placed him close to the crime scene at around the time of the murder. We can also place him pretty much exactly at the spot where Angelica Reyes' mobile phone was recovered, and explain how it got there. Not only that, he has dried blood on his collar.'

Morovi looks surprised.

'How do you know this?'

While I recount the exploits of Larsson and Leifby and the cancelled parking ticket, Morovi looks resolute.

'Well I fucking never,' she says. 'Larsson and Leifby might just've saved a murder investigation. I didn't see that coming.'

'Wester claims that he's there on duty, but we've checked SGS duty logs. There's no mention of any operations on Kungsholmen at that time of day, which means we can assume that he is lying. He parks up at eleven and returns about forty minutes later. That fits. He also has a rucksack with him. My guess would be that it contains a laptop. While at Reyes', he removes the list from the memory stick before returning it to the hole in the wall.'

'Why does he put it back? Why doesn't he take it with him?'

I hesitate.

'I think at that point he felt like he had a chance to throw us off the scent, deflect attention from what he deleted. Instead of looking for something that's *missing*, he wants us to focus on what is *visible*. The pictures. It worked, to an extent — those photos were shown to every last relative and friend. That must've used up an awful lot of man hours.'

Morovi bites her bottom lip.

'Alright,' she says. 'Borderline, but I'll buy it.'

She turns to Birck for the next instalment.

'Yes,' he says. 'That's what we've got.'

'Is it?'

'Yes.'

Morovi is pale with exhaustion.

'You haven't got him.'

Birck flings his arms wide.

'But it is him.'

'You can't prove it. You've got a motive. You've got Wester on Kungsholmen at the time of the murder, with blood on his collar. You've constructed a hypothesis that makes the link between him and Reyes' mobile phone. That's all. You can't put him inside the apartment, you don't have a single witness statement indicating that he was even inside the building.'

'We have not been able to …' says Birck.

'I know that. But are you *going* to be able to put him at the scene? If so, how? You haven't got a weapon, no confession. What you can prove is that he once paid for sex, but it's so long ago that it's covered by the statute of limitations. You cannot even say how the list fell into Reyes' hands — it's all assumptions and guesswork.'

She shakes her head. 'It won't stand up.'

Birck is staring purposefully at the floor in front of his shoes.

'What do you want from us? We've hoovered a five-year-old murder investigation, studied three years' worth of documents from a whole fucking unit — we've looked at every bloody last scrap of paper. We've checked whether there are CCTV images from the night of the murder, captured by one of the nearby cameras. They've either been destroyed, deleted, or they simply don't show anything. We've located and eliminated the cars in the area, sat up all night reading SGS inquiry files, incident reports, personnel lists, gone through their budget, outgoings, we've counted manually, month by month, to see whether any money is missing, I've sat there myself looking at *receipts*. There are no stones to turn. We're not going to get any further. This is what we've got. Everything else has been destroyed, or was never written down to begin with. Everyone is either dead, knows nothing, or doesn't want to talk. This is what we've got to go on, or nothing.'

Birck wipes his lips. Saliva has been raining forth along with his words. The echo of his voice hangs in the air.

'Are you done?' Morovi asks.

'He's the one who did it,' he says, almost pleadingly. 'We've got him paying for sex, the extortion, the list, we can put him close to the scene with blood on his collar. We've ...' He clears his throat. 'We've got the phone, it's, it exists, we've ...'

He starts looking in his pocket, a piece of paper, I'm not sure which. He unfolds it with trembling hands. It's a copy of the note Sköld left.

'Gabriel,' I say.

'An officer took his own life. *He shot himself.* We can't ...'

'Gabriel.'

He looks at me, surprised.

'Yes?'

'We haven't got him.'

Birck makes his way over to one of the chairs and crumples into it. A little sliver of saliva glistens on his chin.

You get close, but not quite all the way there. That's often the way. Triumphs aren't the norm. Perhaps we should've sensed the defeat, felt it coming.

It's late. So much time has passed. There's something I want to be out of the way. *The funeral.* Jesus. How am I going to cope?

Birck tips his head back, eyes closed, and says to Morovi:

'Are you scared?'

'Sorry?'

'Are you scared? About what's going to happen to you, to the force, if the truth gets out? Is that what this is about?'

Morovi approaches Birck slowly, stands next to his chair and stares down at him.

'You know that it was him,' she says quietly. '*I* know that it was him. But that's not enough. It *shouldn't* be enough. Not even with a crime like this, with a perpetrator of this kind. Am I scared? Yes. I'm scared of what will happen if we start bending the rules.'

'Everyone bends the rules,' Birck mumbles.

'We're not everyone. We're not Social Services or the Inland Revenue. Our arsenal of weapons to use against citizens is much heavier. And you know this,' she says, somewhat more loudly. 'You have taught yourselves this. You were trained in it once. I want to bring down Wester, too — what the hell do you think of me? But in a case like this, one that branches right up to the top, it's even more important that everything is done right. They'll shoot the thing to pieces otherwise. And based on what you've told me, you haven't got him.'

Birck wipes his chin.

'But there's nothing more we can do,' I say. 'Gabriel is right, we've … We've done all we can. We're not going to get any closer. And even if we could, we're suspended.'

'You're not suspended.'

'But you know what I mean.'

'I know what you mean. Is there a question coming?'

'It's this, or nothing. Are we going to drop it?'

'Have you spoken to him?'

'Wester?' I shake my head. 'We never did, so as not to frighten him. Because we were only ever likely to get one chance. We wanted to be ready when it came.'

'Ready,' she repeats thoughtfully. 'It's late. The registrar has gone home, so the papers won't be fed into the system until tomorrow. That means that for the time being, you're not tied to your desks.' She gives Birck a stiff nod and starts heading towards the door, but then says, over her shoulder: 'It couldn't hurt to take a trip out to have a look at Wester. Or something.'

'Now?'

'What have you got to lose? And remember what you've got from the scene ...'

Her words linger inside the room as the door slams shut behind her. Birck stares into space.

'What we've got from the scene ...'

He stops himself mid-sentence and his eyes meet mine. It hits us both at exactly the same time.

DNA.

72

Unsolved murders are mazes. I do think that's true.

Within this maze, though, the signs are no longer indistinct. They are forming a pattern on the walls. If you look at them all at once, you can make out a glimpse of what went on, what must have happened. Not everything, that's never the way. So long afterwards it's a question of likelihood, not objectivity, we all know that. Parts of the past always need to be reconstructed, supposed, assumed.

Yet still, the signs are finally clear.

The DNA register that the police have at their disposal is in fact four separate databases. First of all, the Trace Register. A record of any DNA profiles collected from crime scenes that have not been tied to a particular person. It contains, for example, the sample obtained from Angelica Reyes' apartment. The second is known as the Investigations Register, comprising individuals suspected of crimes that would carry a custodial sentence. Part three, DNA profiles of convicted criminals, primarily those sentenced to jail terms. The fourth and final database is the one known as the Elimination Register. It comprises DNA profiles of police personnel and others, and is used to compare and eliminate possible contamination that might occur when the individuals in question have had direct or indirect contact with a certain exhibit.

Jon Wester was on that database. Not anymore — we checked that on the night Sköld died. The database is regularly screened according to the laws governing personal information and integrity, with individuals' information being removed at regular intervals. When an employee retires or leaves the force for any reason, the profile drifts off into space and disappears. It is permissible to keep the sample for up to two years *from the date on which the circumstances that necessitate the taking of samples cease to apply*. That's what the rulebook says. Jon Wester disappeared from the database more than two years ago.

Birck looks at me.

'We'll have to do it the old-fashioned way,' he says.

'You mean ...'

'Yes.'

'After what Morovi just said to us?'

'Yes?'

'I don't think that's what she was getting at. And besides, that could make the sample inadmissible.'

'Leo, *we* would know for sure.'

'And you think that's worth it?'

'Don't you?'

I look out through my office's little window.

Stockholm glitters as we roll out onto Götgatan, where the neon signs shine bright and clear.

'I'm sorry that I got like that ...' Birck begins.

'It's okay.'

'No, it isn't.'

'But I know how you feel.'

'It's not the first time I've felt like this. Admittedly, several of those involved are police officers, but that's happened before, too.' He hesitates. 'But I've never acted like that towards my boss before.'

'So there is something there.'

'Yes.' He stops at a red light on Ringvägen. 'Yes, there's something there.' The lights change, we move off. We're getting close.

This doesn't feel right. We are about to cross a line.

It'd been such a lonely time, and then, suddenly, Grim reappeared. He slung me back into the maze. Now he's gone for good. And that makes everything else blurred, uncertain.

'What do we do if ... I mean, if this does work, what the fuck do we do then?'

'Well ...' Birck slows down. 'I doubt it's going to be that straightforward. But yes, then we will have got him, I suppose. Is this the place?'

'Next junction.'

'I hope he's home.'

73

More than five long years have passed since the murder. Five years, but the same city, the same tarmac. Suddenly I am at one with it, the city, the street — it comes as a surprise to me, but the sensation is clear. I have become part of it, or perhaps it has finally sunk into me. Perhaps it's yet another sign.

He lives on Timotejgatan, a flat little piece of tarmac lined with pale three-storey buildings. We park up a little way away, a spot that gives us a view of the entrance, but where the car won't be easily identified. Up in Jon Wester's window, white curtains frame a sad-looking pot plant and an Advent candle. It's on.

Birck adjusts his uniform. Both his and mine are borrowed.

'Christ, it's been a while since I wore this get up. It's so bloody impractical.'

'You've got too comfortable. Concentrate now. Make the call.'

We don't have much time to play with. It needs to happen tonight, preferably this evening, before our new restrictions start to apply and the straps are tightened around us. We need to lure him out.

Birck takes a deep breath and then puts the phone to his ear, waits for the call to be answered.

The number he's calling is a company phone, the only number we've been able to get hold of. It maybe one and the same as his private number, but that's unlikely. Perhaps there's a phone ringing in a desk drawer somewhere, in some office. Perhaps we've hit a wall already, in which case …

'Hello?' says Birck. 'Who am I speaking to?'

Sound leaks from Birck's phone. Inside the quiet car, you can just about hear the words of the other voice:

Who are you looking for?

'Jon Wester.'

And who's asking?

'My name is Jonas Almqvist and I'm … I need your help, I work as a security guard for G4S. My round tonight includes the cash service depot in Åkersberga. I'm covering for the regular guard here, so I'm a bit unsure of how it's usually done here.'

What's this about?

Birck clears his throat.

'I'm in my van right now, pretty sure that I'm sat looking at a cash depot with no active alarm.'

Eh?

'I know that the alarm is supposed to be activated,' he goes on, 'but I'm pretty sure it isn't, I've been in touch with the control room. They couldn't see anything either. I'm the last one here and I can't activate the alarm. Plus I have to keep moving. The next chance I'll have to come past is in two hours' time. It's an empty depot, but still, it doesn't look too fucking great.'

No, it certainly does not.

'I don't suppose you could come down here, could you? Because … You're the one who's responsible for security here, aren't you? I mean, the way it's set up and everything.

No, I'm not … Well, I was responsible for the planning and implementation.

'Exactly. The control room gave me your number. I'm sure it wouldn't take you very long to sort out. I would really appreciate it, I mean otherwise I'm going to have to tell my boss tomorrow that *I* followed *my* instructions — and called you — but that you …'

Alright, alright. [sigh, crackling on the line] Åkersberga. I'll set off in a few minutes, should be with you in half an hour or so.

'Great. I'll try and hang around. I'll let the others know to cover the rest of my round for the moment. But the sooner you can get here the better, because ...'

I'm on my way.

Birck hangs up and puts his phone away. I look at him.

'Jonas Almqvist?'

'It was the first thing that popped into my head. I'm reading *The Queen's Tiara* at the moment.'

We look up at his window. The light goes off. Seconds later, the front door opens and he emerges. He looks annoyed, and who could blame him?

'We'll have to do it soon,' Birck says. 'Before he makes any calls and realises that he's been duped.'

'Are you sure you want to?'

Birck looks hesitant.

'Yes, although it is crossing a line.' He looks at Wester, who is closing the driver's door of a low, dark-coloured Mercedes. The rear lights shine through the night as he turns the key in the ignition. 'That's if there ever was a line.'

74

It's dangerous to get too close — just as risky as falling too far behind. We mustn't give ourselves away, but we mustn't lose him either.

Wester's Mercedes takes the expected route, through Södermalm and out onto the northbound motorway towards Täby and Åkersberga. We are three or four vehicles behind throughout. Birck is driving, and I'm keeping tabs on the Mercedes. Neither of us wants to talk. Darkness fills the car.

At one point, the police radio crackles. Birck turns it off.

'A patrol car could've done this for us,' I say.

'Would you be happy handing this over to them?' Birck coughs. 'They would never have pulled it off.'

The question now is whether *we* will pull it off.

'There's a risk that it could turn,' he goes on, 'rather physical.'

I look down at my legs, my own chest. Dressed in uniform, my body seems unfamiliar, as though it belongs to someone else.

It's approaching midnight. The motorway sweeps over the city and into Solna. We drive past Karolinska, and I avoid looking at the buildings towering above the road.

It starts as we pass Haga Park, the frozen silhouettes of its trees in tight, tight rows. Birck put his foot down and tucks in behind Wester's Mercedes. You can almost see his eyes darting up towards the rear-view mirror, clocking the liveried car behind. His shoulders probably hunch slightly.

Birck turns on the blue lights. They bounce off the Mercedes' black paint. Sirens wail. Birck indicates right, exhortingly: *Slow down, stop at the roadside.*

Wester ignores the signals. He increases his speed.

'Oh, shit,' Birck hisses, repeating the signal, sirens and lights on once more.

Nothing happens. Wait: the Mercedes' indicators flash, and he starts to slow down, glides over to the right, and comes to a halt on the verge. Birck sighs loudly. He's been holding his breath.

We proceed past the Mercedes and pull in in front, stopping a car's length ahead and stepping out into the cold December night without looking at each other. The damp finds its way inside the uniform and makes you shiver. I realise that I'm longing for the first snow of winter. It hasn't arrived yet.

Birck has the breathalyser, a standard Dräger model, in one hand and the standard-issue flashlight in the other. Wester is studying us through the windscreen. He's kept it dark in there: all you can see is a pale face against dark clothing, a pair of darker holes — his eyes behind his glasses. Birck approaches the driver's door and leans towards it.

'Lights on in there.'

Wester does as he says. As the light comes on, I look at him, his eyes. Everything looks different up close, even people. Wester looks older, friendlier somehow. More open.

With one finger, Birck points down towards the tarmac. Wester undoes his seatbelt and opens the window, which slides down with a buzz. Behind us, the cars are sweeping past along the motorway, at short intervals. Headlights clip my peripheral vision.

'Good evening,' says Birck. 'Where are you heading?'

'Why do you ask?'

'Do you have some ID?'

'Yes.'

'Can I see it?'

Birck puts the torch in his mouth and extends his free hand. Wester drops a driving licence into his fingers. Birck studies it with a mute stare before returning it.

'Both me and my colleague feel that your car was weaving about a bit too much. When did you last drink alcohol?'

Wester stares at him. Birck raises an eyebrow. I'm surprised at his calmness.

'Weaving, you say. Okay.'

'When did you last have a drink?'

'I am sober.'

'Can you answer the question?'

'The day before yesterday. I had a beer with my dinner.'

Birck shows him the Dräger.

'Do you know how one of these works?'

Wester rolls his eyes.

'What are you on about? My car wasn't weaving.'

'You know you're being a bit aggressive now?' Birck says, taking a step towards Wester as he checks the device's settings.

'Let me blow then, so I can get going.'

Birck holds out the breathalyser. Wester closes his lips around the mouthpiece and blows. The Dräger emits a beep, which is soon drowned out by the noise of a passing heavy goods vehicle. The wind is cold and hard as ice, it bites at your face.

The display shows NEG.

Negative.

'Hmm,' says Birck, then puts it away. 'This thing only reacts to alcohol, not narcotics. We would like you to come and sit in our car, so that we can have a little chat. Bring your driving licence.'

Wester doesn't reply. Instead, he just stares at me.

'Shouldn't your colleague stay in the car?'

'Do we really need to make things difficult?' says Birck.

'I'm not leaving my car.'

'Do you want some help?'

That's not a question. He puts one hand on his truncheon. I take a step forward.

'I have been breathalysed. It was negative. You've done your job. If you don't let me leave now, I will be reporting you.'

'Where are you off to?'

'That is not any of your business.'

'My colleague and I maintain that your car was weaving alarmingly. As we were passing the park it was shocking — another half a metre, and you would've ended up in the ditch. We would like to take a blood test, down at the station. Solna's not far, we can do it there.'

'What the hell is going on?' Wester squints in my direction. 'I think maybe I recognise you. Have we met … ?'

'We're the ones asking the questions here,' Birck interrupts, adjusting his beret as he does so. It looks weird. 'I asked you whether we need to make things difficult, or are you going to come with us?'

Wester smiles weakly.

'I am going nowhere until you tell me what this is really all about.'

Birck closes his grip around the driver's door handle and opens it abruptly.

'Get out.'

'No.'

Wester makes an attempt to pull the door shut, a sudden movement that makes Birck grab hold of his arm. Wester struggles to break free, but Birck's grip is too firm and he can't. He flails with his free hand instead, striking Birck in the face.

Birck drags him out of the car, down onto the cold tarmac. Wester grunts something indecipherable and squirms as he does so, but Birck forces him to lie face down, with his hands pinned up behind his back.

'Resisting arrest. Assaulting a police officer.'

'For fuck's sake,' Wester hisses, his face dotted with gravel. 'What the fucking hell do you think you're playing at? I'm an ex-cop, do you think I don't know what you're up to …'

'Swab him, would you please,' Birck interrupts. 'Might as well.'

That's the signal. I pull the little kit from my inside pocket.

'Swab me? In your fucking dreams — I'm going …'

A heavy groan is expelled through Wester's mouth as Birck pushes a knee into his back, forcing the air from his lungs.

I've broken through barriers before. In my line of work, I've pushed the limits further than you ought to, in fact — how many times have I *breached* them, even just with Grim?

I don't feel the slightest sympathy for Wester, but I do, perhaps, for the idea of the presumption of innocence. For someone who has yet to, beyond a reasonable doubt, be shown to be the murderer. He did it, but we can't prove that. We still don't have the right to act like this.

I thought that I had changed. That I had, at least partly, become someone else.

For a second, I'm somewhere else entirely, alongside the man who was once my best friend. He's lying in a hospital bed, and I'm asking him, coldly, why he tried to trick me.

Because I never learn.

I stare down at Wester, then crouch in front of his panting face. Thin, white clouds escape his mouth in snappy puffs.

I see my hands working, watch them manage to prise open Wester's jaw and ram a cotton bud into his mouth. Wester lies perfectly still, until he bites down hard, like a dog. The cotton bud breaks off between his teeth.

313

I wrench it out.

'Fuck's sake,' Birck hisses. 'We've got a couple of hundred of those in the car, don't you know that? We've got as long as it takes. If you don't have anything to hide, why are you resisting? Get another one.'

My hands retrieve the next kit from my pocket and repeat the whole procedure. As I prise open Wester's jaw again, he groans with exertion. Maybe he's giving up, realising how futile resistance is. I swab the little tool once, twice, three, four times, keep going for almost a minute before I return it to its protective case.

'Thanks for that,' says Birck, as I lean over Wester and cuff him. 'Let's go for a drive, the three of us.' He hauls Wester to his feet. 'And perhaps introduce ourselves. My name is Gabriel Birck.'

Wester looks at me quizzically.

'Leo Junker,' I say, and take off my beret. 'Violent Crime Unit.'

'What the hell is this about?'

'Angelica Reyes,' says Birck, making something happen in Wester's eyes.

They sparkle, for a split-second, with fear.

75

I take out the kit and inspect it. By the light inside the car I can see the top of the little stick glistening with saliva.

DNA.

We've put Wester in the back seat. He's yet to say anything beyond grunting that he's been the victim of an assault.

'You claimed to be traffic cops,' Wester says. 'That's not allowed.'

'We've been working on the murder of Angelica Reyes for a while now,' Birck says, easing us back out onto the motorway.

We leave his Mercedes behind, waiting for a recovery truck. A taxi overtakes with its top sign glowing through the darkness.

Wester squirms. It isn't possible to sit comfortably in a car seat with your hands behind your back.

'What happened between the two of you?' I ask.

'I won't be saying a word to you two. I know what you're trying to do. Drop it, before I report you to the Ombudsman.'

'And what are you going to report us for?' says Birck. 'We're just talking.'

'We mean it,' I say. 'We want you to tell us what happened.'

'You are a fucking disgrace to the force. I've got nothing to say to you.'

'Are you sure about that? You may remember that DNA was recovered from the crime scene.'

'Are you trying to threaten me?'

'Absolutely not,' says Birck. 'But you know how this works. Everything will be so much easier if you talk.'

Wester doesn't talk, though. As we park up outside the remand centre in Solna and take care of practicalities, he maintains his silence. The only thing he says to us before we're separated as a guard leads him away is:

'When you wake up in the morning, you'll have an official complaint against you.'

'When you wake up in the morning, you'll be remanded on suspicion of murder,' Birck replies.

76

Doing this is not allowed. It's about the principle, our room to manoeuvre. You need warrants for this kind of thing. Only in bad crime novels will you find police officers who can do exactly as they please with no reprimands or consequences of any sort.

It's not impossible to add illegally obtained evidence to a case file. Fingerprints, for example, are straightforward. You just need to get hold of them, and have a contact in Forensics who's happy to do a professional comparison and analysis. That's enough. DNA is different. DNA *is* basically impossible, because the test has to go to the National Forensics Centre. To even get something sent off there, every step of the process must be done exactly by the book — labelled, recorded, and documented. You need to attach prosecutor's decisions and all kinds of shit, or it won't happen. Illegally obtained DNA is pretty much unusable.

That is, unless, you can obtain it under false pretences, like a routine traffic stop that leads to violent resistance. Everything is then entered into the system, where a DNA-matching check is conducted. The problem is that NFC's analysis will take some time, perhaps weeks.

'In the meantime …' I said, in the car on the way to Wester's earlier on. 'Well, I don't fucking know.'

'Yeah,' said Birck. 'But. Do you remember about a month ago, at the beginning of all this, when I had lunch with a friend who works at National Board of Forensic Medicine? His speciality is DNA. I'll ask him to compare the samples under the counter. If I show the prosecutor the results, they'll be able to draw out the process against Wester. In which case, he'll stay on remand until the results come back from NFC and then ... BOOM. Assuming you think it's worth it, that is?'

He posed the question so simply, so naturally, despite the words puncturing me from the inside out.

The end sometimes justifies unconventional means, that was SGS's motto. It's more of a feeling than an insight as such — the fact that, in moments like these, something bigger than your own hopes can steer the course of events.

Now, afterwards, the regret hits me in the chest. We've committed a violent act, there's no denying it. I look at my hands. I can feel Wester's face in my palms, his cold cheeks and his hard jaws, how they creak as I prise them apart and force him to open wide.

'So?' Birck asks again. 'Do you think it's worth it? I mean, your *friend* died because of this.'

'Yes,' I say. 'But ...'

'I know.'

'Hi,' Birck says into the phone. 'It's me. I know that it ... Yes, I know, I was about to apologise, but we ... I need your help.' Short pause. 'A murder.' More silence. 'Yes, Angelica Reyes. I can ... I don't know. That's for you to decide.'

They end the call. I stare out the window. We're heading towards Bromma.

'He's going to do it,' says Birck.

'*Now?*'

'No.' He changes lanes. 'But as soon as he can. Probably tomorrow night.'

We keep talking through the journey, but Birck never says his friend's name, and that's probably deliberate, to protect him. Before long, we stop outside a house in Bromma. It's in the heart of a leafy suburb, identical to so many others.

'Stay here,' Birck says, and takes the little tube with him.

Birck stops on the doorstep and knocks on the door. A man opens it, and takes a step outside. He's our age, and he's wearing a dressing gown. I glimpse his profile, sharp and angular. He holds out his hand. They exchange a few words, but I can't discern which ones, then the door closes and Birck returns.

'Who is that?' I ask. 'What's his name?'

'His name's Birck.'

'What do you mean, Birck?' I feel like I've lost it. 'You're Birck.' Birck smirks.

'His name's Daniel Birck, and he's my big brother.'

'You've got a *brother*?'

'Haven't I mentioned that?'

'No, you haven't.'

We leave Bromma. The night is as thick as smoke.

'What are you thinking about?' he asks.

'Grim's funeral.'

77

Two days later, a few hours before a court is to decide whether the decision remanding Wester into custody needs to be reviewed, the test results come back from National Board of Forensic Medicine. It has no sender, and no addressee. It is delivered by hand. Birck shows it to me, standing in my office.

The new sample, collected at an unknown location at an unspecified time, is a match with the unidentified DNA recovered from Angelica Reyes' apartment on the night of the thirteenth of October 2010.

'We got him,' says Birck.

'Yes.'

I start laughing, but I don't really know why.

I think about the swab, its little protective sleeve, the glistening saliva, and I wonder where it is, whether Birck's brother held onto it. For a second, I see myself holding it in my hand, then throwing it away, then destroying the whole kit.

It feels shameful, like trying to cover up a crime. As though I'm trying to convince myself that I were a more honourable cop, *a better person*, than I actually am.

Because I do want to know. It was worth it.

As if this force, too, ultimately took a firm grip on me.

People don't change. They adapt. *Because I never learn.* Maybe that's the truth.

78

The bells chime in Salem Church.

It's the twenty-second of December, a Tuesday, and the priest is an older woman with short silver hair and round glasses that remind me of John Lennon or Harry Potter. The fact that there are no more than eight people present, of whom only seven are alive, seems to make her take the task in hand even more seriously.

I'm in the front row. Behind me, a few lonely souls; one of them is Nikola Abrahamsson. He was already sitting there when I arrived, and I tried to make eye contact, but he avoided it. I don't blame him. At least, I don't think so. I see Ludwig Sarac and a few others; we don't say much to each other either during or after the ceremony.

The priest stands where she's meant to, the man from the undertakers is somewhere in the background, and in a simple wooden coffin is my friend John Grimberg.

My suit feels stiff. Before I left, Sam fixed my tie and pushed a roller across my back to get the dust off — I haven't had time to get it dry-cleaned — and then she asked me if I wanted her to come with me. I regret saying no.

The priest starts talking, and our eyes meet, but I hear only snippets of what she says. The organ begins to play. The priest sings beautifully; I grasp a book of psalms in my hands and follow the words, studying the text.

Trusting in my Father's wise bestowment,
I've no cause for worry or for fear.

We could've been something big. I convinced myself of that, I think, that we had that potential. We could've broken free, like the music that streamed from the rolled-down windows of the cars those nights in Salem.

I hear his voice, his *Leo, have you ever thought about ...* and that billowing laugh, I can see that serious stare. He should still be around, should be here now, next to me.

Instead, he disappeared before time, and I'm already starting to forget how his skin felt against mine.

When the ceremony is over, I walk to the water tower. I'm drawn to it, cannot resist.

Leo, have you ever thought about how it sometimes feels like life hasn't even started yet? As though we're ... I don't know. As if we're waiting.

Yes, and while we were doing that, waiting, time passed and life-changing tragedies occurred. We hurt each other in small ways and big ones, and once real life did kick in we could never share it.

I lie down on my back again. It feels good to be back. The ground is cold and wet. This, here, is the end of something.

In my inside pocket, I still have the list I got from Jonna Danielsson. I'm reminded of it and I pull it out, I want to touch it, to have something tangible, *him*, to hold on to.

I hold it in front of my face, read the names once more. Such a tiny list, really, such a shitstorm of consequences.

It might be the light from the sky shining through the thin sheet of paper, it might be something else. Here by the water tower, it feels like he's so close, but there's no way I can explain it. On the paper, small indentations emerge, like when you write something on one piece and the pen's movements leave marks on the page beneath.

No ink, but an impression.

I laugh.

It's a name, written in Grim's handwriting. Perhaps it was more of a suspicion, a hunch. If it was, where did it come from? Or perhaps he really did know — but how? I will never know.

It was him Grim was on his way to see, that day when it all came to an end, under the bridge. Lansec Security's offices are located on Vasagatan, not far from there. That's why he was out.

Jon Wester?

That's what it says. One last mystery.

79

On the twenty-eighth of March 2016, he is convicted of the murder of Angelica Reyes, having pleaded not guilty. By that time, he has reached fifty-two years of age. The time on remand has hollowed him out, made him grey. You can see that from a mile off.

It's the DNA that ties him to the deed. It is noted that the method by which it was obtained was questionable, but that the analysis and processing of the DNA sample has been handled according to NFC's rules and guidelines, and as such it should be permitted to form part of the evidence. The court spends a full day on the question of the sample. Birck and I give evidence. As soon as the name Carl Hallingström is mentioned, the questions dry up.

Besides that: testimony from two beat officers, Larsson and Leifby; a cancelled parking ticket; a video clip found on a dead cop's computer; and other supporting evidence, including a mobile phone picked up by a child the morning after the crime. The court rules that as a whole, the evidence is sufficient to prove beyond reasonable doubt that Jon Wester took Angelica Reyes' life. Wester, meanwhile, claims that he was in Kronoberg Park as part of an SGS operation, an assertion only supported by flimsy circumstantial evidence.

The only point at which the prosecutor's version of events is seriously called into question is in connection with the list of informants. It is shown behind closed doors, and after the fact it emerges that the defence have managed to insert a large question mark in the middle of the chain of events: how did the list end up in Angelica Reyes' hands? Who did she take it from? Was it from Wester, and in that case, why was he carrying it? The prosecutor counters that this has no bearing on whether or not Wester was guilty, since Reyes was demonstrably in possession of the list and used it against Wester. The defence claim that it has a crucial role in explaining the relationship between Reyes and Wester.

The court accepts the prosecution's version. Wester immediately declares his intention to appeal.

Birck and I leave the courtroom side by side.

Morovi never did report me. The month I spent restricted to administrative duties was punishment enough, she felt. I spent the time tying up loose ends surrounding the Angelica Reyes case, before returning to regular duties at the end of January. I visited Salem several times a week.

For so long, I was looking for a home. For a while, I convinced myself that it was with Sam; after that, it was in work; and then when everything seemed to be falling apart after the shot in Visby harbour three years ago — the shot that killed Markus Waltersson — it was in my ties to Grim.

I think I have recently started to understand something about the place where I grew up and the people who have shaped me, but for now it remains more of a feeling than an insight, difficult to express.

It's been over three months since Grim's funeral. Sometimes I think about my image of the future, how we were going to meet under blazing sun on Norr Mälarstrand. Maybe it is only in their thoughts, their memories, that certain people can meet. That isn't a melancholy thought, it doesn't feel like that anymore.

It feels redemptive.

Maybe I'll never learn. It could be that people don't change, just adapt. I don't know. What I do know is that I feel different.

Me and Birck head for the entrance. The reporters can sniff a headline; they want a quote. It's not our job to give them one. It's Monday, the end of March, and the new year is just a quarter old. We walk back to HQ.

'Are you coming up?' I ask.

Birck shakes his head.

'I'm meeting my brother.'

'You've never really talked about him.'

'Our relationship is ...' he says, seeming to look for the right word. '... complicated.'

'Aren't all sibling relationships complicated?'

Birck laughs.

'True.' He turns serious. 'How are things? How does it feel?'

'Good,' I say.

'Really?'

'I think so. What about you?'

'Same here.' He gives me a cautious smile. 'See you tomorrow?'

'See you tomorrow.'

Up in the Violent Crime Unit, everything is quiet. There's a man outside my door who I recognise, more a shadow than a person, with two plastic cups in his hands and a troubled expression on his face.

'I thought,' says Carl Hallingström, 'that I could treat you to a coffee. In your office,' he adds, offering me one of the cups.

The man's posture is slumped; he's pale and gaunt, with bloodshot eyes. I take the cup and open the door, and Hallingström walks in ahead of me. The coffee burns the palm of my hand in a nice way, making me more alert. I take a little sip.

Hallingström sits down and looks perturbed.

'What are you doing here?' I ask.

'Sit down, would you?'

'This is *my* room.'

Hallingström waves his hand dismissively.

'Of course. Of course, sorry. I am a bit tired.'

'What's it about?'

I stay standing. He stares at the cup in my hand.

'Have you tasted it?'

'Yes.'

'Nasty, isn't it?'

'Yes.'

'Huh,' Hallingström says and stares at his own coffee, as though he's weighing his words carefully: 'Nasty. Yes, that's the word.' He takes a gulp, then grimaces and clears his throat. 'So ... about your questions. The ones you put to me in this very room, back in the winter. We haven't had the chance to talk since then, you see. And I want you to understand that I didn't know that much.'

'You must have known quite a bit.'

'Yes, over time, I came to. But by then it was too late.'

'Too late?'

'To be able to do anything.'

'You're trying to wriggle out of it.'

'No,' Hallingström says, determined now, without blinking.

'How much did you know at the time?'

'That a young woman was dead. That it was probably one of her punters who'd done it.'

'And when did you realise it was Wester?'

'Only last winter. Patrik Sköld told me.'

'And you suspended him.'

Hallingström looks resolute. He drinks some of his coffee. I drink some of mine. Hallingström crosses his legs.

'I was forced to. I had no choice.'

'You always have a choice.'

'No,' Hallingström says, his voice heavy. A solemnity that can come only from having experienced that many times over. 'You do not.'

'This wasn't a theft or fraud case you were dealing with here. This was a murder, and you knew it was him.'

'Hmm.' Hallingström, his mouth full of coffee, raises an index finger. He swallows. 'Not exactly. *Sköld* claimed that he *thought he knew* who it was. There's a huge difference.'

'For a lawyer, perhaps, or NPA. Not for me, though. You, in fact, attempted to *hamper* our efforts.'

'I know.' Hallingström gets to his feet again. 'That is … Well, that was everything. I just wanted to say that for a long time I didn't know much, and when I did find out I simply did what was deemed necessary.'

'Deemed necessary?' I repeat. 'By whom?'

'Oh, you know how it is. Someone. There's always someone.'

Hallingström opens the door and walks out, disappears.

80

It's evening. I'm in my office. It's all over, but it doesn't feel that way. The most difficult crimes might always remain unsolved.

I think about all those who are no longer with us. The way we live without them, and yet still we live with them.

I stand up from my chair, and walk around the desk. It's going to be a long, warm spring, you can almost smell it in the air in the mornings.

I am glad that I get to be part of it.

For the very first time, I realise, I am going to try to hold on to that feeling.

I put my coat on, switch off the light, and walk out into the corridor. Sam's just coming back from the toilet, and she smiles when she sees me. She's come straight from the gallery, to pick me up. We're going to the cinema.

'Are you done?' she asks.

'Yes,' I say. 'I'm done.'

'Let's go then.'

I lock the door, take her by the hand, and walk over to the lift. And, from that moment on, you know nothing about me.

THE LEO JUNKER SERIES

Four gripping crime novels that cut to the corrupt core of Swedish society — and show one damaged police detective's struggle to do the right thing.

THE INVISIBLE MAN FROM SALEM

Officer Leo Junker and criminal John Grimberg grew up together in the housing estates of Stockholm. Both men want to escape their past, yet its violence binds them together.

THE FALLING DETECTIVE

Hate stalks the streets of Sweden. But there are links from the lowest street to the highest office, and Leo's murder investigation soon runs afoul of the national security service, SEPO.

MASTER, LIAR, TRAITOR, FRIEND

What fires forge the men who stand in the shadows of all police forces, intelligence agencies, and governments? Leo's boss Charles Levin knows — a knowledge that will prove fatal.

THE THIN BLUE LINE

A final reckoning with the past, with truth, with lies, with *the official version*, and with what it takes — even breaking the law — to uphold the law.